MYSTERY

Giroux, E. X.
The dying room.
11/93   19.95

The
Dying
Room

Also by E. X. Giroux

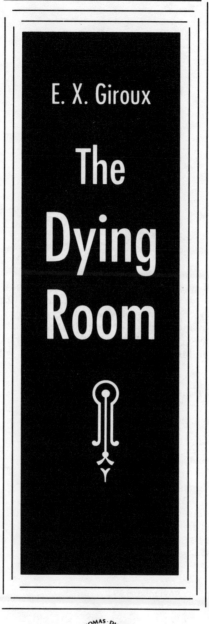

E. X. Giroux

The
Dying
Room

St. Martin's Press   New York

Mystery
Giroux

Design by Lynn Newmark

Library of Congress Cataloging-in-Publication Data

Giroux, E. X.
 The dying room / E.X. Giroux.
  p. cm.
 "A Thomas Dunne book."
 ISBN 0-312-09791-3
  1. Women—Ontario—Crimes against—Fiction. 2. Mothers and daughters—Ontario—Fiction.   I. Title.
 PR9199.3.S49D95   1993
 813'.54—dc20   93-24388
                                                    CIP

First Edition: November 1993

10 9 8 7 6 5 4 3 2 1

This book is for Don Reed, one of the good guys in the white coats.

Prologue

RECTANGULAR PANES OF glass framed the ebony velvet of the night sky. The woman who stood in front of the window pressed one hand against the cold surface of the countertop; the other one held back a gay curtain. Her eyes searched the darkness as though hoping to see the first opalescent flush of dawn.

Her pajamas clung damply to her body, and she hugged her robe closer as she turned away from the window. Her nightmare still lingered, not dispelled even in the safety of this familiar kitchen. A powerful dream, powerful even by the standards of bad dreams, a mixture of youthful memories and more recent ones thrown into a terrifying sequence. One moment she had stared at the cold dead face of her grandfather as he lay on the bed in the dying room; the next moment she was beside the same bed but the hand she touched was warm, as warm as the blood on her own hands.

Horror and sickly fear still clung to her, so tightly she fancied she could smell them. How long had the horror been waiting? Had it been growing even while she attended school? Under the lush canopy of the maples had it grown and strengthened, waiting for her return?

And she had returned. Nothing had warned her. Where were the premonitions other people boasted about having? She had felt not the slightest stirring of fear. At the time it had even seemed a good idea. The house was waiting, relatives and old friends were waiting—and, she now knew, the horror had been waiting.

Nothing had warned her, and she had been content and even eager as the tires of her car hummed away the miles—miles taking her back to Hampton. Taking Jamie with her back to Hampton. Taking both of them to what waited in the brick house beneath the scarlet and golden leaves of autumn. . . .

KAREN DANCER SHIFTED behind the steering wheel, trying vainly to find a more comfortable position. Perhaps it would have been better to have flown from New York to Toronto and taken a train to Hampton. Driving the entire distance had been tiresome. She glanced at her daughter, sitting bolt upright beside her, turning her head from one window to the other, trying not to miss a thing.

"Tired, Jamie?" she asked.

"A little. But look! That sign—Hampton, four miles. We're nearly there!" She squirmed around to face her mother. "It really *is* named after you."

"Not me. My ancestors."

"Your grandfather?"

"Farther back than that. A very remote grandfather. Great or great-great or—" Karen gave up the greats and laughed. Jamie, not to be outdone, laughed too. She was still pale, Karen thought. Her big honey-brown eyes looked even larger in a face that was too thin, the bone structure showing too clearly. Well, a couple of weeks of autumn in Southern Ontario should correct that. September was one of the best months here, warm enough to be pleasant but past the stifling heat of midsummer. And the trees! Clumps of maples had caught their eyes, the massed dark green of their foliage spattered liberally with patches of colored leaves that later in the season would spread and make the trees tall pillars of red and gold.

"Are you greatly anticipating this visit?" Jamie asked.

Darting an amused look at her, Karen wondered, not for the first time, how the Hampton family would view an eight-year-old child who used the vocabulary that Jamie did. An unusually bright little girl, her teacher had told Karen last spring.

"In fact," the teacher had stated, "we would be inclined to worry about Jamie's accelerated development if she weren't so well rounded in other ways."

Karen had looked anxiously at the other woman. "Are you saying she's a child prodigy?"

"Not at all. Simply an acutely intelligent little girl."

"You don't feel she's spending too much time reading and studying? Her vocabulary is—"

"Outstanding." The teacher laughed. "Right at present Jamie's putting it to good use—lettering placards."

"What for?"

"Jamie is sparking a protest session complete with slogans. A sit-in, I believe. They're protesting the cafeteria food. Last month she had them agitating for a longer recess."

"Perhaps," Karen suggested weakly, "she'll end up majoring in political science."

"Or anarchy," the teacher had said darkly.

Jamie was tugging at her mother's sleeve. "Karen, that sign ahead. Town limits—population twenty-nine hundred."

"Yes, I see it."

4

"But a sidewalk starts right beside the sign and there're no houses here. Why is the sidewalk here?"

"It always was that way. I'll stop and we'll have a look at the town from the top of the hill."

She pulled the car over, and by the time she slid out from under the wheel Jamie was already standing on the sidewalk, morning sunlight gleaming on her long flaxen hair, a soft breeze blowing the brief pink dress against her body. Joining her daughter, Karen stared down into the valley.

"I can't see a thing," Jamie protested. "Only trees."

"But look at it, dear. The leaves are beginning to turn. In a few days it will look like a scarlet and golden ocean. Those spires there, see, those are the three churches."

"Let's drive down, Karen!"

Again the child moved faster than her mother and was in the car before Karen.

"Let's drive all over town," Jamie cried. "Look, there the houses are. What's this street called?"

Karen glanced at the old brick houses set well back from the street among clusters of tall trees. That one was where her closest friend, Dinah, had once lived. Would Dinah still be in Hampton or had she moved away? Karen recognized another one; her English teacher had lived there.

"Karen?" Jamie repeated. "What's the name of this street?"

Her mother's brows knit. "The real name is . . . I should remember . . . oh, yes, Richelieu, but it was never called that. This part we're on is called Lofton Hill, after the family that owns the factory. See, that's their house." She pointed at a sprawling white house behind a high box hedge. "Farther down where the shops are it's called Main Street, and then when it reaches the other side of town it becomes Factory Hill."

5

"Wouldn't it have been simpler to call it Richelieu all the way through?"

Much simpler, Karen agreed silently, but nothing had ever been simple in Hampton. All the street names once so familiar sounded strange now: Elm, Cypress, Oak, Arbutus. . . . The only trees that grew on those streets were maples, many of them a couple of hundred years old.

"Has it changed much?" Jamie was asking.

Karen shook her head. She'd seen no changes so far. The small grocery they were passing had the same sign hanging over its door that had been there when she had left Hampton twenty years before.

"And you weren't much older than me when you left," Jamie said.

Reaching out an arm, Karen hugged the child's shoulders. "A great deal older. Sixteen."

"Can we drive through town?" her daughter asked again.

"A little way, and then we'll have to go to Uncle Alfred for the keys." She pointed a finger. "Look, honey, there's the library and the park beside it."

Jamie twisted her head toward a squat brick building with a trim of gray stonework around the windows and door. Beside it was a small park divided into four grassed triangles by walks leading inward like the spokes of a wheel to the center. "What's that funny thing in the middle, Karen?"

Taking her eyes from the road, Karen looked at the open wooden structure with ornate gingerbread trim. "A bandstand."

"A what?"

"The town band used to play there every Saturday night during the summer."

They were now driving slowly along Main Street. As Karen gazed down the line of buildings—the small department store, a florist, a greengrocer, a hardware store—she felt her eyes widening. The names over them were the same ones that had been there two decades before. "It doesn't seem possible," she said aloud.

"What?"

"Time seems to have stood still here. You'd think after all these years . . . oh, here's where we turn. You can see the post office at the end of the street, Jamie, and here, two doors away from it, is where your uncle lives."

"Great-uncle," Jamie corrected.

"Great-uncle," Karen agreed, and pulled the car up to the curb. She tried to recall who had once lived here. Of course, the Lovatts. Her uncle had married their only daughter. It looked much like all the larger houses in the town: square, rose-red brick, ivy crawling up the walls, a white painted stoop shielding a solid oak door. The grounds were well kept, and mauve and bronze chrysanthemums bloomed profusely in neat beds. Karen took a deep breath. Even the smells were familiar: late flowers, freshly cut grass, and the elusive smoky tang of autumn.

"It's very big, isn't it?" Jamie said in a hushed voice.

"Not as large as the house we'll be staying in." She took the child's hand. "Come along and meet your uncle."

"Great-uncle." Jamie glanced over her shoulder at the other side of the street. One young woman was wheeling a pram and another one had just stopped and was bending over the baby. The sounds of their voices drifted across the street. "Do you know them, Karen?"

"I don't think so, but it's been so long. I may even have trouble recognizing Uncle Alfred."

She didn't. The moment the oak door swung open she recognized him. He was much older, of course, and frailer, but still the same spare erect figure who had dominated

7

her childhood. His small gray eyes went from the woman to the child.

"Well, Karen, so here you are. And your little girl. Come in, do come in." He shut the door behind them. "You didn't say exactly when you were arriving, and I had no time to get a letter back to you."

Jamie, still clinging to her mother's hand, was gazing around the square hall, up the steep flight of polished steps. It wasn't a graceful staircase. On its outer edge a sturdy hand rail ran; on the other side a rather ugly maroon wallpaper came down to the treads.

"It was rather a sudden decision," Karen told her uncle. "We left in a rush—"

"No harm done. Come into the parlor. My eyes aren't as good as they once were, and I can't see you properly in this dark hall."

He ushered them into a long narrow room that didn't appear much brighter than the hall. The thick foliage of the trees planted squarely in front of the house shaded the windows. The room had tall ceilings and was furnished with graceful antiques. The gleaming wood floor was partially covered by a silky old Oriental rug. Jamie was staring from one piece of furniture to another.

Alfred Hampton looked around with complacent pride. "You like my home?"

"I don't know," Jamie said.

"Good girl. Not going to make any definite statement until you've thought it over. Over there—that lady's desk—that's a fine piece of Chippendale. The table next to it is Queen Anne. Both of them belonged to my wife's family. Excellent taste!"

Walking over to the Queen Anne table, Jamie examined a chessboard on top of it. Alfred followed her and picked up a chessman. "Ivory and ebony," he told her.

8

"Notice the inlay on the board. Must be two hundred years old."

Her brown eyes went from the chessmen to the old man. "How old are *you?*"

He smoothed a crisp gray mustache. "Not nearly that old, if that's what you're thinking, young lady. How old are you?"

"Eight years and two months."

"Well, I'm over ten times that old."

"Over eighty?"

"Eighty-three, to be exact." He noticed Karen still standing near the door. "I forget my manners. Sit down, Karen, yes, right over here."

Taking the chair he indicated, Karen gestured to her daughter. Jamie cast another look at the chessboard and perched on a footstool near the old man.

"Now." He leveled his eyes at her mother. "Let's look at you. Hmm, you haven't changed as much as I thought you might. Your hair is much darker. It used to be the same shade as your daughter's." He swung his eyes toward the little girl. "What's your name?"

"Jamie."

"That's no name for a girl. That's a boy's name."

Jamie opened her mouth and Karen said hastily, "That's what she called herself when she started to talk. It just stuck. Her name is Jennifer."

He nodded approvingly. "Now that's a good name, has a solid ring. I'll call you Jennifer."

The girl cocked her head, her long straight hair falling over one side of her face. "If you'd like to, I'll allow you to."

"Thank you. You not only look much like your mother once did, but you seem to have a similar temperament. Precocious!"

Jamie sounded the word. "Pre-co-cious. I like it."

"You *like* being precocious?"

Again Karen intervened. "She collects words. It's her hobby."

Under the trim mustache the old man's mouth twisted into a wintry smile. "Jennifer and I may get along. I'm fond of words myself. Do you play chess, child?"

"A little."

"You don't play a little. You either play chess or you don't."

"I play chess, Great-Uncle Alfred."

"Uncle will do. Hmm, we'll play a game sometime."

To Karen's relief the elderly man and little girl appeared to be getting on famously, but she decided it was time to move things along. "About the house—"

"What about it?"

"I was wondering whether it was ready for us—water, electricity, that sort of thing. And if I could have the keys."

He cocked a cold eye at her. "You haven't really had any interest in your property, have you? You insisted I take charge of everything, and when I tried to give you accountings—"

"I was so rushed. I knew you would do a good job."

Under his cold glare she winced. He'd tried to give her accountings all right, pages and pages of meticulous details on rent and taxes and drain tile to be renewed. Finally she had written to him and told him to go ahead and use his own judgment. She knew she'd offended him because from then on his only communication had been an annual Christmas card.

"Our family home, and you neither know nor care about it!" he said tartly. "I'd better bring you up to date. Your cousins Ashley and Sybil moved into it years ago, shortly after their father's death."

"Ashley and Sybil are living there? I thought that we—"

10

"You needn't worry. Plenty of room for all of you. When you were growing up, that roof sheltered sixteen members of our family. Don't you remember even that?"

"I remember," Karen told him.

"Sixteen people!" Jamie exclaimed.

"Sixteen," he told the little girl. "And there's only five of us left. My eldest brother, John—he was your grandfather—died just before your grandmother and your mother left Hampton. Since then, my other brothers and sisters have passed on. The family is narrowing down; old families do. I'm the last of my generation." With a certain amount of relish, he added, "Still alive and kicking and the rest of them dead and buried." As though the thought reminded him of something else, he brushed at his mustache and said quickly, "I was sorry to hear of your personal losses, Karen: your mother and your husband."

"Were you?"

"Still thinking about your mother, aren't you?"

"Yes."

"Still bitter. I rather thought so, when you didn't bring her home to the family plot for burial."

Karen regarded him bleakly and for a moment forgot the child on the footstool beside his chair. "Mama didn't belong with the family in life, why bury her with them?"

"A Hampton—"

"Mama was never a Hampton! She was Maria Rossetti."

"She was Mary Hampton!"

A faint flush colored Karen's cheeks. "You tried to make her that, but thank God she stayed as she was— warm and gentle and human! An Eye-talian," she mimicked, "a little waitress John Hampton was fool enough to marry."

"Karen, Karen." He extended a hand to her. It was so thin the skin looked transparent, and bluish veins knotted

11

the back of it. "I'm too old for quarrels. I'll admit your mother didn't have an easy life with us. The marriage was injudicious. John was over fifty and she was so young—"

"How old were you when you married?"

It was his turn to flush. "Over sixty, but that was different. Lottie . . ."

As his voice trailed off, Karen considered his marriage. Charlotte Lovatt was different. She belonged to another of the old families of Hampton and was completely acceptable—an Anglo-Saxon and a Protestant. As she remembered the woman, Lottie was also a bitter old maid. But there was nothing to be gained by arguing with Alfred Hampton.

"I didn't come here to talk about Mama," she told him.

He folded both hands in his lap and looked down at them. "Let me say this, and then we'll drop the subject. I know Mary had a poor time with us, but I wasn't responsible for it. None of the men were. It was the females: my sisters, my cousins." He hesitated. "Women can be . . . deadly." He lifted his eyes. "You won't need keys for the house. In Hampton no one locks doors—"

Jamie looked up into his face. "No one locks doors? Why, there're *five* locks on our apartment door."

"New York." He pursed his lips. "Not in Hampton. No reason to. Now, about the farm. Nice young couple renting it now. Nat and Maudie Jenks. They have two children near Jamie's age—"

"My age!" Jamie cried.

"You must get over this deplorable habit of interrupting, child!"

"De-plor-a-ble," she echoed.

"Definitely precocious!" he snapped.

"Precocious . . . deplorable . . ."

"Jamie." Karen tried to keep from smiling. Jamie

12

meekly dropped her eyes, and her mother turned back to Alfred.

He was watching her closely. "Karen, why did you decide to come back to Hampton?"

"As I explained in my letter, Jamie has been ill. Just measles, but she had a bad case and hasn't picked up as well as she should have. Her doctor recommended a change, somewhere quiet, away from the city."

"The child does looked washed out. But you mentioned something about your own health."

"Nerves. I've been working too hard, and then all the worry about Jamie—"

"Working too hard. At what?"

"De-plor-a-ble," Jamie said clearly.

He swung his white head toward the child. "What are you talking about?"

"You interrupted Karen. Deplorable."

"Jamie," her mother snapped, "would you like to wait in the car? One more word and that's where you'll be." She smothered a smile at the look on the old man's face. "She's always called me Karen."

"A child calling a parent by the given name is reprehensible," he declared icily. "Utterly reprehensible." He looked suspiciously at the little girl, but Jamie, her lips pressed tightly together, looked silently back at him. "She confuses me. I must admit I don't recall what I asked you."

"You asked about my work. I'm in advertising—pictorial layouts. I've just received a promotion and I suppose I worked too hard getting it. Anyway, the doctor said it was time for both Jamie and me to get away, and I thought of the old house and the farm and Hampton . . . and autumn in Ontario."

"So you do have some feelings for your home town. But you've picked a poor time to return."

"Why?"

Instead of answering her question, he bent over the quiet little figure beside him. "And what do you think of living next door to a farm with playmates and cows and horses, Jennifer?"

She gazed demurely up at him, her lips still pressed together.

"Answer your uncle," her mother prompted.

Pointing at her lips, Jamie shook her head.

"Answer him!"

"You told me if I said one more word I'd have to sit in the car."

"Jamie," Karen warned softly.

"All right, Karen. Well, Uncle Alfred, I think I will find a farm and horses and cows rep-re-hen-si-ble."

He slapped one hand against the arm of his chair. "You don't even know what that word *means.*"

"I'll find out," Jamie promised.

Throwing back his head, he laughed. Karen was startled. She'd seldom seen him smile, let alone laugh. He wiped his eyes. "I hope Lottie gets here in time to see this young minx."

"Lottie is here," a voice said from the doorway.

His wife stood in the doorway. Karen recognized her immediately. The tight bony face and sour mouth hadn't changed. She was much younger than her husband, probably in her late fifties, and her suit and small hat were expensive but dowdy.

Alfred got stiffly to his feet. "Karen and her daughter got here ages ago, and I haven't even had time to offer them tea."

Lottie Hampton nodded at Karen. "Lunchtime now. Always come home to make lunch for Alfred and see he's bedded down for the afternoon. Needs lots of rest. Have to

14

shut the shop down for an hour, but it's easier than trying to hire someone."

What shop? Karen wondered, and then remembered. "Do you still run the wool and yarn shop on Main?"

"Same place, Lovatt's Wools. Put some new lines in lately, novelties and hobby crafts. Heard you were in advertising. I was thinking maybe you could think up something catchy for my newspaper ads."

Karen laughed and shook her head. "I'm only in the pictorial part. I'm afraid I won't be much help with slogans."

Jamie cocked her bright head to one side. "What about Darn 'n' Yarn at Lovatt's Wools?"

"That isn't half bad," Lottie muttered and then turned her head sharply. "Did you say that?"

"Yes," Jamie told her.

"What's your name?"

Before Jamie could reply Alfred said quickly, "Her name is Jennifer, my love. You wouldn't believe this child, she's—"

"Time for your lunch," Lottie interrupted crisply. "I only have an hour."

"Deplorable!" Jamie muttered.

"What'd she say?"

Alfred again spoke quickly. "She's trying out a new word. I've been teaching Jennifer words. She learns quickly and is excellent company."

It was evident that Lottie wasn't about to extend a luncheon or tea invitation to them, Karen decided, as she got to her feet. She was right. Lottie gestured toward the hall. "I'll see you to the door, Karen. Now, Alfred, I don't want you sneaking down those stairs while I'm gone this afternoon. You know how nervous it makes me. You wait till I get home and I'll help you down."

He passed one hand over his sparse white hair, parted

neatly on one side and brushed over the lines of a finely shaped head. "I get so tired of being up there, Lottie. I'll hold the railing and take my time."

Karen had a fleeting vision of the frail old man on that steep staircase. "Why don't you set up a bedroom downstairs?" she asked him.

He gave her a horrified look. "Never!"

Karen turned puzzled eyes on her aunt. Lottie's tight mouth creased in a meager smile. "Don't remember much, do you? The only bedroom on the first floor of these old houses is the dying room."

"The what?" Jamie asked.

"The dying room," Lottie repeated. "Your mother must remember, there's one in the family house. People don't care much for that room, particularly someone Alfred's age."

"What's a dying room?" Jamie demanded.

"Never mind that now," her mother said. "We really should be getting along."

"I'll see you to the door," Lottie said again. "You stay right here, Alfred. I'll fix you up in a minute."

Ushering Karen and Jamie out, Lottie shut the parlor door firmly behind her. She stood close to them in the hall, her bright eyes fixed on Karen's face. "Awful trial your uncle is. Have to watch him like a hawk. Claims the afternoon nap keeps him from sleeping at night. Would you believe the old fool sometimes wanders out of the house at night after I go to sleep? To get his exercise, he says."

"He looks in good shape for his age," Karen said.

"Looks better than he is. I tell you he's an awful trial." Lottie swung open the heavy door, and Karen found she welcomed the sunlight spilling across the stoop. She felt a hand touch her arm and looked around. Lottie lowered

16

her voice. "That's the reason I don't want you upsetting him."

Karen stiffened. "I have no intention of upsetting anyone."

"What'd you really come back to Hampton for?"

"I explained all that to my uncle. Jamie has been ill and I'm not too well myself. We're here for a rest."

Her words appeared to amuse the other woman. "Rest!" Lottie chuckled. "You came to Hampton for your health? Landsakes, that's comic!"

Alfred Hampton's dignified head appeared over his wife's shoulder. "Glad I caught you, Karen. If you need a sitter for Jennifer, call on me. I'm sure we can amuse each other."

"That's very kind of you," Karen said warmly.

"I really have a great deal of time on my hands."

Lottie swung around. "Not now you don't. You get in there, and I'll bring your lunch tray."

Without giving them a chance to say goodbye, she nudged her husband into the hall, stepped in herself, and shut the door firmly behind them.

"An inch more and she'd have had my nose," Karen said indignantly.

Her daughter caught her hand and squeezed it. "I'm hungry."

"So am I. I'll race you to the car."

They flew down the walk with Jamie in the lead. She banged open the door and jumped in. "Beat you!"

Karen reached for the ignition. "How did you like your uncle?"

Her daughter didn't hesitate. "He's nice."

"And your aunt?"

"Great-Aunt Lottie is rep-re-hen-si-ble."

This time Karen felt Jamie had found the correct meaning for the word.

17

THE CAR SWUNG over to the curb on Main Street and Karen gathered up her tote bag and gloves. "I'll pick up some cigarettes at the drugstore, Jamie, and then we'll see about lunch."

At the curb, Jamie hesitated. "Where is the drugstore?"

"Right across the street. It used to be Hopper's . . . good Lord, it still is."

They crossed the street and passed a clothing store. There were few pedestrians. An old man, hobbling on two canes, was limping along behind Karen and her daughter. Directly ahead of them a middle-aged woman, with a bulging shopping bag pulling one shoulder down, plodded along looking in the store windows. In front of the poolroom three boys lounged and Karen gazed incuriously at them. Two of them were tall and gangling, the other one was shorter and heavily built. They were uniformly dressed in dirty T-shirts, baggy jeans, and scrubby running shoes. Their hair was shoulder length and all three sported scraggly beards, those of the two taller ones a carroty color, the shorter one's dark brown. Their eyes roved boldly over Karen, taking her in from the crown of her dark blond head to her sandals. She half expected one of them to whistle, but they did a little better than that.

"Looka the purty li'l lady, Chuck, now ain't she something?" one of the carrot-topped youths muttered.

"That ain't no lady, Danny, that's a broad," the dark one sneered.

Very funny, Karen thought. Jamie turned indignant eyes up to her mother.

"Pay no attention," Karen told her, opening the door of Hopper's Drugstore.

A bell tinkled over the door and Karen halted, transfixed. She was willing to bet it was the same bell that had signaled a customer's arrival during her own childhood. The interior of the store was unchanged. One side was still dominated by a soda counter with a marble top and a few white-painted metal stools. The other side held shelves covered with a stock of cosmetics and boxes of chocolates. Into the darkest corner a prescription counter was squeezed, and at the rear was a small wooden counter with an old cash register at one end of it and racks of cigars and cigarettes behind it. Lounging with one hip propped against this counter was a scrawny young man with a bad case of acne. As they entered the door, he glanced up, stared at them, and then appeared to lose interest. Picking idly at a pimple, he returned to his comic book.

"I'd better get a few other things while we're here," Karen said, but Jamie had already crossed to the corner where magazines and paperback books were displayed.

Karen found what she was looking for, a jar of hand cream, a box of tissues, and a bottle of nail polish. By the time she'd gathered them up, Jamie had returned clutching a comic book and a paperback. Karen read the paperback's title: *How to Increase Your Word Power.*

19

Taking it from her daughter, she flipped through the pages. "You already have two of these."

"Not this one. This is a new one."

"Very well." Her mother sighed. "Thank goodness for the comic book anyway."

She carried their purchases back and arranged them on the counter beside the boy's elbow. He didn't raise his head or even bother to move his arm out of the way while she did it. The bell tinkled over the door but she paid no attention until she felt Jamie tugging at her skirt. Then she turned slowly. The youths from the poolroom were standing a few feet behind them. An unpleasant-looking trio, she admitted to herself. The two with red hair looked enough alike to be brothers. They had small pale blue eyes with almost white lashes and brows.

"Lookee here," one of the redheads said, "Same purty lady we seen outside. Small world, ain't it, Tim?"

"Sure is," the other one said. "Need any help with your shopping, lady?"

"Told you once she's no lady," the dark boy sneered.

Tugging Jamie closer to her, Karen turned back to the clerk, expecting him to order the three boys out of the store. Instead he was grinning, one hand still investigating a raw red lump on his chin. No help there, she decided.

She pointed at the cigarette rack. "Two packs of Players, cork tips, please."

"Get the li'l lady her cigarettes, Bob," a voice said from behind her.

She was beginning to recognize their voices. Without turning she knew this had to be the one they called Danny. Taking his fingers reluctantly away from his chin, the clerk half-turned toward the cigarette rack. His hand wavered past the pile of Players and then stopped in mid-air directly above them.

"Out of Players," he mumbled over his shoulder.

20

"They're right under your hand," Karen told him.

He bent his head and appeared to peer at his hand. "Don't see any. You see any, Chuck?"

This time it was the dark one. " 'Pears to me you're out of them, Bob. Better put some on order."

"Shame to disappoint such a purty li'l lady." Danny chortled. "Better give her another brand."

The clerk grabbed two packages at random. "Here." He threw them down beside her other purchases. "These will do you."

Karen's fingers were digging into the leather of her tote bag. She found she was listening for the bell over the door, hoping another customer would enter the store. Along with the odors of the drugstore, medicinal mixed with the perfume of talcs and powders, she could smell the bodies of the youths surrounding her. It was a menacing smell, rank and fetid as animals.

"Li'l girl got hair as purty as her mommy," Danny said, an edge of ugly humor in the high-pitched voice. "See how long it is?"

Karen swung around but she was too late. Giving a sharp squeal, Jamie clapped one hand to her head. Danny slowly opened his hand and released several long flaxen hairs.

"You pulled my hair!" Jamie cried, her face flushing with rage. "It hurt!"

Without warning she pulled her foot back and drove the sharp toe of her small shoe into Danny's ankle. It connected with a satisfactory crunch, and he stopped grinning abruptly, uttered a howl of agony, and bent over to grasp his leg.

"You little brat!" he shouted.

"Good work!" Karen told her daughter. She turned back to the pimply youth. "If you don't have my brand of cigarettes you can keep all this. I don't want it." She swept the pile of bottles and the box toward him. The paperback and the comic book teetered on the edge of the counter, but the rest crashed on the floor at his feet. There was the splinter of broken glass and then the smell of acetone. The nail polish bottle had broken. He looked down in dismay.

"My pants!" he yelled. "You've ruined my good pants!"

"Fine," Karen said sweetly. Tugging Jamie along, she stepped toward the other three. For a moment she thought they would bar the way, but the dark one grunted something and they fell back. Taking their time, Karen and Jamie made their exit.

"What about my pants, Mrs. Dancer?" the clerk shouted after them.

With difficulty she restrained herself from telling him what to do with his pants. The last thing she heard as the door shut behind them was a husky voice muttering, "You're goin' to pay good, bitch."

"Hoodlums," Karen said as they reached the sidewalk.

"He knew who we are." Jamie's blond brows drew together. "How did he know who we are?"

"It's a small town, honey. Word gets around. Forget it, their types are everywhere." To divert her daughter, she pointed. "The restaurant we're going to is just down the street. I used to spend half my life there."

As they walked, Karen glanced at the other people on the street, wondering if she would recognize a face. The old man with the canes was halfway up the block and the woman with the shopping bag was just entering a store. When they reached the restaurant she paused and looked into the window. Over her head a sign spelled out THE CASBAH, and the window display valiantly tried to live up to the name. The trunks of two dusty artificial palm trees protruded from a gravel base, and a pineapple leaned drunkenly against one of them. Plastic garlands of flowers

22

were flung helter-skelter over the gravel, their colors faded from long exposure to the sun.

"The food is better than the decor," a voice said in her ear, "but you probably remember that, Karen."

She turned and looked into the face of a tall, fair man. "Jim!"

His lips parted over even teeth. "I didn't know if you would recognize me."

"You haven't changed at all!"

"And neither have you. I'd have known you anywhere." He smiled down at Jamie. "Even if I hadn't recognized you I'd have known who it was when I saw this child. She's the picture of you." His smile faded. "Karen, it's a long time since your mother took you away from Hampton. I saw you off that day. Do you remember?"

She did. She remembered the loss she had felt and the loss she had read on his face as he'd waved goodbye from the station platform. She had hung from the window of the train, looking back, as his figure became smaller and smaller.

"Your mother," he said hesitantly. "I was going to write when I heard about her death. And then . . . your husband. I should have written, Karen, but I didn't know what to say. Two deaths, and so close together."

She took a deep breath. "A long time ago, Jim. It was over eight years ago." Aware of Jamie again, she said, "This is Jamie. Jamie, this is Jim Miles, an old friend."

Jamie held out a small hand. "You may call me Jennifer, if you like that better."

Putting down the black satchel he was carrying, he bent gravely over her hand. "Jamie's a fine name. Would you call me Jim?"

She nodded, and her face broke into a radiant smile. Karen nudged his satchel with the toe of her shoe. "So

23

you did get your wish and followed in your father's footsteps. I suppose you're Dr. Miles now."

"I did and I am and the doctor prescribes some nourishment. You both look hungry."

"Will you have lunch with us?"

"I've eaten and I should really be on my way to my next house call, but I'll steal a few minutes and have some coffee with you."

The interior of the Casbah had changed somewhat. The old wooden booths were gone and in their place were chrome and plastic ones, but the candy counter was still in the same place and at the back of the restaurant she could see the red, green, and blue lights of the jukebox.

When they were seated in one of the rear booths, Jim Miles leaned over the table. "Remember—" Breaking off, he laughed. "That's one word we're going to overuse. I was going to ask if this was familiar."

She gazed around. "Hot chocolate and doughnuts after skating parties. Coke and sandwiches after swimming. French fries and hamburgers to spoil our dinners. Yes, Jim, it's familiar."

"And above all, Karen Hampton and Jim Miles, together."

Jamie had been reading the menu. She glanced up at him. "Were you Karen's boyfriend?"

He grinned. "Her best beau, after stamping out heavy competition."

A young waitress had arrived and was standing silently, her pencil poised over an order pad. Karen ordered soup and sandwiches.

"I'd like a chocolate sundae too, Karen," Jamie said.

Karen nodded. "And milk and coffee. Jim?"

"Coffee for me, Jessie. How's your mother?"

She took time out from scribbling on her pad to beam

at him. "Much better, Doctor Jim. Says the pills you gave her make her feel twenty-five again."

"Why the Doctor Jim bit?" Karen asked as the girl headed toward the kitchen.

"To distinguish me from Dr. Miles."

"Is your father still—" she stopped. She had almost said alive. "Is he still in practice?"

The waitress was back, balancing two cups of coffee. Jim waited until she set them down. "Barely. He's over eighty now. But he still treats some of the older patients, if they can make it down to the office."

"Does he take care of Uncle Alfred?" Jamie asked.

"Indeed he does. Have you met your uncle?" When Jamie nodded, he asked, "What do you think of him?"

"He knows some lovely words."

Jim was peeling the wrapper off sugar cubes. He gave her a puzzled look, dropped the cubes into his cup, and said to Karen, "I saw you when you came out of the drug-store, but you were bolting along so fast it took awhile to catch you."

Karen put her cup carefully in its saucer. "Jamie and I had rather an unpleasant experience there."

"Hoodlums," Jamie explained. "Would you say they were reprehensible, Karen?"

"Extremely, and deplorable too."

"What about precocious?"

Jim was looking from one to the other. "Is this some sort of game?"

"Jamie collects words."

"Oh." He winked at the little girl. "Now I understand, I collect rocks." He turned back to her mother. "What happened at Hopper's?"

As she told him his face became serious. She could see the changes twenty years had wrought. He was heavier, his waistline had thickened, and there were diagonal lines

25

across his brow and deep furrows at the corners of his mouth. I wonder what changes he sees in me? she thought.

When she had finished, he pushed his cup back. "The redheads were the Dimwiddie brothers, Tim and Danny. I would expect something like this from them, but—"

"But what?"

"Young Bob Hopper getting in on it too. Ordinarily he's a rabbit."

She felt in her bag, remembered she had no cigarettes, and took out her lighter. "Have you a cigarette?"

He shook his head. "Gave it up," he said.

"Bob Hopper didn't seem rabbity today, but then he had lots of support," Karen told him. "Just who are Tim and Danny?"

"Their dad runs the poolroom. I never figured they were bad lads, but they can be ornery."

"What about the dark boy, the one they called Chuck? I had the impression that he was the ringleader."

He hesitated a moment and then said slowly, "I don't know. But I do know I'm going to have a word with the Dimwiddies."

"Don't bother. It's not really that important, and—" breaking off, Karen chuckled. "Jamie and I protected ourselves very well. Bob is minus a pair of trousers, and Danny will probably have a large bruise on his ankle."

The waitress was back with a loaded tray. She distributed sandwiches and soup bowls, smiled brightly at Jim, and let the tag end of the smile drift over to Karen.

Karen picked up her soup spoon. "They sounded like hillbillies."

"An act," Jim told her. "They've all graduated from high school. In fact—" He broke off abruptly.

"In fact what?"

He got to his feet. "In fact I'm going to do my good deed for the day."

Jamie twisted around and watched him walk briskly toward the front of the restaurant. "I hope he goes over there and . . . and smears them!"

"That doesn't sound like a nice little girl."

"I'm not a nice little girl!"

"You certainly aren't," her mother told her dryly. "But your thirst for violence isn't going to be satisfied. He's coming back."

Handing her two packages of Players, Jim slid back into his seat.

"Thank you—how nice. But aren't you going to be late for your call?"

He glanced at his watch. "It can wait a few minutes. No doubt the bed-rest-and-aspirin routine as usual. To change the subject, Karen. Do you remember Cassie Saunders? She was in our grade all through school. Her father had that filling station over on Fir Street."

Karen started to shake her head and then she squeezed her eyes shut. Cassie . . . Cassie Saunders . . . filling station. She did remember the girl vaguely. Tall, ungainly, a head that looked too small for the big doughy body. Limp cotton dresses and eyes almost buried in rolls of fat in a flabby face.

"Yes," she told Jim Miles. "I remember Cassie."

"I just thought of it when I was buying the cigarettes. She's having a party tomorrow night and everyone will be there. Good time for you to get reacquainted."

"Cassie? Cassie is having a party and everyone will be there?"

"You're thinking of the old Cassie. This is the new one."

Now Karen really recalled the girl. Cassie, always on the fringes of any group; no skating parties, swimming parties, or dancing for Cassie Saunders. She only went back and forth to school and then faded away to the house where her parents lived beside the library.

"When did she become the new Cassie?" she asked curiously.

"About two and a half years ago when her mother finally died," he said grimly. "Terrible thing for a doctor to say, but I have never signed a death certificate that gave me as much pleasure. You can't have forgotten Laura Saunders?"

"Who could?" A big woman, Karen thought, layers of blubber and a mouth like a steel trap. "A tyrant," she said aloud. "Mac, who kept house for us, used to call her That Holy Terror."

"Mac was quite right. Holy and terror described Laura. A religious fanatic who nearly drove both her husband and daughter mad. Stan Saunders died shortly after you left town, but Laura still had Cassie to prey on." He paused. "I can still see Cassie when I went downstairs to tell her that her mother was dead. She was hunched on a sofa in that grim parlor hung with religious pictures, and she looked like a bag of oats tied in the middle. When I told her, she looked up and smiled. She smiled and said, 'Jim, could you put me on a diet?' "

"A diet?"

"Another of Laura's whims. She stuffed the poor kid with her own favorite foods: mounds of potatoes, greasy pork, gravy. When Cassie protested she was whipped—"

"Whipped! And she never rebelled?"

"Laura dominated her. But Laura's death . . . well, that was poetic justice."

The waitress appeared at his elbow. She had a coffeepot in one hand and Jamie's sundae in the other. Putting the sundae down she bent over Jim. "More coffee?" she asked sweetly.

Reaching over, he picked up Karen's cup. "Please. For both of us."

Karen noticed that the girl managed to brush her hip against Jim's shoulder as she poured the coffee. As she left the table, Karen lifted her brows at her old friend. "One of your conquests?"

"Jessie?" His teeth flashed in a wide smile. "That's one hazard doctors and ministers have in common. Every young girl in town."

"And some of the older ones, I'll bet. What does your wife think of it?"

"I've never married. Been waiting for Karen to come back to town."

His tone was light but his eyes were serious. Too serious, she thought, and changed the subject. "How did Laura Saunders die?"

"The same way she lived—like a swine. She had a heart condition, of course; anyone that obese can't escape one. She must have weighed over three hundred. I had her on a strict diet, and somehow she came up with a big roast of pork with all the trimmings. Ate most of it at one sitting. She had what she termed heartburn afterward, doctored it with baking soda, and dropped dead."

Karen tore the plastic wrapping from one package of cigarettes. "And Cassie went on a diet?"

"Dieted, bought new clothes, got a job here as librarian. In fact, she blossomed." He held up a hand and started counting on his fingers. "Right now she's also president of the Hampton Literary and Drama Society, director of a health, exercise, and diet club held every Thursday night in the high school gym, volunteer worker at the hospital—"

"Hospital?"

"Oh, yes, we have a new hospital. You passed it on your way into town: the old Lofton House on Lofton

29

Hill. Amos donated it to the town when his wife died. It's rather small but better than nothing. Now, back to Cassie—"

"I get the idea." Reaching across the table, Karen tugged his hand down. "Cassie has made up for all those nightmare years. Good for Cassie! But about this party. Shouldn't I have an invitation? I can't just crash it."

He caught at her hand and captured it in both of his. "I'll phone Cassie tonight. She'll be delighted."

"Does she still live beside the library?"

"Uh-huh, but don't worry about getting there. I'll pick you up about eight, eight-thirty. Okay?"

Jamie spooned up the last bit of ice cream. She had a dab of chocolate syrup on her pointed chin. "May I go to the party?" she asked.

"No," her mother said. "Wipe your chin off, honey."

Sliding back his sleeve, Jim glanced at his watch. "Good Lord, I'll have to be going." He patted Jamie's head. "Here's something to make up for missing the party. A new word—pulchritudinous."

She dabbed at her chin. "Thank you. What does it mean?"

He grinned. "It describes your mother."

He nodded, picked up his bag, and walked toward the door. The little waitress ran out from behind the candy counter and pulled it open for him.

"Karen." Jamie was tugging at her mother's arm. "What does pul-chri-tu-di-nous mean?"

Karen was still staring after the doctor. "I think it means beautiful."

Putting her arms around her mother's neck, Jamie whispered in her ear, "Then he's right, you are *beautiful.*"

Karen hugged her close. In her arms the thin little body was warm and comforting, the silky hair brushed softly across her cheek. You're all I have, she told the child silently, all I have left.

Jamie moved away from the circle of her mother's arms and looked up into her face. "Karen," she said, "pulchritudinous is a *beautiful* word."

3

FOR THE FIRST time since they'd reached town Karen truly felt she was coming home. The last brick house and the cement sidewalk that ran to the town limits had dropped behind them, and the blacktopped ribbon of country road wound its peaceful way through grainfields and pasture-land. Fat dairy cows munched lush-looking grass near the fence that paralleled the road. She glanced at a white frame farmhouse with a red-painted barn and a tall silo looming behind it.

"That's the farm Uncle Alfred mentioned," she told her daughter.

"Where is your house?"

"About a quarter of a mile farther on. You'll see it in a minute. Yes, there it is."

While Jamie leaned forward for a better look, her mother guided the car through an open ornamental gate-way and eased it up the length of a long narrow drive. Maples stood on both sides, their bright leaves littering the ground beneath them and blowing crisply across the gravel. At the end of the drive was an old coach house converted years before into a garage. On its peaked roof a weather vane in the shape of a deer swung in the wind.

Karen pulled the car into the garage and turned to speak to Jamie, but the child was already out of the car and running toward the house.

"There it is, Karen," she called back. "My, but it *is* big."

Karen decided against getting their luggage out until Jamie had seen her fill. Her daughter was nowhere in sight. She strolled over the smooth lawn that swept from the three-story brick house down to the road. It was dotted with lilac bushes, and two magnificent maples stood guard. Sunlight glinted from the panes of the row of long narrow windows and burnished the leaves of the ivy climbing the rose-red walls. Behind one of the lilac bushes Jamie was standing, her eyes wandering from the slate roof and the slender chimney pots to the wide oak door.

"Come around to the back," Karen called.

Obediently the child trailed her around the side of the house, past a grape arbor, to the rear garden. It looked much the same as it always had, the kitchen garden in the same spot, its rows of vegetables bordered with a bed of marigolds and nasturtiums, the lawn, green and neatly clipped, sloping back toward the barn. In the middle of the plot of grass, three metal lawn chairs and a white enamel table were shaded by a large blue-and-white umbrella. A clothesline stretched from the back porch to the barn, with a long clothes pole leaning against it. At one side was the toolshed, built of unpainted wood with a sloping tar-paper roof. Another maple blazed behind the shed. Karen could recall dropping from the tree onto the shed roof when she was younger than Jamie.

"This is nice," Jamie cried. "That barn—are there horses and cows in there?"

Karen laughed. "I'm afraid not. It hasn't been used for years except for storage."

"Can we go over to the farm?"

"Not now, maybe later. Let's walk around behind the barn. There used to be swings there."

Jamie tore off around the barn, and her mother followed more slowly. When she reached the back she found that not only were the swings still there but Jamie was already perched on one, pumping her legs and trying to get it in motion.

"Would you push me?" she called.

"Not that one. Out of it!"

"Why?"

"Come over here and I'll show you why."

The tree that supported the swings was the largest one on the property. The trunk had a large circumference, and the two branches supporting the chains were enormous. The tree grew on the edge of a deep ravine that cut through the meadow. On the far side of the tree a child-sized swing hung over smooth ground. The larger one that Jamie had been on was so close to the ravine that with a few strong pushes it would swing right over the edge. Karen pointed. Jamie looked down a steep slope with the glint of water at the bottom.

"See that creek down there? The water is deep and it's filled with rocks. If you fell out of the swing that's where you'd land. So . . . you use the one on the other side of the tree, hear?"

Jamie looked a bit mutinous, but under her mother's unwavering eyes she finally bobbed her head. Karen didn't blame her; she'd stolen many hours on the forbidden swing as a child herself. The element of danger, she told herself, that sweet hazardous feeling that all humans seek, the reason mountain climbers clamber up sheer cliffs, why sky divers plunge into drifts of white cloud,

34

perhaps why men had been willing to journey from earth through space and stand on the alien surface of the moon. . . .

Her reveries were interrupted by Jamie. "Shouldn't we go back to the house and meet your cousins? What are they like, Karen?"

"Much older than I am. They were young adults when I was your age. I doubt they'll be there, honey; they used to work downtown and probably still do."

"Let's go in anyway. Uncle Alfred says no one locks doors here."

"Very well, Jamie. I suppose you're curious to see the inside."

Strangely enough, now that they were there Karen was in no hurry. What's the matter? she asked herself mockingly as they turned back to the house. Still afraid of it, still afraid of the dark halls and the dying room? She wished Lottie Hampton hadn't mentioned the room in front of Jamie.

As though to dispel her unease she set a good pace and, without knocking, turned the handle of the white-painted rear door. It led directly into a cavernous kitchen, three times the size of any kitchen found in modern homes. Through dotted curtains, afternoon sunshine slanted in through two long windows across the plastic surface of the table and fell in pools of amber on brown linoleum. The ranks of tall oaken cupboards over the sink were unchanged, but the black wood and coal range that had squatted in the corner had been replaced with a white enamel stove topped by an imposing battery of controls. A tall refrigerator towered over the stove on one side, and on the other side was an upright freezer. Karen eyed a shining new dishwasher with a chopping-block top. Uncle Alfred must have taken her quite literally and spent the rent money lavishly. The walls had been papered in a

35

gay red-and-white check, and the color was echoed in the potted geraniums that were massed on both windowsills.

Jamie hadn't wasted any time. She had found the pantry door beside the refrigerator and was gazing at the baked goods aligned along the shelves. An iced cake sat beside a loaf cake, and a dish of cookies was flanked by three loaves of home-baked bread. The odors were mouth-watering. Karen put a fingertip on the brown crust of one of the bread loaves.

"Still warm," she told her daughter. "Perhaps Sybil is home, after all."

Returning to the kitchen, she pushed open the swinging doors and looked down the shadowy hall. At the far end she could see the massive front door and the fanlight over it, stained glass throwing bright patches of yellow and red and blue on the dun-colored carpeting.

"Is anyone home?" she called its length.

She waited but there was no answer, so she went back to the pantry where Jamie was still standing, gazing yearningly at the cookies. The smells took Karen back years, a mingling of spices and fresh bread and the odor of geraniums drifting from the kitchen.

"May I have a cookie?" Jamie asked.

"You had lunch only a little while ago, honey, and you don't want to spoil your dinner."

"The doctor said I should eat a great deal, Karen; he said I was underweight," the child said eagerly.

"You sure are," a deep voice drawled behind them. "Look scrawny as a picked chicken. And you're no better, Karie."

Karen whirled around. "Mac!" she cried. "What are you doing here?"

The woman was short and almost as broad as she was tall. An ample bosom billowed over a starched apron, and round owlish eyes twinkled behind round owlish glasses.

"Waiting for you to kiss me," the woman said and held out plump arms.

"Mac!" Karen repeated and, flinging her arms around the woman's shoulders, she kissed her heartily. Tears welled up in her eyes.

Holding her away, Mac peered up into her face. The eyes behind the heavy lenses looked damp. "Ain't we a couple of fools." She laughed, lifting her apron corner and dabbing at her eyes. "Taking on like this! Well, don't just stand there hanging on to me. Introduce me to your daughter."

"Jamie, this is Mac, short for Mollie MacLean—"

"Who raised your momma from a pup," Mac broke in.

Jamie smiled up at the old woman. "Hello, Mac, you have a boy's name too."

"Not shaped much like one." Looking down at her massive bosom and wide hips, she bellowed with laughter. Karen found she was laughing too, and she heard Jamie giggling. Mac lifted down two plates and piled cookies on them.

"Gotta feed the child, Karie. You too. Skin and bones, both of you. What they been feeding you in New York?"

"Nothing like your baking," Jamie said, eyeing the cookies.

"Flattery will get you everywhere," Mac told her as she led the way to the kitchen table. She put the plates down and got a jug of milk from the fridge. "You keep paying compliments, and I'll keep feeding you till you're as plump as I am."

"Her dinner—" Karen began.

"Few cookies won't bother either of you. Oatmeal, same as I used to bake for you. Got a pound cake in there too. Recollected as how you used to relish it." She lowered her bulk on one of the chairs. It squeaked in protest.

Picking up a cookie, Karen took a bite. "Delicious as

ever, but you didn't answer my question. What are you doing here?"

"Here to look after you, you and Jamie. Minute I heard you was coming back I came up to the house and told Sybil I'd be here to help out. No way I'm sitting at home with you here by yourselves."

"Not by ourselves, Mac. Ashley and Sybil are here."

"Out more than they're in. And Sybil's cooking—" Mac made a face. "Hog slop and worse since she got mixed up with that dieting club Cassie Saunders got going. Sybil's idea of a meal is carrot juice and a piece of lettuce."

"What does Sybil do now?"

"Still works at the law office where she always did. Old Mr. Gaines is pretty much retired now, but his son's carrying on for him."

"I meant what does Sybil do with her life?"

Mac looked approvingly at Jamie. She had devoured her cookies and her glass was empty. Reaching across the table, Mac refilled it. "Keeps house for her brother, sings in the choir, and does church work. B'longs to nearly every woman's club in town."

"Is she still as pretty as she used to be?"

"Handsome woman. Good-looking pair, Ashley and her. Got the Hampton height and bones and their mother's coloring. I like Ashley, but Sybil's a dried-up prune—all the juices gone. Never did cotton to her."

"And Ashley?"

"Was on the town council after his clothing business went bust, and now he's mayor."

Jamie had finished her second glass of milk. She wiped off the white ring around her mouth. "May I go outside, Karen?"

"All right, honey, but stay in the yard."

The child paused beside the door. "Mac, where is the dying room?"

38

"Right off the dining room. Want me to show it to you?"

"No!" Karen lowered her voice and said to Jamie, "You run along now."

Light reflected from the other woman's glasses, obscuring the look in her eyes. "Still feel the same about that room? Yes, I can see you do. Nothing to fear there, Karie, just a room where people sickened and some died. You're still recollecting that time your dad and uncle forced you to—"

"Don't, Mac. I don't want Jamie in that room. And I don't want you filling her head with tales about it. She's a high-strung child and she's been ill—" Karen broke off, looked at the old woman, and saw her lips tucked tight to hide the hurt. She reached out and took Mac's hand. "I'm sorry. I'm acting high-strung myself. Nerves. That's why I'm here—for a rest."

"Is that the only reason you come home?"

The question sounded familiar. Both Alfred and Lottie had asked the same question. And Lottie had laughed unpleasantly when told the reason for her return. Karen's brows drew together. "That's the reason, but I've had that question asked three times today. What's the mystery, Mac?"

Mac averted her eyes. "I guess you really *don't* know. Better ask Ashley; after all, he's mayor. Not my place to gossip about things that don't concern me." Ponderously, she moved her bulk around to face the younger woman. "You planning on getting married again?"

Bewildered by the change of subject, Karen shook her head.

"High time you do. Some women need a man. Maybe Sybil don't but you do."

"I have all I want. Jamie, my work—"

"Not enough. Youngsters grow up, and work's not

enough for a woman like you. Sure, you're a fine-looking female but so is Sybil. Now you're a plum, but later you may be a prune like her."

Karen tried to think of a way of changing the subject. For someone who didn't meddle in others' affairs, Mac was doing a good job with her personal life. She was droning on about men, love, and marriage.

She cut across the old woman's words. "We had lunch with Jim Miles today."

"Young Jim, huh? Nice boy." Her eyes brightened. "Jim's not married, and he has a good practice. Maybe he's the one to make you a husband and Jamie a father—"

"Mac, Mac." Karen was laughing helplessly. "Stop being a matchmaker."

Mac heaved herself to her feet. "All right, be a prune. Now I got to get dinner on. You want I should help you get settled? Was up getting your room ready when you arrived. Put you in your momma's room and Jamie in the little one opening off it you used to have. Figured the youngster would feel better in this big barn of a house if you was close to her."

Jumping up, Karen hugged the old woman around her ample waist. "You're wonderful. Jamie and I will get the bags. You go ahead with dinner."

The screen door banged open. "Mac! Karen!" Jamie called. "Come and see what I found."

At the foot of the steps a large cinnamon-colored cat was stretched full length on the grass, one forepaw lazily poking at a tiny heap of gray fluff.

"Old Ruby and her kitten," Mac told the little girl. "Ashley gave all the rest away. Cute little fellow, isn't he?"

Jamie scooped the gray kitten up carefully. "He's a boy kitten?" When Mac nodded she spun toward her mother. The kitten opened its tiny mouth and yawned pinkly.

"Isn't he lovely? Can I keep him, Karen, can I keep him?"

"He isn't ours. He belongs to—"

"Oh, Ashley won't mind a bit. Be glad to get rid of him," Mac said.

"You're a big help," she told the older woman. To her daughter, she said, "He can be yours while we're here, honey, but you can't keep a cat in an apartment."

Jamie clutched the kitten to her chest. "Susie has a cat. She has a Siamese cat, a big one. Why can't I have a cat? He won't be any trouble."

Rubbing her brow, Karen suddenly realized she was tired. "Later, Jamie, we'll talk about it later."

"Everything is later. The farm, this kitten. . . ." Jamie's voice trailed off and her lower lip trembled. "I'll name him anyway. He has to have a name that fits, a good name."

"Now don't you go bothering your momma," Mac said sharply. "Time enough for what you want to do. Can't have everything right now." In a gentler tone she suggested, "Why don't you call him Fluffy?"

"A real name, Mac. Fluffy's not a real name."

"You go ahead and think one up. Now, Karie, you come back in here. Talk to me while I stir up a batch of biscuits. Your luggage will wait."

While Mac reached for flour, a bowl, and a sifter, Karen sat at the table, her chin propped in one hand, and watched. As she worked the old woman talked.

"How come she doesn't call you Mother or Mama or Mom, Karie?"

"She never has. When she was younger I tried to break her of calling me Karen but I couldn't. It seemed simpler just to let her go ahead. What's in a name, anyway?"

Mac measured flour into a blue bowl. "Never knew her daddy, did she? He was killed before she was born."

"Four months before she was born," Karen said dully. "I'd rather not talk about it."

Light glinted from round lenses as Mac lifted her head and directed a long look at the other woman. " 'Pears to me part of your trouble is you never want to talk 'bout anything. Keep it all inside to fester. Now, you tell old Mac. You were in Italy seeing to your momma's funeral when it happened, weren't you?"

Karen found she was talking, telling the old woman what had happened over eight years ago. "Mama insisted on the trip to Italy. She had a terminal illness, and she wanted to see the village her parents had come from. Funny, Mac, it was the first time Mama had been abroad."

Karen had argued against it and so had Jeff, but Maria Rossetti Hampton had a gentle strength. She didn't display it often, but when she did—

"Neither Jeff nor I could change her mind. I wanted to go with her, but both Mama and Jeff said no. I was pregnant with Jamie and I'd lost a baby the year before. Jeff would have gone with her, but he'd just been posted to Georgia—"

"He was in the army, wasn't he?"

"A captain in the reserves. Anyway . . ."

Maria had her way and left for her parents' country, and Jeff was in Georgia. Karen remained in their apartment in New York. When the wire arrived she phoned Jeff, and this time he didn't attempt to dissuade her. Maria was dying.

"In a little village in sight and sound of the Ligurian Sea. Piavo, it was called. Mama was there on a narrow bed in a room with whitewashed walls and a black crucifix over her bed. Gathered around her were her aunts and uncles and cousins. She died . . . quite peacefully."

Her coffin had been lowered into the hot rocky soil on the slope behind the village. An olive grove stood guard

42

on one side of the small cemetery, a citron grove was on the other side, and brassy sunlight glared down, but even the sunlight couldn't warm Karen.

She had wired Jeff that she was coming back to Georgia and to him. His answer was six words long: WILL BE WAITING AT THE AIRPORT. He wasn't. His commanding officer was there instead, a tall man with a craggy face and the broad *a* of New England in his deep voice. A tall man with a craggy face, trying to be kind. An automobile accident, he told her, a bad night, bad visibility.

Karen looked at Mac. "And there wasn't even someone to blame. The other car . . . a family . . . they were all dead too. I went back to New York and Jamie was born. Then—"

"Then you found a job and brought Jamie up," Mac finished for her.

Karen's face was in her hands. Tears trickled saltily down her face, seeped out between her fingers, and dripped onto the table.

"Cry, child," Mac whispered and put a warm hand on Karen's heaving shoulders. "Cry for the dead and then let them rest."

"I never . . . never really cried for them. I felt . . . frozen, beyond grief."

"I know, I know."

"And that was that." Karen made vague motions with her hands, motions as though searching for something— the life she had lost, the security of mother love and man love, all gone, everything gone but a thin little girl with long light hair and big honey-brown eyes.

Mac's calloused old hands caught hers, gathering them up and holding them still. "Go up," she ordered, "upstairs to that horrible newfangled tub, and take a bath, a hot one. Jamie and me will get the bags, and I'll see the youngster is settled in."

"Your biscuits," Karen sobbed.

"They'll wait. Bath and lie down. Rest a bit, Karie."

Karen, her cheeks damp and salty, went down the long hall, up the steep staircase, and toward the room her mother had slept in long ago, before she slept her last sleep in the warm soil of Piavo, on the shore of the lazy blue Ligurian Sea.

4

Karen slept for two hours after a quick shower in the pink
tub with the glass doors that Mac had referred to so con-
temptuously. There was nothing wrong with the tub itself, but it contrasted strangely with the remaining old
marble fixtures and clashed with the bright blue carpet
that covered the floor of a spacious bathroom that had
originally been a bedroom.

She was wakened by a hand shaking her shoulder.
Groggily she looked up at the face close to her own, so
close that Jamie's hair spilled across her neck and cheek.

"They're here, Karen, both of them. They came home
in the queerest old car. Mac says it belonged to their father—"

"Who?"

"Your cousins, Ashley and Sybil. They're downstairs,
and dinner is all ready."

"All right, honey, stop shaking me." Swinging her feet
over the side of the bed, she sat up. Her head ached dully.
"What have you been doing with yourself?"

"Unpacking and helping Mac cook dinner," Jamie

said importantly. "Mac's going to teach me to make bread."

The child chattered on while her mother dressed, brushed her hair, and hastily dabbed some lipstick on. Through the doorway beside the antique dressing table she could see the little room her daughter would sleep in. A yellow spread covered the single bed, and on it sprawled Jamie's black-and-white panda. It was three feet long. The round face was soiled and dingy, the ears were bedraggled, and one button eye was missing.

"Caesar looks very much at home on your bed," she told Jamie.

"Mac said I'm too old for him. I told her I don't *play* with him, he's my mascot, and she said—"

Karen laughed. "Come along, honey. If I remember Mac, she'll be steaming if we let her dinner get cold."

In the hallway, Jamie was still talking. "Mac showed me all over up here. Nine bedrooms, Karen, think of it, *nine*. And she showed me the back stairs, and the flight that goes up to the attic. Can I go up in the attic, Karen?"

Her mother nearly said "later" and stopped herself just in time. "We came here for sunshine and fresh air, Jamie. Attics are for rainy days."

"I'll wait, it may rain. Mac says she can always tell by her elbow; her elbow aches when it's going to rain."

"Here the stairs are. Watch your step, they're steep." She smiled down at the child. "Taken quite a fancy to Mac, haven't you?"

"She's—" Jamie seemed to be searching for a word. "She's be-nev-o-lent."

At that moment Mac appeared at the foot of the stairs. "Hurry up, you two, want your food to get cold?"

When she ushered them into the dining room, two people were already waiting at the long walnut table. Behind it was a breakfront buffet, displaying a fine array of china and silver behind glass doors. To the right of this piece of furniture was a closed door. Karen cast a glance at the door and then turned her attention to her cousins. Mac was right, they were handsome people. They were tall and finely boned with dark chestnut hair and dark blue eyes.

Ashley hurried over to take her hand. "Karen, my dear, welcome home."

"So sorry," his sister murmured, "we weren't able to be here to greet you."

"Mac did that just beautifully," Karen assured them and slid into the chair Ashley was holding for her. Jamie took her place beside her mother. "You've met Jamie, of course."

"Of course," Sybil said with no sign of enthusiasm.

Ashley made up for his sister. He beamed at the little girl and closed one eye in a wink. "I had a call from Uncle Alfred this afternoon. You made quite a hit with the old gentleman."

Mac bustled into the room with a large tray and started to set plates of food out. Sybil looked the dishes over.

"Really, Mac, there's not a single thing here I can eat. My diet," she explained to Karen. "Cassie Saunders has a club and—well, I never realized before how we can injure our health with our forks and knives. Look at this." She pointed to a platter of golden chicken. "Fried chicken— grease. Rolls—starch. Potatoes—more starch. Gravy— more grease."

Putting both fists on her solid hips, Mac glared down at Sybil. "You don't need to diet, you're skin and bones now. Cassie weighed two hundred pounds when she started. Now she's got every featherbrained female in town diet- ing and exercising even when if they turn sideways and stick their tongues out they look like dang-blamed zip- pers!"

47

Sybil's blue eyes flashed. "I feel a hundred percent better. Ashley, don't you feel better since we started our health plan?"

"Indeed I do," Ashley agreed heartily, piling his plate high and reaching for a roll.

"I simply can't eat a single thing—"

"What do you *want?*" Mac snarled.

"There's lettuce and some cottage cheese in the fridge. And no tea, Mac."

"I know, I know. Carrot juice!" Mac thundered out of the room.

Sybil turned wide eyes to Karen. "I can't understand why your mother kept Mac on. She's impossible."

At this remark Jamie lifted hostile eyes from her plate, and her mother said quickly, "She was part of our family, Sybil, a much-loved part."

Sybil jerked her head around and saw her brother reaching for the platter of chicken. "Ashley, stop that. You're going to poison your system."

Mac entered the room in time to hear the last few words. She thumped a dish of lettuce and a glass of juice down in front of Sybil. "Poison, is it?"

"Ladies, ladies," Ashley intervened. "You eat your lettuce, Sybil; Mac, don't pay any attention. You cook like an angel."

Mollified, the old woman smiled at him, patted Jamie's head, and walked toward the door. "Poison cake and ice cream for dessert, folks," she called back sweetly.

After that dinner progressed more amicably. Ashley dominated the conversation, assisted occasionally by his sister. He spoke of his own position as mayor and its responsibilities and covered the various weighty problems it entailed—a new road to be paved, a system for garbage disposal. Karen listened, murmuring something appropriate occasionally, but wasn't very interested until Ashley

48

said in an entirely different tone of voice, "Has Roy got to you yet?"

"Roy?"

"Conroy Paul, our dear cousin."

How could she have forgotten Roy? Karen wondered. A brash, talkative boy a few years older than she was. Repulsive, as she remembered him, a fat sloppy youth with a squeaky voice.

"Got to me?" she repeated. "I don't know what you mean. I slept this afternoon. Perhaps he was here while—"

"Not here," Sybil said icily. "He knows better than to step inside this house."

Karen shrugged. "I haven't seen him." She eyed Ashley. "We should have a talk, Ashley. There's so much—"

He interrupted, glancing at his watch. "I have a meeting, and this is Sybil's night for choir practice. In an hour we'll have to leave."

She pushed back her chair. "That should be time enough."

Jamie popped out of her seat, but Karen looked at Mac.

"Not you, young one," the old woman said. "If you're going to learn to cook you better learn to do dishes."

"Oh, Mac!"

"Wanta learn to make bread, don't you? Start piling them dishes up. Be careful, this here is the good set." To Karen she said softly, "I'll be going home directly I clean up. Want me to stay with you and Jamie awhile tonight?"

Karen shook her head. "As soon as Ashley and Sybil leave we're going to bed. We'll be fine."

She followed Ashley along the hall, with his sister close behind her. Opening the door of the front parlor, he beckoned her. Sybil perched on a chair by the door and Karen took another high-backed one opposite Ashley.

"What can we do for you?" Ashley prompted.

Karen took her time answering. She gazed around the huge room, similar to Uncle Alfred's parlor in the Lovatt house and at the same time quite different. The room hadn't been changed very much since her own childhood. The same heavy Victorian furniture lined the walls, and mahogany chairs upholstered in dull brocade sat on a modern broadloom rug the color of sand. Opposite her was a gilt-framed oil, dark with age and grime, a portrait of a man with the finely boned face and small gray eyes of the Hamptons. Except for the luxuriant beard he could have been Uncle Alfred.

Ashley and his sister fitted in perfectly. He leaned back in his chair, one long fine hand resting gracefully on the table beside him, a lock of rich chestnut hair falling over the high Hampton brow. Sybil had picked up a knitting bag, and her steel needles sparkled in the lamplight. She looked the picture of an English gentlewoman, with her twin set, a small string of pearls, well-cut tweed skirt, and low-heeled leather shoes. Her hair, parted in the middle and drawn in looped braids over her ears, framed a lovely but cold and lifeless face. Once a plum, Karen thought, but now all the juices gone. Why had neither of them ever married? she wondered, and then the sound of Ashley's voice broke through her thoughts.

"We haven't much time, Karen."

"Why didn't either you or Sybil ask why I was here?"

He reached for the pipe rack and humidor sitting on the marble-topped table. "Uncle Alfred told us about your letter. We knew the reason."

"And yet Uncle Alfred questioned me about it. So did Lottie and then Mac. What's going on that I don't know about?"

Deftly he tamped moist tobacco into the bowl of a pipe. "I suppose we should have told you, but Sybil and I talked it over, and—well, frankly we hesitated to bother you about such nonsense. And we had no idea you might take it into your head to come back to town at this time."

"What time?"

"A concern—a large and powerful one—wants to buy the farm and this house."

Karen sat up straighter. "What for?"

Holding a match to the bowl of the pipe, he got it going, exhaled fragrant blue smoke, and carefully broke the match before dropping it into the ashtray. "A nuclear power plant."

For a moment Karen was speechless. She felt anger welling up within her, anger compounded by Ashley's casual air, by the steady click of Sybil's needles. "This is my property," she said slowly. "Why wasn't I told?"

"They came to us," Sybil said quickly. "To Ashley and me. They thought we were the ones to deal with because we lived on the property."

"And you didn't tell them otherwise?" Karen asked.

"Roy Paul did it for us," Ashley said sourly. "I figured he'd be hounding you as soon as you got to town."

"Why is Roy interested?"

"Commission. He runs the realty here and hopes to cut himself in on a piece of it. The town is up in arms at the idea. Town council has been fighting for weeks to find some legal method of stopping the concern—"

"What is its name?"

"Allied Nuclear Power Plants. Or, as they prefer, ANPP."

Karen looked from the man to the woman. "But if it's for peaceful purposes, to produce energy, why is the town fighting it?"

Sybil's mouth twisted, and she moved so quickly the ball of purple wool tumbled off her lap. "It is still a *nuclear* plant they're talking about. In Hampton! Can you imagine what would happen? Scum from all over flooding into town, building houses. Hampton children with the danger of radiation right in their midst. Fallout—"

"Sybil," her brother snapped. "Karen understands all that. She's not a child."

"It would appear you have been treating me like one," Karen said coldly. "Has the town council found the legal means to block it?"

He shook his head. "We can't. This land is outside the town's jurisdiction. It's the province's decision, and the provincial government is ready to go along with it."

"What does the government care about Hampton?" his sister asked bitterly. "About our town, our children? This house that's stood here for nearly two hundred years?"

Fumbling in her pocket, Karen found her cigarettes and lit one. Her fingers were shaking slightly. Don't let yourself get excited, her doctor had advised. Stay calm. She forced herself to ask quietly, "Were you afraid of my decision? Is that why you tried to keep me out of this?"

"Of course not!" Ashley exclaimed. "We were only trying to protect you, not to have you bothered. We knew what your answer to ANPP would be."

"I'd be interested in hearing it."

Sybil moved restlessly. "You're a Hampton. There can only be one answer."

The other woman raised an ironic brow. "Half Hampton, as you well know. Also aware of many facts. One of them is that this world of ours is getting very short of the fuels and energy we require. Our oil and—"

"Do you mean you would actually consider selling this land for a nuclear plant?" Ashley asked incredulously.

"I don't know. But I do know the decision is mine to make, not yours, or the towns, or the town council's."

Ashley, his movements slow and deliberate, knocked

52

the ashes out of his pipe into the ashtray. "This land was cleared by a Hampton. This house was built by one. This town was named after our ancestor. No nuclear plant is going to endanger it. Hampton is never going to—"

"Ashley!" Karen's voice slashed across his. "This is the twentieth century. You're thinking and talking about the past. The world is starved for power, and it can only become worse. This plant will heat your homes and light your houses. We can't live on dead dreams."

Sliding back the sleeve of her cardigan, Sybil looked at the slender band of gold on her fragile wrist. "I'll be late for choir practice."

Ashley carefully laid the hot pipe bowl across the ashtray. "I know you don't mean what you said, Karen. You're worn out from your trip. Sleep on it. We'll be home about eleven. We can talk more then."

"I'm tired and I'll be asleep. Perhaps tomorrow."

At the door, Sybil turned. "Keep one thing in mind, Karen. The town is upset. Some of the people are in an ugly mood. Don't wait too long to make up your mind."

Long after they had left the house Karen sat on in the quiet room, staring down at her shaking hands. She thought of her mother and remembered that Sybil had followed the rest of the women in making life a hell for Maria Rossetti in this house. She wondered which half of her would make the decision, the Hampton or the Rossetti?

By the time Sybil and Ashley arrived home, Karen was sleeping soundly in her mother's bed and Jamie, her hair tangled around the giant panda she clutched in her arms, was dreaming in the adjoining room.

Karen had left a light in the hall for her cousins. After the light went out two figures entered the garage. They circled the aged Buick and stopped beside Karen Dancer's car. One of them held a flashlight while the other lifted a hatchet. Slowly and savagely, he shredded the tires on the car.

5

ASHLEY HAMPTON, HIS heavy brows drawn together in a puzzled frown, looked from the garage floor to Karen. He kicked away one of the shreds of rubber. "I can't for the life of me believe it!"

Sybil chimed in. "When we came in here this morning to get the car—well, I just said to Ashley it doesn't make sense. Vandalism! There've *never* been vandals in Hampton."

"I assure you I didn't bring any with me." Karen clutched her housecoat around her. Her feet felt damp; the thin soles of her slippers must be soaked with moisture. During the night there had been frost, and where the morning sun was striking, the crusty white layer had already melted into puddles of water.

Opening the door of his venerable Buick, Ashley allowed his sister to slip in. "I'll phone Jake's Garage and have him send someone up to put new tires on." He got in behind the steering wheel and rolled down the window. "And I most certainly will mention this to Chief Barnes."

"Is Theo Barnes still chief of police?" Karen asked. "He was an old man when I left."

"He's well beyond retirement age," Ashley admitted. "But he's still as sharp as ever. We hired an assistant, a young chap, to be Theo's constable about a year ago. Even Theo isn't going to last forever."

He started up the motor and Karen left the garage and started back across the lawn, trying to avoid the wetter spots. Turning, she watched Ashley pilot the car in reverse down the driveway. It looked like an ancient dowager on wheels but, as she admitted, whoever had wreaked mayhem on her car had spared the old Buick.

"Karen, what are you doing out here in your housecoat?" Jamie called from the stoop.

The child looked trim and fresh in diminutive jeans, a white blouse, and her favorite pink angora cardigan. Running down the steps, she held her face up for a kiss.

Karen kissed her cheek, pushed the fine hair back from her face, and said, "Tire trouble, honey, nothing to worry about. It should be fixed later today. Ashley's sending someone out to do it."

"There's Mac!" Jamie darted down the driveway.

"Morning," Mac called. She wore a wool shawl and carried a string shopping bag. "That the way you dress in New York, Karie?"

Karen took the heavy bag. "Did you walk all the way out here?"

"Good exercise. Better than going to the school gym with those idiot females and doing push-ups." Swinging open the door, she plodded down the hall. "Leave their cars at home, and none of them would need to get together to grunt and groan." Putting a copper kettle on the stove, she shrugged off her shawl. "After breakfast you two can do some walking. Want you to go over to the farm and get two dozen eggs from Maudie Jenks. Mind you ask for brown ones."

*　*　*

56

"Brown eggs, brown eggs, nothing but brown," Jamie chanted as she skipped along ahead of her mother. "Why couldn't we cut across the fields to the farm?"

Karen turned her ankle on a rock, swore under her breath, and moved over to the blacktop surface of the road. "Because they have Jersey cows, honey, and there's nothing meaner than a Jersey bull."

"Brown eggs, brown eggs, nothing but brown. A bull wouldn't bother us, we aren't wearing red."

Karen watched the child skipping along, bright hair streaming out behind her. Despite the fact that her tires were ruined she felt fine. The crisp smells of autumn floated on the soft breeze, the sun was warm across her shoulders, and her daughter was happier than Karen had ever seen her.

As they neared the farm buildings, Jamie turned a puzzled face to her mother. She wrinkled her nose. "What's that smell?"

"Barnyard," Karen told her.

Turning through the gateway, they strolled up the winding drive toward the white frame house. Two large mongrel dogs came pelting down toward them, barking at the top of their considerable lungs. Karen grabbed Jamie's arm and they stopped. In the next field a man in overalls and a wide straw hat was climbing to the seat of a tractor. He turned his head, bellowed at the dogs, and jumped down.

"Want something?" he yelled.

Karen waited until he reached the fence, and then she gestured at the wickerwork basket on her arm. "Mollie MacLean sent us over for eggs. I'm Karen Dancer, and this is my daughter, Jamie."

Putting a hand on a fence post he vaulted over the fence. "Nat Jenks." He extended a hand, noticed it was smeared with grease, and pulled it back. "Come around to the back of the house. Maudie will see to it."

She glanced sideways at her tenant. Under the brim of the straw hat, his face was lean, with a pug nose and a tanned skin covered with freckles. His expression either was naturally morose or he was in a surly mood. The corners of his mouth slanted down.

Behind the house a young woman was pinning a wash on the clothesline. A girl about the same age as Jamie was handing the garments to her, and a boy who looked about ten was peering around the barn door. He slid out and moved toward Jamie. He was a carbon copy of his father, right down to the freckles.

"This is Mrs. Dancer," Jenks said gruffly. "My wife, Maudie. And these tykes are Betsy and Dave."

"Pleased to meetcha," Maudie said politely.

She looked much pleasanter than her husband did. Short curly black hair framed a wide ruddy face.

Jenks, having disposed of the amenities, turned back to Karen. "Decided what you're going to do yet?"

Karen stared at him and he elaborated. "About that plant and this here farm."

"We only arrived yesterday, Mr. Jenks. I heard about it last night for the first time."

"Wanted to tell you about us. We're hard-luck people—"

"Nat!" his wife interrupted.

"Keep out of this, woman! Don't get the idee I'm begging, Mrs. Dancer. Nat Jenks never begged for nothing. But we're making out good here, got a fair herd built up." He thought this over, the corners of his mouth dragging down even more and added, "People need milk too, don't they?"

"Of course they do," Karen said. "I promise when I make up my mind you'll be the first to know."

His wife smiled first at her husband and then at Karen. "You're taking on over nothin', Nat. Mrs. Dancer here—well, she was a Hampton."

"Right you are." His mouth relaxed a trifle. "Mollie MacLean wants some eggs, Maudie."

He started to turn away, and Karen touched his arm. She had better ask him; it was obvious who the boss in the Jenks family was. "I was wondering if your children could come over and play with Jamie."

He looked from the freckled boy to the curly-haired girl. "Don't see why not. You tell 'em to mind their manners, Maudie."

With his departure, things eased up. Maudie took the basket and went off for eggs while Betsy and Dave edged up to Jamie. The children were soon chattering away, and they chattered all the way back to the house. This time, with Dave assuring them that the bull was securely penned up, they walked along a winding lane that led between the fenced meadows.

As they neared the house, Jamie said to the other two children, "We have swings. Karen, would you show us how you swing on that big one?"

Her mother set the basket down on the table under the blue-and-white umbrella. "Let's go."

She tried to race the children around behind the barn but they easily outdistanced her, and by the time she reached the swings the children were already ranged in a semicircle to watch her.

Dave cocked a cynical eye at her. "Ladies can't swing worth nothin'."

"My mother can," Jamie defended loyally. "Without being pushed, either. Show them, Karen."

With the honor of the Dancers at stake, Karen exerted every effort. Soon she had the big swing curving in long arcs over the ravine. Jamie clapped her hands, and her two new friends watched open-mouthed. After a time Karen stopped pumping and let her legs dangle while the swing slowed.

With a flourish she jumped off the seat. "Still think ladies can't swing, Dave?"

"Not bad," he said and immediately qualified it. "For a girl."

Karen didn't know whether she'd been promoted or demoted. One moment a lady, the next a girl. Having re-marked on Karen's prowess, Dave proceeded to outdo her. He had barely planted his feet on the swing seat and grasped the chains in grubby hands than Karen reminded him sharply who was boss.

"No standing up and never that swing. You three use the one on the other side of the tree."

"Kid stuff!" The corners of the boy's mouth turned down in a manner reminiscent of his sire, but he jumped off. "Aw, this is no fun. Let's play something else."

Leaving the two little girls trying to placate their lordly male, Karen returned to the house. As she entered the kitchen Mac was pushing through the swinging doors, a broom in one hand and dustpan in the other.

Putting the egg basket on the counter, Karen told her, "Brown eggs and jumbo size. I'm afraid there will be two extra for lunch. The Jenks children are playing with Jamie."

Mac beamed. "No trouble. Lots for all of us." Her smile faded. "Just saw Roy Paul's car pull up out front. Better get out into the back yard and see what he wants."

"Back yard? Won't he come to the front door?"

"Not Roy. He'll be sneaking around to see if Ashley's home. Too bad he isn't. If anyone ever needed a bashing, it's that Roy."

Karen stepped out onto the porch and looked around. She could see no sign of her cousin.

"Psst!"

She turned and saw him; at least she saw his head and shoulders. A balding head and meaty shoulders were thrust around the corner of the house. He gestured frantically at her.

"Is Ashley home?"

"No, he isn't."

"Good." He stepped out of concealment.

The years hadn't improved him any. He was still repulsive, and his voice still tended to squeak. He advanced on her, holding out one sweaty paw. She barely touched her hand to it and then withdrew it with unseemly haste. Roy didn't appear to notice. "Got some people to meet you, Karen. Damn important. Be right back."

When he returned, shepherding two men in front of him, Karen was sitting in one of the chairs under the umbrella, having a much-needed cigarette. She examined Roy's companions. The one in the lead was a handsome middle-aged man in expensive clothes. Executive, she pegged him. The other was younger, homely, with a wild shock of brown hair. He was harder to place. He wore jeans and a suede jacket, casual but well cut.

She started to rise, but the man in the lead lifted a beautifully kept hand. "Don't get up, Mrs. Dancer. We hate to intrude without warning like this, but Roy insisted it was the best time to see you."

"Karen," Roy said, oozing perspiration and bonhomie. "Like you to meet Vincent Halloway and Calvin Trent." He paused and added impressively, "ANPP."

The one he'd called Halloway sat down on one of the remaining chairs and Roy squeezed his bulk into the other. Trent glanced around and then sank to the lawn near Karen's feet. He grinned up at her. He looked awkward sitting there, all elbows and knees, and he had a long, rather doleful face. On his chin was a crescent-shaped scar.

Halloway cleared his throat. "You're probably wondering about our visit, Mrs. Dancer."

"Not really. My cousin, Ashley Hampton, told me about your interest in my property last night."

Roy had been mopping at his wet brow. Now he stopped abruptly. "Don't believe a word he says, Karen. Do you know he falsified records so Mr. Halloway wouldn't know who really owns this—"

"Come now," Halloway interrupted, "that's not quite correct." He turned placid eyes on Karen. "Hampton managed to keep us away from the land registry office, and he did lead us to think this land was his and his sister's, but he definitely didn't falsify." He turned a reproving glance on Roy. "You better watch the terms you use, Roy."

"Well, anyway, I wised up Mr. Halloway and told him I'd get an interview with you—"

It was Karen's turn to interrupt him. "What is your interest in this, Roy?"

He looked faintly aggrieved. "You'll need someone to handle the sale." One pudgy hand patted the briefcase in his lap. "Got the facts and figures right here. ANPP is being more than generous."

Karen decided to ignore him. She turned toward Halloway. "I'll need more information on this and I'll need time." She moved her legs and felt something under one foot. Looking down she saw she had placed one sandal squarely on Trent's hand. "Sorry," she told him. He nodded and smiled again. She revised her opinion of his looks. Under thick eyebrows, Trent had good hazel eyes and when he smiled his face was charming.

"Think nothing of it," he said and added, "Mr. Halloway's the business manager and I'm a consulting engineer, in case you're wondering."

"We're not here to pressure you," Halloway assured her. "And we're not about to go into details today. I've persuaded Mayor Hampton to call a meeting tomorrow afternoon at the town hall. ANPP feels it's time to bring this out in the open. Cal and I are going to try to explain to the citizens that they will be in little or no danger." He smiled, displaying excellently capped teeth, and continued ruefully, "Right at present they appear convinced that the very least we'll do is drop an H bomb on their community."

"You've had problems?" Karen asked.

It was Trent who answered. He had a slow deep voice. "Understatement, Mrs. Dancer. They haven't got around to stoning us yet, but we're pariahs. We found it wiser not to try to locate in town. We're in a motor hotel between here and Katoma, which makes for a lot of unnecessary driving."

"I'm wondering if some of this feeling has spilled over on me."

Trent raised his eyes to her face. "What do you mean? You only arrived yesterday."

"My daughter and I had rather a nasty time in the drugstore with a group of young hoodlums, and last night someone went into the garage and slashed all the tires on my car to ribbons."

"Unbelievable!" Roy exclaimed. "What a bunch of savages there are in this town!"

Halloway bent forward. "Just a minute, Roy. Let's not build this up too much. It sounds like vandalism, and these days there are vandals everywhere."

"Not in Hampton," Roy said stoutly. "Do you think I'd live and raise my boy here if there was a chance he could associate with that sort of trash? This is a case of spite, a pure case of spite directed at Karen."

Trent gave the man a look of active dislike. "Rather stupid, don't you think? More apt to inspire the opposite result from what the townspeople want. Mrs. Dancer might get spiteful in return and sell her land to a concern they all loathe. And the people here *aren't* stupid. Look at the way Ashley Hampton blocked us for weeks."

Halloway waved his hand. "Right at the moment all I'd like to do is to invite you to attend the public meeting tomorrow, Mrs. Dancer. Come and listen and judge for yourself." He pulled himself out of the low chair and smoothed down his jacket. "Will you do that?"

Karen stood up and faced him. "I'll think about it."

Her cousin stepped forward, his little eyes ugly. "Come on, you can do better than that."

Trent unfolded himself from the ground, coming erect so quickly that he caught Roy's big paunch with his shoulder and sent him reeling back. "Oops, sorry, Paul," Trent said insincerely. He added, "That's up to Mrs. Dancer."

"Entirely," Halloway agreed. Nodding at Karen, he led the way back around the house. Trent winked at Karen and followed him.

Rubbing his stomach, Roy Paul bent to pick up his briefcase. Karen watched him curiously. "Roy, isn't it going to be unpleasant for you and your family in Hampton if this deal does go through?"

He gave the nasty little snicker she remembered so well. "With the money we'll clean up from the sale, who cares about this dump? Vi—you must remember her—will be tickled pink to locate somewhere else. Do the boy good too." His face brightened with pride. "Lad's going to university now in Toronto."

"That's funny." Mac's voice came from the open

kitchen door. She stepped out on the porch. "Heard he was home from school. Expelled, someone said."

"Malicious libel," Roy snarled. "The lad's taking a sabbatical."

"In his first year, two weeks after classes started?" Mac asked innocently.

He darted her a venomous look. "Busybody, aren't you, Mollie? Like everyone else in this godforsaken place!" He stomped away and then stopped at the side of the house. "See you at Cassie's party tonight, Karen," he called back. "Vi will be tickled pink to see you again, and you can meet the boy."

Karen was taken aback. "Are you going?"

"Sure enough, see you."

She stood gazing after him until she felt Mac touch her arm. "Better come in and have a cup of tea, Karie. You look right tuckered out again."

A small figure dashed between them. Karen reached out and grasped an arm.

"Slow down, Jamie. Where are you going in such a rush?"

"Going to get Caesar," Jamie panted. "We're going to play hospital. Dave's going to be doctor and Betsy and me are nurses."

Dave came cantering up, with his sister trailing along behind. He pulled to a halt. In his mouth he held a long strand of grass that bobbed up and down as he said, "I gotta be doctor 'cause I watched my paw butchering a hog. Betsy didn't see. Maw said she was too young."

"And a girl, of course," Karen said. "Great credentials for a doctor, Dave, butchering hogs. Who are your patients?"

"We got a couple of cats in the barn—"

"Ruby and the kitten," Jamie explained.

Betsy waved a doll at Karen. "I found this in the shed, Mrs. Dancer, can we play with it?"

It was a good-sized doll. The head and the long yellow hair was still intact, but it lacked an arm. Karen nodded. "I don't see why not, Betsy. She looks like she could stand to go to a hospital."

"Let's get Caesar," Jamie told the other children, and the three of them raced into the house.

Mac said indulgently, "They're getting along fine and Jamie's having fun."

Karen put her arm through the older woman's as they walked into the house. Mac was talking on at a furious rate, but Karen wasn't listening. She was wondering about Cassie Saunders's party that night and what kind of reception she'd get.

6

LIGHTS GLOWED FROM every lower window of the Saunders house, spilling softly in yellow rectangles over the lawn and flower beds in front. The door stood hospitably ajar, and drifting from it was the strumming of a guitar, voices raised in song, and a mixed hubbub of party noises. Karen, recalling the grim façade of the house in her youth, didn't quite recognize it. She couldn't remember the inside, but from Jim Miles's description, she'd pictured a gloomy dark interior. The hall he ushered her into was far from gloomy. The wainscoting had been sanded down to its original mahogany and glowed a lustrous red-brown against stark white walls. A colorful hanging in an Aztec motif blazed against one wall, and the staircase that led to the upper floor was carpeted in bright orange.

The hall made a vivid impression, and so did their hostess as she hurried to greet them. Karen was braced for a change in Cassie Saunders, but the woman warmly shaking her hand was an utter stranger. A black velvet jumpsuit, acting as a foil for heavy gold jewelry, clung to a tall svelte figure. Her hair had been cut cunningly to set off a deep widow's peak, fine dark eyes were emphasized by skillful makeup, and in the face of a madonna that could have been painted by Raphael was only one odd note. Cassie's lower lip was heavy and full, what an earlier generation would have described as bee-stung. Its size and shape was frankly sensual and had been made more so by an application of dark red lipstick.

"Wonderful," Cassie was telling her. "I was so delighted when Jim phoned and said you were able to come." She looked doubtfully from the door to her right to the arch to her left. "Both drawing rooms are being used; the party's just spilled over. Should I take you around and recite names or would you rather . . . ?" She put one long dark red fingernail to her dark red lips. "I think it would be better if you just wander around. You'll become reacquainted in no time."

Jim draped an arm around Karen's shoulders. "I'll take the girl in hand and shepherd her around."

"No, you won't." Taking his free hand, Cassie tugged him toward her. "I have a job in the kitchen for you." She made a little moue with the lovely mouth. "Mrs. Jasper insisted on bringing something to help with the refreshments—"

"Meat?" Jim asked hopefully.

"A horrible roast of beef. I couldn't hurt her feelings, but I really can't deal with it." The dark eyes swung to Karen. "I'm a strict vegetarian. So . . . Jim will have to carve. Do you mind, Karen?"

"Not in the slightest."

And that was a lie, Karen told herself, as she watched Jim and Cassie walking away. She felt deserted. Would she be able to recognize the people in those rooms or not? Squaring her shoulders, she turned toward the archway and stood in it for a moment, her eyes making a wide sweep of the room. The drawing room was big but hardly

68

large enough for the number of people in it. Some were sitting on divans and chairs, all Swedish modern, others were lounging on cushions scattered over the beige carpeting, and more were standing in groups. They were all young people, in their late teens or early twenties. She recognized Jim's admirer, Jessie, the little waitress from the Casbah, now clad in denims and a fringed shirt. At the far end of the room, surrounded by a ring of boys and girls, was the guitar player. She felt her mouth tightening. Two of the boys had carrot-colored hair and she recognized their profiles. It was Tim and Danny Dimwiddie. When Danny shifted to the right, she could see that the boy strumming the guitar was Chuck. The only concession she could see that he'd made to the party was to change his T-shirt. The one he wore wasn't much cleaner, but across his chest was lettered *Work Is a Four-Letter Word.*

Wrong room, Karen told herself, and retreated toward the other door. This room was just as large, furnished again with Swedish modern, scattered this time over a green rug, but the occupants were much different. The Establishment, she muttered under her breath, and stepped into it.

A tall old gentleman with snowy hair and an overbred face running to a great deal of brow and very little chin moved majestically over to her and held out his hand. She recognized him immediately. He was not only the wealthiest man in town but also the acknowledged social leader.

"Mr. Lofton," she said.

"My dear Mrs. Dancer." He bent over her hand with old-world courtliness, and for a moment she thought he was going to kiss it. "I heard you had returned to Hampton." He pronounced the name of the town as though he might have been saying heaven.

"Yesterday," she told him.

"Come along, my dear, and I'll get you a glass of

punch." Taking her arm he lowered his voice. "It is absolutely necessary to carry a glass of it around with you." He held up his own glass of pale yellow liquid. "Under no circumstances drink it! It's a mixture of grapefruit and lemon juice with some mysterious ingredient I think might be carrot."

Karen laughed. "What on earth do you do with it?"

He bent toward her ear and said in a conspiratorial whisper, "Cassie's plants appear quite used to it. I generally—ah, dump mine in that philodendron over there. We all have our own means of disposal. I understand many of the ladies arrange to take theirs into the—ahem, powder room with them."

He ladled out a glass of punch and presented it to her as though he were handing her a bouquet. Karen was charmed. He took her free arm in a firm grasp, his hand dry and papery against her skin. "I would imagine you may need a little help in—ah, sorting out your old friends."

"Indeed I do." She gazed around the room. "Oh, there's Sybil and Ashley over there. Who is that they're talking to? Why, it's Lottie Hampton. Is Uncle Alfred here?"

"Dear me, no. Lottie keeps him wrapped in cotton wool for fear he may break. And Alfred is far from fragile; he's as tough as I am." He beamed down at her. "Alfred phoned and was positively ecstatic about your little daughter. He tells me I must meet her. He's planning on playing chess with her, and I understand he's hoping for a game of war."

"War?"

"Oh, just with toy soldiers. Alfred has quite elaborate setups for wars—the older ones, of course. The War of 1812 and the Plains of Abraham. Doesn't go for more re-

70

cent ones. Alfred seems to feel all the magic has now been taken out of war."

"It sounds like a game Jamie would enjoy."

Amos Lofton was looking over her shoulder. "We'll start over here." He waved his glass at a group of older men. "Ernie, Bruce, Peter, here's someone you must remember."

She shook hands with Ernie Cross, the editor of the *Hampton News*, Peter Hawkins, a retired grocer, and diminutive Bruce Gotham, who at one time had cut her hair. Then Amos called their wives over, and she shook hands with Mrs. Cross, Mrs. Hawkins, and Mrs. Gotham. Miss Pierce, her literature teacher, was next on the list. Miss Pierce dived into the crowd and returned with Miss Olsen, a tall and hairy woman who had been the bane of Karen's existence in physical education classes.

More followed and Karen's right hand became nearly numb from handshakes, her other clutching the warming glass of punch. She heard her voice repeating endless phrases: "Lovely to be here"; "Yes, we arrived yesterday"; "Jamie? She's eight"; "Yes, at the old house on the farm."

There appeared to be some sort of unspoken agreement on the topics to discuss. The weather—New York versus Ontario—proved popular. Memories in common were allowed. Relationships were discussed and then rediscussed, but one subject was not mentioned. Nuclear power plants were sternly avoided.

Karen appreciated this but it was too good to last. As she was chatting with Mabel Becker, who rejoiced in being the only hairdresser in town, she felt a hand grasp her bare arm. She didn't have to look to know its owner. It was pudgy and damp with perspiration.

"Lovely to be home," she told Mabel, and reluctantly glanced at her cousin.

" 'Lo, Mabel; hi, Karen," Roy said heartily. "Hate to break in on this here tête-à-tête, but Vi is just dying to see Karen. Come on, luv."

Karen tried to shake him loose, but his moist grip was tenacious and he propelled her away from the hairdresser, almost into the arms of a tall statuesque blonde. If Vi was dying to see her, Karen thought, she was concealing it admirably. Her smooth, lacquered face was vapid and her voice matched it.

"How nice," she said, extending a limp hand. The voice denied that anything was nice. It was whispery and languid.

"Very nice," Karen said, just as falsely.

"I don't suppose you remember me."

"Of course I do," Karen answered untruthfully, searching hastily back through the years. "You used to work at—now, it's on the tip of my tongue."

Roy came to the rescue. "The coal and wood office."

"I wanted you to know," the whispery voice went on, "how hard Roy has worked for you, how much it has cost our family as a whole, this unswerving loyalty he has shown you."

While Karen stared speechlessly, Roy chimed in. "Standing foursquare with you, Karen. Nothing I wouldn't do for my favorite cousin." Quite carried away, he waved his glass of punch. Yellow liquid swirled over the rim of the glass and splashed onto the cuff of his shirt.

In his wife's vapid face unexpectedly shrewd eyes scanned Karen's face for her reaction. "Yes, Roy and I, and our boy for that matter, have—" Breaking off she noticed that her husband was trying to hold on to the punch glass and wring out his cuff at the same time. "Oh, for heaven's sake, Roy, give me that stuff." Without even looking around, she tossed the contents of the glass in the large pot behind her. "I swear Cassie's plants thrive on it.

72

Look at the color of that fern. Should try it on my be-
gonias." She appealed to Karen. "Now, what was I saying?"

"I haven't the faintest idea," Karen confessed.

"People are avoiding us," the whisper continued.
"Even tonight, I can see them turning away as we ap-
proach."

I don't blame them, was Karen's agonized thought. I
wish I could have. Aloud, she said, "Just what does this
have to do with me?"

Vi leaned closer. "ANPP!"

Taking a step backward, Karen stared from Roy's
sweaty face to his wife's empty one. She opened her
mouth to make a sharp retort but Roy forestalled her. "Do
you realize, Vi, that Karen's never seen the boy? Go look
him up, will you?"

As Vi languidly swayed off toward the door, Karen
looked around for rescue. There seemed to be no help in
sight. She stared at Amos Lofton's slender back, willing
him to turn around, but he was deep in conversation with
Ernie Cross and his plump wife. At the far end of the room
she caught sight of Jim Miles and waved at him. He was
helping Cassie and Sybil set up a long board over two
sawhorses painted bright orange. When she couldn't
catch his eye she turned back to her cousin. Roy hadn't
stopped talking since his wife had left, and Karen hadn't
caught a word.

"So you have to make up your mind, luv. ANPP won't
wait forever." He gestured. "There's Vi and the boy now."

Vi and a young man were approaching. The woman
had apparently run completely out of energy and was
leaning heavily on her son's arm.

"Our son, Charles," Vi whispered.

Oh, no! Karen thought inwardly, and looked into the

73

eyes of Chuck. He stared insolently back. His lips, in the midst of his scraggy beard, were sneering.

"Well, shake your cousin's hand, Charles!" his father prompted.

Chuck's sneer widened, and he held out a grimy hand. Karen looked icily at it and made no move to take it. "We've met," she told Roy.

"How nice," Vi cooed.

Karen had had enough. "It wasn't nice, or lovely, or charming, at all!" She turned to his father. "We met in Hopper's Drugstore. I was telling you about it this afternoon."

Roy's little eyes widened to their maximum. "The hoodlums?" At Karen's nod he spun toward his son. "If you've queered my pitch, you no-good bum, I'll—"

"Now, now, dear. Don't take on. Boys will be boys. And Karen's too big a person to take a little misunderstanding to heart. Charles didn't even know who she was—"

Roy's wrath descended on his spouse. "You knew about it, didn't you? Why didn't you tell me, Vi?"

While they were engrossed, Karen tried to slip away. Roy noticed her movement and grabbed her arm. The anger faded from his face and he said heartily, "Vi's just dying to have you to supper, luv. Aren't you, Vi?"

"Just dying," his wife echoed and sounded as though she was.

Help, Karen called silently and then help arrived. A small round figure bounced past Chuck, narrowly missed hitting Vi, and flung itself into Karen's arms.

"Karie! Karie Hampton! Welcome home, Karie."

Karen looked down into her best friend Dinah's vivid face. She kissed her warmly and managed to whisper into her ear, "Rescue me, for God's sake!"

Dinah tugged her hand. "Come with me this minute,

74

Karie. We've got twenty years to make up for!" She pulled her past Vi. "Sorry, Roy, didn't mean to step on your foot. Over here, Karie, by the window. This room's stifling."

Thankfully, Karen sank down beside her old friend on a couch next to an open window. Cool air stirred her hair and moved against her flushed face.

Dinah giggled. "I noticed you were pretty flushed up. Heat or the Paul family?"

"A little of both. Thanks!"

"Think nothing of it. I'd have done the same if you'd been my worst enemy. Nobody should fall into their clutches. But forget about them. Tell me about yourself."

"You first."

"Well, for openers, I married Les Gaines. Remember—"

Karen clapped both hands over her ears. "Don't say that *word*. I've heard it several thousand times in the last hour."

"Okay. There he is now. Yoo-hoo, Les!"

Les came over and met Karen. He was Dinah's opposite, as tall as she was short, as gaunt as she was plump, as quiet as she was talkative. Karen liked him immediately. He mentioned he was a lawyer, admitted he had taken over his father's practice, said yes, it was the firm Sybil Hampton worked for, and faded tactfully away to allow the two friends to talk.

Dinah looked after him. "Hopeless situation, Karie, married to the same man for nearly fifteen years, two sons and a daughter, and I'm still wild about him." Turning to Karen, she pointed at the glass she was clutching. "Like to get rid of that?" Karen thrust it into her hand, and Dinah bent over, twitched the curtain aside, and tossed the punch nonchalantly out the window. She grinned. "Each to his own. See Amos Lofton over there sneaking up on the philodendron? Wait until you see the food."

"Does Cassie always serve the same stuff?"

"Always. But she's such a terrific person no one wants to hurt her feelings. She has the stamina of ten people, and if there's an elderly person, a child, or an invalid in town who needs help, our Cassie is right there. She's going to make a great doctor's wife."

"Doctor?"

"Jim Miles. Didn't you know?" When Karen shook her head, Dinah continued, "They have an understanding."

"Are they engaged?"

"Not formally, but they've been going together for two years now and in Hampton that's an open declaration of marriage. What's the matter, Karie, still have something going for Jim?"

Karen glanced at Jim, at his fair head and wide shoulders as he helped Sybil and Cassie with the refreshment table. "I don't know. It was wonderful to see him again but—well, it's all in the past, isn't it? Along with sock hops and chocolate malts and hit records."

Dinah changed the subject. "Tell me about the present. I've been hearing about your little girl. She sounds like a child prodigy."

Karen started to tell Dinah about her daughter. A number of people were now sitting near them, and they fell silent and listened. Sybil and Cassie bustled up to the circle of chairs, each carrying a tall pitcher of punch, and began to refill empty glasses.

"So she's a brain?" Dinah asked.

"Only one side of her. One minute she's trying out five-syllable words, the next she's a third grader again. She carries around an old panda she's had since she was three—"

Cassie put down the pitcher and clapped her hands. "Food, everyone, help yourselves!"

"Oh, Lord," Dinah muttered, and got to her feet.

At the improvised table Mrs. Jasper's roast beef was receiving a rush, the Wheat Thins and carrot sticks were not far behind. As Karen stood indecisively looking at the strange array of food, Jim joined her.

Spearing a slice of meat, he dropped it on her plate. "Avoid that salad and that bowl of mush as if your life depended on it," he cautioned in a low voice.

She looked at the green jellied salad with chunks of pale pink embedded in it. Sybil Hampton was righteously ignoring the roast and spooning up great lumps of the salad. Behind her, Ashley was surreptitiously dueling with Amos Lofton for the last slice of beef.

"What is it?" Karen asked Jim.

"Gelatine flavored with spinach, and that pink stuff is watermelon. In the bowl beside it is yogurt and wheat germ, half and half. Look, is Mac staying with Jamie tonight?"

Karen selected a cracker. "Uh-huh."

He glanced at his watch. "Nearly eleven. Do you think Mac would mind if you stay out a little later?"

"Mac's staying the night. She's probably sound asleep by now."

"Good. We're going to my house and have a steak and a decent drink. How's that sound?"

"Like heaven. But how—"

"Leave it to the doctor." Taking her plate, he set it down on the table and called to Cassie, "Sorry we can't stay, Cassie. Karen just realized how late it is. I'll have to get her home."

Cassie, her madonna face concerned, rounded the table. "What a shame!" She gathered both of Karen's hands into her own. "Come down to the library when you get a chance, and I'll make out a temporary card for you and we can have a chat."

77

Dinah appeared at Cassie's side. "Could you drop by and see Les and me and the kids tomorrow night?"

"I'd love to," Karen told her. "And I'll come in a bit early and stop by the library, Cassie. Thank you so much for the lovely party."

Jim and Karen made their way to the door, saying good night to people as they went. Karen had a warm glow. Everyone was smiling and waving at her. If there was bad feeling among the townspeople, it certainly wasn't evident here.

Outside, the night was clear and cold. Frost was glinting on the grass and their breath came out in little puffs of white vapor. Jim turned his car, drove a block, and pulled up in front of a house with a wide veranda and a cupola. A large modern picture window had been installed in the living room, which made a strange contrast to the narrow windows on either side.

As Jim opened the door, he said, "The big window was Dad's idea and not a bad one. These rooms were so dark before. Come right in, Karen, I'll mix a drink and then broil a couple of steaks I've been saving."

In the lamplight the room was attractively shabby and looked comfortable. Through the big window she could see the frosty lawn and a boxwood hedge. Jim busied himself at a small bar in a corner while Karen wandered around the room. She stopped to look at the family photographs on top of the upright piano and was studying the books in the glass-fronted case when he called to her.

She started over toward him, caught her toe on the edge of the carpet, and cried out. He turned just in time to catch her. She landed in his arms, her head against his shoulder.

"Karen," he murmured. His mouth sought hers in a long kiss before she pulled away.

He smiled down at her. "Should I say I'm sorry?"

"It wouldn't be very gallant," she told him. "And I'm still waiting for that drink."

"Coming right up. Then the steak, then more drinks, then a session with the old school yearbooks, and more drinks—"

"Whoa!"

"Then a session with the old photographs and more drinks. Tonight time doesn't count, Karen."

"One o'clock at the latest," she warned.

It was closer to three when Jim drove up to the brick house outside of town. Climbing out of the car, he came around and helped her out. She noticed he was pulling his jacket tightly around him.

"Where's your topcoat?"

"I must have forgotten it at Cassie's. I'll pick it up tomorrow." He was staring over her shoulder, toward the rear of the house. "There's a light on back there."

"Where?"

"It looks like it's in the barn."

"We'd better check." She walked down the side of the house, avoiding the corner of the grape arbor. "Jamie and the children from the farm were playing out there this afternoon. They might have left a light on."

The barn door was half open and light streamed out from it. Jim cut in front of Karen. "I'll get it." He stepped through the doorway and she heard him exclaim, "My God!"

She peered around his arm. In the center of the floor was a crumpled heap. The tines of a pitchfork glinted in the light, and the handle of the fork made a dark right angle above the bundle. She glimpsed a pink angora sweater and a fall of long blond hair.

"Jamie!" she shrieked.

7

PLANTING A FOOT on the sweater, Jim jerked the fork tines out. "It was driven right through into the boards underneath," he grunted.

Karen stared down at her daughter's old panda. The pink sweater was buttoned over his plump torso and the short legs stuck out ludicrously under it. The toy's round black-and-white face peered sadly out from under the blond wig, the single button eye winking mournfully in the light reflected from the bare bulb dangling over their heads.

Jim shook his head. "God, what a sick joke!"

She shivered. Reaction was setting in. "It's past sick, it's ghoulish. It looked just like Jamie for a moment. That hair—"

"Where in the devil did that come from?"

She pointed to a corner. "Over there."

Striding over, he picked up the one-armed doll that Betsy Jenks had found in the shed. It dangled from his hands, the round head now bald, pieces of loose cotton mesh still glued to it in places. "Took a lot of work to peel that wig off," he muttered. Stooping, he scooped up the panda. "The sweater's ruined, and I'm afraid the toy is too."

She was shaking in earnest now. "Jim, how did they get the panda? Jamie always takes it to bed with her. She—Jamie!"

Suddenly she wanted to see her daughter, to look down at her sleeping face. She hurried across the lawn, tripped over over something, and nearly went sprawling. The clothes pole lay on the ground at her feet. Near it was a white blotch. A handkerchief? she wondered, but she didn't pause. By the time she reached the back door she was running. As she entered the kitchen, the swinging doors thumped open and light from the hall silhouetted Mac's stout form. Karen switched the kitchen light on. Mac was wearing a shapeless robe in a loud tartan pattern and her hair was wound around big plastic rollers.

She clapped one hand to her bosom. "Lawd, Karie, you nearly scared the living daylights out of me."

"Jamie! Is she all right?"

Mac was lifting the milk jug from the fridge. "Just going to get her a cup of hot milk. Woke me up a few minutes ago shrieking loud enough to wake the dead. Had a nightmare."

"She never has nightmares," Karen muttered, and brushed by the older woman.

"Wait up," Mac called but Karen was already going up the stairs, taking them two at a time.

A light was on in the room Mac had been sleeping in and the door was open to Jamie's room. The child was sitting huddled on the side of the bed, her back to her mother, her head turned toward the blank dark rectangle of the window.

Karen took a deep breath. "What's this I hear about you having a bad dream, honey?"

81

Leaping from the bed, the child threw herself in Karen's arms. "It wasn't a dream. Mac said I was dreaming but I wasn't. I *saw* it"—she lifted her face—"as clearly as I see you," she said firmly.

Sinking into a chair, Karen pulled the child onto her knees, brushed the hair away from the pallid little face. "What did you see as clearly as you see me?"

"At the window, Karen! A face, an awful face staring in—"

Karen hugged her. "Calm down, Jamie. Now, start from the beginning."

Behind them the door banged open and Mac came into the room, carrying a mug of steaming milk. At her heels was Jim Miles.

"Jamie, what's all this about a nightmare?" he said.

"It wasn't . . . I wasn't dreaming!" Jamie said, and burst into tears.

Picking up the little girl, Karen sat down on the bed, cradling her in her arms. Jamie buried her head against her mother's shoulder. Mac held out the mug, but Jim shook his head. "Give her a few minutes," he told the old woman.

Mac sank down beside Karen, the springs creaking under her weight. Jamie's sobs were the only sounds in the room. Karen stared at the child in her arms, thinking of the fall of blond hair across the barn floor, the pitchfork protruding from the pink sweater. She closed her eyes, and when she opened them Jim was gently wiping the child's damp face. "Can you tell us about it now?"

She nodded and gulped. "I woke up, and there was something tapping on the window. I got out of bed and went over and looked out and this face . . . this awful face was pressed right against it, and I started to yell and Mac came in . . . she came in and said I was dreaming. I saw it, Jim, right outside the window!"

"Stuff 'n' nonsense." Mac grunted. "This here window's twenty feet from the ground. Youngster's had a nightmare. Dreamed she saw a face."

Karen straightened. "Jim, the clothes pole. I fell over it. There was something white near it. Do you think—"

"I think I'm going down and have a look." He patted Jamie's head. "I think someone played a joke on you, young lady, not a very nice joke."

Mac stared after him. "What's this all about, Karie?"

Karen was holding tightly to her daughter. "You said Jamie yelled pretty loud. Where are Sybil and Ashley? Aren't they home yet?"

"Came in before I went to bed, just after eleven. But there's no way they'd hear anything from this central section in the wing where they sleep." She looked around the room. "Really knew how to build in the days this house went up. Thick walls and two hall doors between here and their bedrooms. Want I should get them?"

"No. No, don't get them." Karen looked down at Jamie.

Jamie put a finger to her mouth. "Karen, I forgot Caesar and my good sweater. I left them outside."

Mac sniffed. "Saw them when I put the milk bottles out."

Karen looked at her. "Where?"

"On the umbrella table. Careless child. I left them there so she'd remember next time to bring them in."

Jamie dabbed at her eyes. "I want Caesar."

Helplessly, Karen looked down at her. "Caesar's had an accident, Jamie. I'm afraid he's . . . look, honey, we'll go downtown tomorrow, and we'll buy a nice new panda—"

"I don't want a new panda! I want Caesar, and I want him *now!*"

"That's enough!" Mac snapped. Her eyes slid to Karen

and behind the heavy lenses the other woman could see tension. Mac's voice softened. "Why don't you ask your momma about that gray kitten again?"

A sudden look of calculation erased the threatened tears from Jamie's small face. "Could I have the kitten?" she asked plaintively. "To take Caesar's place. Please, Karen."

Karen squeezed her. "Yes, you may have the kitten."

"I'll have to name him, and he'll have to be trained. Susie's cat has a litter box. Karen, can I have a litter box and keep the kitten right here in my room?"

"I'll fix it up tomorrow," Mac promised. "Now, don't you go bothering your momma no more."

Jim's heels clicked along the hall. He stepped on a loose board outside the room, and it squeaked in protest. In one hand he held a scrap of white rubber, which he showed to the little girl. "There's your awful face, Jamie. Someone did play a trick on you." He handed it to Karen and she stretched it out in her hands as Jim explained. "It's a white balloon, with a face drawn on it in black ink or paint. It was tied to the top of the clothes pole. Whoever did it tapped on the window with the pole and then held that thing up against the glass."

The balloon had heavy brows and slanted eyes drawn on it. Under a round nose was a wide mouth full of jagged teeth. Take a sleepy little girl, she thought, hold it up a few inches from her eyes in the middle of the night . . . Karen shivered.

Jamie said it for all of them. "It wasn't funny!"

"No, it wasn't," Jim agreed. "It was a lousy thing to do. Now, I'd better get along home. Want to walk me to the door, Karen?"

Standing up, Karen handed the child to Mac. "Would you put her back to bed, please?"

Jamie pulled at her arm. "Can I sleep with you tonight, Karen, can I?"

"Yes, you may, this once. Hop into my bed and I'll be up directly."

As Karen and Jim left the room, they heard Mac scolding the child. "Taking all the advantage you can get, aren't you? That's the trouble with youngsters. Offer a hand and they take the whole arm. But go on, get into your momma's bed, and I'll sit with you till she comes back."

As they went down the staircase, Jim laughed. "Sounds as though Mac is accusing Jamie of being an opportunist."

"With good reason. But there's no way I can say no to her tonight."

He stopped by the front door. The ceiling light cast heavy shadows downward across his face, emphasizing the lines across his forehead, the deeper ones bracketing his mouth. "You're pretty shaken, aren't you?"

"Yes."

"Don't be. A couple of stupid practical jokes—"

"Aimed at a child." Her mouth hardened. "A deliberate effort to terrorize a little girl. And that thing in the barn. I was meant to think just what I did, that it was Jamie there, pinned to the floor by that fork." Her eyes searched his face. "And you, Jim. You knew yesterday that Roy Paul's boy was the one called Chuck. You could have told me."

"I nearly did. I nearly blurted out when you were talking about their hillbilly speech that one of them was going to university. Put yourself in my place. Would you want to tell someone their own cousin had been in on that harassment?"

"Harassment," she said slowly. "Ever since we drove into Hampton. That's the right word. First those boys, then my tires, now this . . . this foulness." She glanced up at his intent face. "Are you going to the meeting to-morrow?"

"ANPP? No. My afternoon schedule is full. My advice to you would be to stay clear of it also."

"I hadn't intended to go, but now nothing could keep me away."

8

THE HAMPTON TOWN hall was located on what at one time had been a market square. Now the hall stood in solitary grandeur at the end of a long raised cement ramp. For the size of the town it was rather an imposing structure. The brick and gray stone used in many of the other buildings had been ignored when it came time to build this one. The original clapboard had been stuccoed over, and the front had a high peaked roof supported by six Grecian pillars based on a wide portico. On both sides of the ramp leading to it, vehicles of all makes, models, and ages were nosed in.

Gazing up at the building, Karen thought of the difficulties she had encountered so far that day in getting to it. When she had gone to check her car that morning she found that although the ragged pieces of rubber had been swept off the garage floor her tires were still mangled.

She had stormed into the house, where Mac had clapped a hand to her mouth. "Dad-burn it," she muttered. "Clean forgot to tell you. Jake Squeers phoned yesterday to say he didn't have the right size in stock and would have to send for them. Said to tell you it'd take a couple of days." She brightened. "Solves one problem. Guess you won't be able to get to that meeting, eh?"

"Wrong," Karen told her grimly. "You walk farther than that every day. So can I."

The next obstacle had proved to be Jamie. Karen had been dressing when the child came upstairs to check on the gray kitten, now shut into her little room with bowls of food and water and an improvised litter box.

"Where are you going?" she asked her mother.

Pulling the amber dress over her head, Karen knotted the leather tie around her waist. "To the town hall for a public meeting, honey."

"I want to go with you."

"Sorry, it's strictly for adults. You'll have to stay here with Mac. Perhaps Betsy and Dave can come over and play—"

"I won't stay here!"

Jamie jumped on her mother's bed and thumped the pillow with hard little fists. Picking up the hairbrush, Karen looked from it to her daughter's set face. It was a tempting thought; Jamie was making too much mileage on the loss of Caesar. She waved the brush. "You'd better behave, Jamie, or you'll get a touch of this on your bottom."

The child looked from the brush to her mother's face. She changed her tactics. "Couldn't I walk in with you and stay with Uncle Alfred? The other day he said he'd be glad to have me."

Sighing, Karen started to brush her hair. "I'll phone him, but—"

"If he says no I'll stay here with Mac," Jamie said eagerly.

Uncle Alfred proved to be willing. "By all means bring her in, Karen. Come a little early." His voice dropped to a

88

conspiratorial whisper. "I have a bottle of port that Lottie doesn't know about. Amos Lofton brought it to me. He has a fine cellar. We'll have a small glass."

The small glass proved to be a good-sized cut-glass goblet. Alfred served it in his library. Holding the goblet up, he looked approvingly at its contents. "Fine color," he told his niece. He turned to Jamie. "Now, Jennifer, let's look the battlefield over. I made it myself of plastic and papier-mâché. It's true to scale and as authentic as the real thing. These are the Plains of Abraham, and here is the spot where General Wolfe led his gallant men up the cliffs."

Both mother and child looked admiringly at the battle-field spread out on the long plywood table. Alfred was lifting cardboard boxes down from the shelf over it. He opened one and took out a tiny soldier in a gaily painted red uniform. The figure was mounted on a miniature prancing white horse.

"Did you make these too?" Jamie asked, lifting up a foot soldier.

"No indeed, these are antiques. Quite fragile, so we must handle them with care." He produced two sheets of closely written script. "Here are all the moves in the bat-tle: Montcalm and the French troops against the English under General Wolfe. You take this one, Jennifer. It de-scribes General Montcalm and the French—"

"I want to be General Wolfe," Jamie said firmly.

This time the child had met her match. "Nonsense. I'm *always* General Wolfe!"

"Why?"

"Because of this." He held up the soldier on the white horse. "This is the general, and I have him."

"Does Wolfe win?"

"Of course." He lowered one eyelid in a wink. "But you'll give me a fight, won't you?"

Finishing her wine, Karen said goodbye to the two bending over the table, received a nod from her uncle and an abstracted wave from her daughter, and left the house. She took her time walking over to the townhall, and when she arrived she stood outside for a few minutes, looking up at the building and the people mounting the shallow steps. She knew she was trying to put off the minute when she must enter herself. Finally she shrugged and walked across the ramp, up the steps, and through the wide doorway.

Two women were slightly ahead of Karen, and she followed them up the staircase to a narrow hallway and a set of double doors standing open. Under a NO SMOKING sign a group of young men were gathered, watching the people filing past. The Dimwiddie brothers were there, and near them was Bob Hopper. Directly under the sign that forbade smoking Chuck Paul lounged, a cigarette drooping from his mouth. She expected the Dimwiddies to make some remark. The one called Danny opened his mouth, received Chuck's elbow in his ribs, and snapped it shut. Lifting her chin, Karen walked past them into the room beyond. She now had her bearings. This was the place used for meetings and for dances. Folding wooden chairs, showing signs of long use, were drawn up in rows with a wide aisle between them. The room was crowded with people.

Pausing inside the doors, she looked for an empty chair. Six young girls were sitting in the last row. Jessie, the waitress from the restaurant, was one of them, and next to her were several empty seats. Karen was about to take the one on the end when she heard her name called. Sybil Hampton was standing in the aisle about halfway down the room. She waved to her cousin.

"Down here," she called. "We saved a seat."

The "we" turned out to be Dinah Gaines and Cassie

Saunders. As Karen took the aisle seat beside Sybil, Cassie smiled at her and Dinah leaned across the librarian's knees.

"We'd just about given you up, Karie."

"I had to walk in, and then I dropped Jamie off with Uncle Alfred."

"Walk?" Cassie echoed. "What's wrong with your car?"

"It's a long story," Karen told her, and sat back in her seat.

She was conscious of the heat. Several of the long windows were open, but with the number of people crowded into the room they didn't help much. It was a curiously quiet crowd. Any conversations appeared to be taking place in whispers. Almost everyone was staring at the platform at the front of the room. Three chairs and a low table were positioned at the right side of the platform, and the same setup was on the far left. At an equal distance between them was a lectern supporting a large jug of water, a glass, and a wooden gavel. The lectern appeared to be the division between two enemy camps. On the left-hand side Vince Halloway was seated between Roy Paul and Trent. On the right side Amos Lofton was flanked by a burly middle-aged man and a shriveled little figure who bore a marked resemblance to a mummy. Leaning gracefully against their table was Ashley Hampton. Ashley looked as though he were in mourning. His well-cut suit was black, and a narrow black tie bisected a snow-white shirt.

Karen's eyes moved back to the representatives of ANPP. For a moment she thought Roy was talking to Halloway. His jaws were moving rhythmically. Then she decided he must be chewing gum because Halloway was turned away from him, speaking rapidly to Cal Trent.

91

Trent looked as though he were dozing. His eyes were half shut, but as she watched he nodded.

Who are the two men with Amos Lofton?" she asked Sybil.

"Doc Jarvis and—"

"Who?"

"Doc Jarvis, the vet. You must remember his son, Jack. You went to school with him. Jack married Leticia Graves. She's sitting right up there."

Karen followed her cousin's eyes. A number of young matrons were sitting two rows in front of them. The one Sybil was looking at was a stout woman with ruddy skin and untidy brown hair.

"The one on the other side of Amos is Mr. Evans."

"Not the one with the hardware store? He was over seventy when I lived here."

Sybil nodded. "Still going strong. Little hard of hearing, but he opens his store every morning. Amos and the other two are on town council."

Karen wondered silently how the old man could open anything. His face looked like a skull, with tufts of mossy hair clinging to it here and there. She gazed around the room. In one corner she spotted Nat Jenks and his wife. Maudie wore a bright cotton print and her husband had deserted his overalls and was attired in an old serge suit that looked two sizes too small. He had been staring at her, but as she met his eyes he looked away, his lips dragging downward even more. Across the aisle she met another pair of eyes, those of Miss Olsen. The former physical education teacher gave her a hostile glare but Miss Pierce, who was beside her, leaned forward and waved a tiny hand. Karen waved back. A voice spoke from the platform and she looked up. Ashley was now at the lectern.

Clearing his throat, he called, "All right, boys, choose one side of that door or the other but get it closed."

Necks craned around, and Karen darted a quick look over her shoulder. Bob Hopper, red-faced and flustered, was leading the way into the room with the other boys trailing along. Chuck Paul was the last one to enter, and he shut the door and slid in beside his friends, who had taken seats beside the young girls at the back.

The gavel banged and Ashley cleared his throat again. "This meeting will now come to order."

The whispering stilled immediately. Leaning one elbow on the lectern, Ashley swept the room with his dark blue gaze and started to speak.

"Just to clarify the issue, this meeting wasn't my idea. Mr. Halloway requested it be called. Now you all know Mr. Halloway." He paused while his audience acknowledged this fact by throat clearing and a few isolated hisses. The gavel banged smartly down. "This will be an orderly meeting," Ashley stated firmly. He thought this over and then continued. "Mr. Halloway is not a stranger in town. He wants to speak to you people about the power plant his company is trying to force on Hampton. A nuclear plant." He appeared to think this over, liked his wording, and repeated more forcefully, "A *nuclear* plant." More hisses greeted this, but Ashley didn't reach for his gavel. "I think, fellow citizens, that Mr. Halloway may be going to tell you that this plant is going to be good for you. A little radiation may even make you feel better." A wave of guffaws swept the room and he waited patiently, a faint smile touching his lips. "Now, with no further ado, I will call upon Mr. Halloway." Vince Halloway started to rise and then sat down as Ashley continued, "Nearly forgot to tell you that Mr. Halloway and his associate represent ANPP. In case you don't know what that stands for, it's Allied Nuclear Power Plants. I figure the reason they prefer initials is so they don't have to say *nuclear* too often."

Sybil hissed in Karen's ear. "Isn't Ashley wonderful at public speaking?"

Apparently the audience agreed. As Ashley made an ironic little bow toward Halloway, a storm of applause broke out. Three men in the front row were so carried away that they leaped to their feet to give him a standing ovation. Karen recognized Ernie Cross as one of them. She wondered about the lead story Cross would write for the *Hampton News*.

Vince Halloway waited until the noise died away, got slowly to his feet, and approached the podium. The audience was now quiet. Not coughs, throat clearing, or shuffling of feet could be heard. The very silence was unnerving. It must have been even more so to the man standing facing the ranks of quiet people, but Halloway showed no signs of nervousness. He positioned a notebook in front of him, opened it, poured a glass of water, and took a sip. Then he began to speak, his voice deep and resonant, carrying to the back of the room.

"Mr. Mayor, members of the town council"—he inclined his head to the right—"and citizens of Hampton. After Mayor Hampton's stirring introduction, anything I have to say may sound anticlimactic."

"Speak English!" a voice shouted from the rear of the room.

Halloway continued as though he hadn't been interrupted. "However, there are a few points Mayor Hampton didn't touch on." He looked earnestly around. "I am not going to try to tell you that there is absolutely no danger from a nuclear installation—"

"Damn right you aren't!" shouted the same voice.

"—but I *am* going to tell you that every safety device known to modern technology will be installed in this plant. I will call upon Mr. Trent in a few minutes to explain what this entails. I also feel it important to dwell on

94

the need for what this plant will produce. You are all aware that our resources are being rapidly exhausted. The world of today needs light and power; the world your children will inherit—"

"Children!" a harsh voice growled from his right. Doc Jarvis was on his feet. "I got a couple of grandchildren I'm concerned about right now. They're not going to live in a town with danger from fallout and radiation. They're not going to grow up going to school and rubbing elbows with every ragtag foreigner you people pull into this town." Doc Jarvis tore his angry eyes from Halloway and beamed them around the room. "You folks all know about Jack; you know these kids are the only grandchildren I'll have. Stand up there, 'Ticia, and tell the folks how you feel."

He pointed a finger at his daughter-in-law, and Leticia Jarvis lurched to her feet. She swung around and faced the rows behind her, her fleshy face as red as her father-in-law's. "My kids aren't going to school with no Hunkies, Spics, Chinks, or Japs," she shrieked and plumped back down on her chair again.

A roar of approval greeted this statement. Charming woman, Karen thought. Aloud, she whispered to Sybil, "Is Jack Jarvis dead?"

"Lordy no, Jack had a vasectomy last year after his third child was born. Doc and 'Ticia have done everything but disown him."

Doc Jarvis strode over to Halloway. "You going to pretend you won't be bringing foreigners in here?"

Halloway looked steadily back. His face was expressionless, but his distaste showed in his voice. "We employ technicians on the basis of their ability, not on their race or national origin."

"Yeah," another voice snarled. Nat Jenks was on his feet, his lips pulled down almost to his chin and his big wrists protruding redly from blue serge sleeves. "I say it

95

too. My kids ain't gonna grow up with no furrin brats!" He considered this before adding, "And what about our cows? Gonna poison them too?"

More clapping mixed with boos and catcalls greeted this clear thinking. Miss Olsen managed to cheer, thump the back of the seat directly ahead of her with an umbrella, and direct a malicious glare at Karen simultaneously.

Halloway made no attempt to shout them down. Turning away from Doc Jarvis, he calmly consulted his notebook. The veterinarian stared at the other man's back for a moment and then stomped back to his seat. Halloway didn't raise his head until the volume of noise lessened and finally subsided. Then he said slowly, "It isn't as though Hampton doesn't already have an industry to set a precedent. The Lofton Factory has been operating in this town for the past hundred years—"

"Closer to one hundred and fifty," a cold voice cut in. It was Amos Lofton's turn. He stood erectly, his hands folded across his chest. Under the high forehead his eyes steadily regarded the man at the lectern. "Don't become confused about my factory. I manufacture fine china and pottery. Lofton products are highly regarded the length and breadth of this continent, but mine is a small concern. Only a hundred employees are on my payroll, and they come from families who have worked at Lofton for several generations." Casting his eyes toward the ceiling, he pursed his lips and added emphatically, "And I will fight to my dying breath to protect the citizens of this town from your dangerous concern!"

Another wild round of applause broke out. Ernie Cross was on his feet, and so was Leticia Jarvis. Karen saw Miss Olsen leap up and haul little Miss Pierce upright. Shouts of "Well said!" and "Tell him, Amos!" and "That's the stuff!" sounded from every corner of the room.

This time Halloway did shout. "Now that you've heard from your feudal lord, perhaps you'll give Calvin Trent a chance!" As they quieted he turned to Trent. "Mr. Trent is an engineer with degrees from both the University of Wisconsin and the University of—"

"Damn foreigner!" a voice bellowed.

"—of Washington," Halloway continued doggedly. "He is here to explain the technical details and to answer any of your questions on safety precautions."

Hauling his long body off his chair, Trent slouched toward the lectern. As Halloway passed the engineer, he patted him on the shoulder. Trent gave him a wry grin. Not too different from throwing another martyr to the lions, Karen thought. Trent didn't step behind the lectern, he leaned against its side, one elbow bracing him. He cut a very different figure from Halloway. He was still wearing the suede jacket over a turtleneck sweater and denim pants.

"Kind of interesting to see a nice orderly meeting and find how fair you people are," he drawled. "I figure it's not much use talking sense because you won't listen to me any more than you did to Mr. Halloway." He paused and added, "Any of you good people got any questions?"

"Yeah," Nat Jenks snarled. "Why don't you go back to the States, furriner?"

Unhurriedly, Trent swung his shaggy head toward the farmer. "I'm home. Right now I'm not too proud of it, but I'm a Canadian."

"Prove it," Jenks yelled.

Trent patted his hip. "Got my voter's registration right here in my wallet. You come up here and I'll show it to you."

"Still a damn furriner," Jenks growled. He spun around and yelled, "We gonna sit here and listen to any more of this shit?"

97

In answer a pop bottle looped over his head and landed on the platform. Trent glanced down, drew back his foot, and booted it away. It crashed at Ernie Cross's feet and shattered. Pandemonium broke loose.

Roy Paul got to his feet, his bulging briefcase clutched to his chest. His face was colorless and Karen expected him to beat a hasty retreat. To her surprise he waddled over to the lectern and stood beside Trent.

"Listen!" he shouted. Despite his pallor his forehead was spangled with beads of sweat. "Listen to me! I'm not a stranger. You all know me. This is Hampton, and my mother was a Hampton!"

"Better believe we know you, Roy!" a female voice shrieked.

"Spit it out, Paul!" a male voice echoed.

Roy took a deep breath. Karen could see his chest rise and then fall. She felt faint from the stifling heat of the closely packed bodies, faint from the feeling of violence generating from those bodies.

"Sure I'll spit it out," Roy yelled. "ANPP isn't going to hurt our town. It's going to bring prosperity to Hampton. The merchants are going to get more trade. This town is going to boom! And you're all going to be in on that boom. Houses will be built, more schools will go up, we'll get a decent hospital. Hampton's got to grow. If it doesn't, it'll die. And you'll die with it." He caught his breath and then called, "What's your answer?"

Almost before the last word was out of his mouth, he got it. Someone yelled, *"You're* going to be the first to die!" and something came flying through the air and hit him on the chin. For one bad moment it looked like a white-colored rock, but it split on impact and liquid dribbled down his chin and onto the pudgy hands clutching the briefcase.

"Roy's got egg all over his lying face," a young voice chortled.

Someone tittered, and then laughter spread from one person to another, filling the hall with sounds that were worse than the shouting and booing had been. The laughter had a bad sound, an ominous sound. Karen found she was biting her lip.

Roy Paul stood there, egg dripping down his face and sweat beading his brow, with a dignity and courage that Karen wouldn't have believed possible. Taking one sticky fist from his briefcase, he extended a forefinger and pointed it straight at her.

"There's another Hampton here," he called, his squeaky voice breaking. "Get up, Karen, and let them know who you are and where you stand."

Karen had no intention of getting up. She shrank back in her chair, cursing Roy Paul silently. As though alarmed that someone might think they were standing up to be counted, the rest of the people hastily sank back to their seats, leaving Cal Trent and Roy the only ones still on their feet. Trent stood as though he'd fallen asleep, held up by an elbow braced on the lectern, and Roy clutched his briefcase with one hand and pointed at Karen with the other.

Sybil tipped the balance. Her fingers closed like a vise on Karen's knee. "Don't you dare!" she hissed. "Sit where you are."

Karen looked from the hand gripping her knee to the fat, perspiring man on the platform. The ranks of people in front of her were turning, like a many-headed monster with one body, and their faces, faces she had known all her life, were suddenly those of strangers. She glanced over the rows of people to her cousin. You poor fool, she thought, and found she was getting to her feet. Sybil clutched tenaciously at her but Karen wrenched herself loose.

She stood erect, her head up, and looked back at the rows of blank staring faces. "My mother," she told them in a clear ringing voice, "was one of those foreigners you're talking about."

"Another bloody furriner," a voice blurted somewhere behind her, and the next moment something thudded against the back of her head.

An egg, she thought incredulously. She felt moisture trickling down her neck. She spun around and something soft squished across the bridge of her nose. It spattered across her eyes, temporarily blinding her. She felt her way out into the aisle, turned to leave the hall, and took two steps. A foot slashed across her instep, another hit her behind the knee, and she fell forward. She put her arms out to save herself and felt the jolt from the fall all the way up through her body as she went sprawling. Whatever had hit her face was trickling into the corner of her mouth. Not egg, she thought detachedly, it tasted like tomato. She groped at her face with one hand, trying to wipe the pulp away from her eyes so she could see. She heard chairs scraping back and fought down panic.

Then there was a hand under her armpit and she was dragged to her feet. "Hold steady," a voice murmured in her ear. "Time for us furriners to clear out before they decide to have a lynching party."

She still couldn't see, but she could walk and she did. Cal Trent slid an arm around her waist and they left the room, made their way down the stairs, and came out into the clear autumn air of Hampton.

9

KAREN WRIGGLED HER shoulders against the leather seat of Cal Trent's sport car and mopped at her face with the handful of tissues he had handed her.

He reached toward the ignition. "Any better?"

"Not much, but at least I can see now." She pulled her shoulders away from the seat. "I'm getting your seat filthy."

"It will wash." He started the car. "Where to?"

Karen shook a dazed head. "Jamie's at my uncle's. I suppose I should pick her up."

"Better have second thoughts on that." He gave her a wide grin. "You have no idea what you look like."

She looked down at the red stains down the front of her dress. "Probably like the tail end of a massacre. You're right, it might frighten both Jamie and Uncle Alfred. Could you drive me home so I can clean up?"

Trent backed the car out from between a dusty pickup and a late-model sedan. "Can do."

To Karen's relief, he made no effort at conversation. I'm still in shock, she told herself, shocked and grateful to this man for getting me out of there. When he drew the car to a stop in front of the garage, she climbed out, looked ruefully at the stains on the seat, and said, "Thanks so much—"

"Think nothing of it." He slid out of the car. "I'll wait for you and drive you back down to get your daughter."

She didn't argue. As they mounted the flight of steps to the front door she found she was limping. The blow on the back of her leg must have pulled a muscle, she decided. In the open doorway Mac stood, her hands on her hips, her chin jutting.

"What's that red stuff all over you, Karie?" she demanded.

"Tomato. Little disturbance at the town hall."

"From the way you're walking I'd say more than a little. Doesn't surprise me. I told you not to go." The round glasses turned toward the man behind Karen. "Who are you?" she demanded.

He grinned up at her. "You know who I am. I saw you with your nose pressed against the screen in the back door when we were here yesterday. You were eavesdropping."

"No other way a body can find out what's going on," Mac admitted shamelessly. "Didn't catch your name."

"Calvin Trent, but you can call me Cal."

"Umph! You can call *me* Mrs. MacLean!"

Turning smartly on her heel, Mac strode down the hall toward the kitchen. Karen hesitated at the foot of the stairs but Trent waved toward them, the grin on his face broadening. "Go on up and clean up. I'll beard the dragon in her lair—or should I say the cook in her kitchen?"

Much to Karen's surprise, when she came down again he was sitting comfortably at the kitchen table, eating a large slice of cherry pie and sipping a glass of milk. Opposite him, Mac watched with approving eyes.

"Lanky men can always pack food away," she told him. "Guess you make good money at this engineering, eh?"

"Fair," he said, around a mouthful of pie.

"You married?"

"Mac!" Karen said sharply.

"Not right at present," Trent told the old woman. "I was for a while when I was young and callow. We got divorced."

Mac shrugged heavy shoulders. "Lots of divorces nowadays." She turned owlish eyes on Karen. "You look some better."

Karen admitted she felt better. She had taken a quick shower, washed the foodstuff from her hair, and put on clean clothes. After running a critical gaze over Karen, Mac turned her attention back to Trent.

She crooked a thumb at Karen. "Good-looking female, Cal."

He pushed back his plate. "Sure is, Mac."

"Mac?" Karen echoed.

But Mac was looking past Trent to the door. "What you youngsters want?"

Betsy and Dave Jenks had their noses pressed against the screen. "Is Jamie home yet?" the little girl asked.

"Not yet," Mac told them.

Swiveling around, Trent looked at the two children. "You two like to go swimming?"

Betsy ducked her head bashfully but Dave said eagerly, "Sure do, mister."

Trent glanced up at Karen. "How about picking up your daughter and we'll take the three of them swimming? There's a good pool at my hotel, and you and I can have a drink on the patio beside it, sun ourselves, and keep an eye on them."

Dave pushed the door open and dragged his sister into the kitchen. "We ain't got our suits here, mister."

"We'll stop by and pick them up. What about it, Mrs. Dancer?"

"I'm not sure Mr. Jenks would like it . . . after what happened today."

Mac got ponderously to her feet. "I'll phone over and fix it up. Nat Jenks's bark is worse'n his bite. Well, what are you waiting for? Get going."

Bending over her, Trent planted a resounding kiss on her cheek. "Thanks, Mac. Don't wait supper."

She smiled widely at him. "I won't. Have a good time, hear?"

All the way to her uncle's house, Karen thought of Mac's rapid about-face. As Trent pulled up to the curb before the Lovatt house, she muttered, "Certainly charmed Mac, didn't you?"

"I have that effect on females over fifty and under fifteen. Want me to come in with you?"

She climbed out of the low seat. "You'd be wasting your time. Jamie's got her own personal charmer in there. I'll only be a minute."

As she walked up to the house, Trent swung around and started to talk to the Jenks children. The girl ducked her head down but the boy was responding. Karen found herself hoping her uncle hadn't heard about the fiasco at the town hall. She had been fighting off the shakes, the alarming tendency for her hands and lips to quiver. Wonderful place to come to restore nerves, she told herself morosely.

When her uncle opened the door, his face was flushed and his hair looked as though he had been running his fingers through it.

He said indignantly, "It would appear, Karen, that the French won the Battle of the Plains of Abraham!"

Jamie peered around his arm, her cheeks pink and her eyes dancing. He gestured at her.

"This daughter of yours brought up all her cannons, caught my men in a crossfire, and annihilated my troops. Of course, she cheated flagrantly and refused to follow the rules of battle."

Jamie smiled up at him. "You told me to give you a fight."

"You cheated, you young minx. I demand a rematch!"

Karen tapped her daughter's shoulder. "Run along out to the car, Jamie. Betsy and Dave are waiting for you. You're going swimming."

The child sped down the walk and Alfred peered over Karen's shoulder. "Whose car is that? It looks like the one that young fellow from ANPP drives."

"It is."

"Do you think it wise to be seen in public with him? The townspeople may start to think—"

"I'm afraid it's a bit late for that, Uncle Alfred."

"What do you mean?"

"When Lottie gets home you'll hear all about it. Now, I must run. Thanks for entertaining Jamie."

He smoothed down his ruffled hair. "I found it most stimulating. Be sure to bring her back soon. I must set history straight and have General Wolfe lead his men to victory."

Waving a hand at him, she returned to the car. Jamie was in the back, squeezed between her two friends. Her hand was on Trent's shoulder and she was talking animatedly to him.

Karen gave him sidelong look. "Another victim of your charm?"

"Well, she *is* under fifteen."

All the way out to the hotel, the children chattered nonstop. The place was a modern complex, sprawling around a central paved area that contained a large pool, cabanas, and a scattering of chairs and tables shaded by colorful plastic umbrellas. Trent found an empty table near the shallow end of the pool, seated Karen at it, and left to help the children change. In a short time the three were splashing around in the water. Dave Jenks immediately established his dominance by ducking both shrieking little girls. As Trent was returning to the table he saw this and strode to the edge of the pool.

"No more of that," he told the boy.

Dave shook wet hair off his freckled face. "Or what?"

"Or I'll wade in there and break every bone in your body," Trent told him pleasantly.

As he sat down opposite her, Karen smiled. "You have an unusual way with children, Mr. Trent."

"Unusual but effective, and forget the mister. If Cal is good enough for Mac, it's good enough for you." He waved at a waitress. "What would you like?"

"A gimlet."

"Make that two." He turned back to Karen. "I've bribed an off-duty waitress to play lifeguard for the kids. Linda's a good swimmer and is crazy about children."

"I take it she's under fifty."

"Barely over fifteen. Here she comes now." He gestured at the girl approaching them. She had a good build and the scanty bikini showed every curve. She wrinkled her nose at Trent.

"Which ones, Mr. Trent?"

He pointed them out. "Keep a wary eye on the boy. He's a handful."

"Will do," she promised, and plunged into the water.

Their glasses were set in front of them and Karen picked hers up. Her hand was shaking again, and some of the icy fluid sloshed over the rim. Raising the glass to her mouth, she took a long drink. "You seem to have everything organized."

"Right. Feel free to get loaded. It wouldn't hurt you at all. Now, to get acquainted. I've given my full pedigree to Mac and I'll do the same for you. I think she was looking me over for potential husband material."

"Not for her. Mac is concentrating on marrying me off. What's the pedigree?"

Without asking if she wanted it, he lit two cigarettes and passed one over. "I'm giving you an extra detail that is top secret. My full name is Calvin Peter Trent—"

"Is Peter top secret?"

"I'll tell you when we get to the secret part. I'm forty-one, reasonably healthy, and fairly solvent. I was born and raised in Winnipeg, but I prefer British Columbia and have a house I built on Vancouver Island that I don't use as often as I'd like to. It looks old, Spanish style, but has all the modern conveniences. There's a central courtyard with a lot of roses and rather a nice fountain—"

"It sounds charming."

"Don't interrupt. Jamie tells me it's a deplorable habit. Where was I? Oh, yes, marital status. I was married for a brief time when I was too young to know better, but fortunately my bride ran off with my best friend—"

"Fortunately?"

"You interrupted again. Fortunately because the girl had the makings of a shrew. It wasn't passion that inspired her to run away but the idea that Dick could offer her more in a material way than I could. She was mistaken about that but only discovered it after we were safely divorced." Breaking off, he looked closely at her. "I wish your lower lip would stop trembling."

"I can't help it." Gingerly she touched her mouth. "One reason I came back here was that I needed a rest. Nerves."

"I know. Jamie told me all about it."

"She seems to have told you a great deal."

He gave her the smile that made his whole face light up. "She talked a blue streak." He motioned to the waitress, and she set fresh drinks in front of them. "Drink up."

"Are you trying to get me drunk?"

"Yes. I will now get to the top secret information, for your ears only. You're wondering exactly why you're here, aren't you? Got a few doubts about my motive."

Shrugging, she turned to watch the children. Linda was swimming along, towing Jamie on her back, while Dave and Betsy churned the water up around them. Karen could hear the sounds of the children's voices, laughter and yells from the other swimmers, and canned music in the background. Trent was quite right; she did have a few second thoughts about why she was there.

"You're with ANPP," she told him frankly. "It occurred to me that you're trying a soft sell."

"I thought so. Allow me to disillusion you. I'm on loan to ANPP, not *with* them. There's a difference. I was hired to pick a site, and as a matter of fact my job is done. I've just been hanging around as moral support for Vince Halloway, who happens to be a personal friend. That part everyone knows. What isn't known is that I picked not one site but two."

"Two!"

He emptied his glass and caught the waitress's eye. "I'll admit that the better one is on your property but the other site will do. And it has the added advantage of being located near a fair-sized city that already has a large amount of industrial development, which means the locals may be more amenable to the idea of the plant than they are in Hampton. So you see I couldn't care less whether you decide to sell to ANPP or not."

"Tell me, if my property is so vital can't the company force the issue? Couldn't they expropriate it?"

Over the rim of his glass, he grinned at her. "That would get you nicely off the hook, wouldn't it?" He sobered. "Not in this case. Only a public body can do that." He put his glass back on the table. "You've sidetracked me. I started to tell you about my motives. My interest in you is purely personal."

Karen looked directly at him. "Why?"

His hazel eyes looked back into hers. "Because, Karen Dancer, from the moment I saw you sitting under that umbrella when that buffoon of a cousin of yours herded Vince and me into the yard, I've wanted to see more of you. Did anyone ever tell you that you have beautiful bones?"

"All the Hamptons have."

"Ah, but the Hampton's don't have eyes and hair exactly the same shade. Did anyone ever tell you that you have amber eyes and hair and that those eyes light up like spotlights?"

"Yes," Karen said.

"To get back to our first meeting. I said to myself, There she is after all these years. Now, I don't intend to rush you into a hasty marriage. You have at least two days to think it over—"

"You're utterly mad!"

"I have company." His voice changed. "Whatever made you do a damn fool thing like standing up as a target at that meeting?"

She dropped her eyes. "So . . . I'm mad too. I didn't intend to, but when I saw Roy standing there with egg dripping down his face and heard all those asinine remarks about foreigners . . . I just jumped up." She added slowly, "My mother was one of the foreigners they despise. She was of Italian descent."

"My mother was Hungarian, and the sweetest woman who ever lived," he told her. "Anyway, that made up my mind for me. Mad . . . possibly. Gutsy . . . definitely. When I saw you standing there with your chin up and your eyes blazing, I told myself, That's my girl!"

"So you fished me out with tomato all over my face. What do you think of Hampton?"

He twisted in his chair to find a more comfortable position. "Hampton is a town full of regressors—"

"What?"

"Regressors. I've hit other towns like this. Generally made up of small inbred groups. Roy Paul was right about one thing: Eventually they die. The families dwindle down, as they are doing in Hampton, and the town dies. I understand you're seeing it for the first time in twenty years. How does it strike you?"

"The same as it was twenty years ago."

"And what was it like twenty years ago?"

"Medieval. I'll admit they're back in the nineteenth century."

"At least. Don't let the modern clothes or appliances fool you. They read about the world, the overpopulation, the pollution, the danger of nuclear war, but it never really . . . touches them. Their lives are bounded by the limits of the town, and anything that happens in it—a marriage, a death, a birth—is more important than civilization going to hell in a handcart."

"Or paving a road or putting in a new system of garbage disposal."

"Exactly. A classic case of regression. And in my opinion they would have fought any company, no matter what it produced, that tried to move in on their precious little world. I think they're seizing on the excuse that this one is nuclear, but they would have resented a company that turned out paper towels."

110

She nodded. "You're right. I remember something I heard years ago. When World War One broke out, the government tried to locate a factory in Hampton to manufacture uniforms for the armed forces."

"What happened?"

"The building was started twice, and twice it mysteriously burned to the ground. Finally they built it in Katoma."

He chuckled. "My guess wasn't too far out."

Stubbing out her cigarette, Karen looked toward the pool. Linda and the three children were sprawled beside it on towels, sunning themselves. Jamie's hair was plastered wetly to her head, and her face was flushed and radiant. At least their visit seemed to be improving Jamie's health, Karen thought. Her color was much better and even her face seemed to have filled out a trifle. At that moment she felt better herself. Her hands and mouth had stopped trembling, perhaps from the gimlets or maybe because of the unorthodox man across from her.

"The people of Hampton," she asked him. "Do you think they could be—well, dangerous?"

He raised heavy brows. "You mean that egg-throwing episode? I hardly think so, Karen. Mainly they were just letting off steam, hollering, clapping, booing."

"What about the pop bottle?"

"It was only tossed on the platform; it wasn't meant to hit anyone. As for the tomatoes and eggs—well, they aren't dangerous weapons. Anyway, it wasn't the old guard who did that. The young toughs at the back of the room were the ones who did the throwing. I had a bird's-eye view, and it was two boys back there, a couple of red-haired kids."

"The Dimwiddies," she muttered.

Dave sprang up, called "Look at me!" and jumped back into the water. Jamie and his sister followed him

111

and Linda got off her towel, hitched up the bottom strip of her bikini, flashed a smile at Karen, and dove in after the children.

"Linda is a nice girl," Karen said.

"She is." Reaching over, Trent took her hand. "Better tell me about it, and don't ask what. If you're thinking of that fall you had you can forget that too. As far as I could see you got caught in a bunch of people moving fast, trying to get out of range of more tomatoes."

"It was something that happened last night. I was at a party at Cassie Saunders's with Jim Miles. Do you know either of them?"

"By sight. And Cassie is a good sight. Quite a woman."

She told him about the face at Jamie's window and the macabre thing on the barn floor. He listened, his eyes fixed on her face. When she had finished, he rubbed his jaw. "Nasty. Damn nasty. I'd like to think it over. Now"— he stood up and smiled down at her—"I'm going to round up that gaggle of young ones and buy you all a gourmet dinner."

She glanced down at her slacks and shirt. "I'm not dressed for a dining room, and I have to be back in Hampton early. I want to stop at the library and then visit an old friend."

"I have a chore in town myself. Have to have a session with Roy. I must admit he stood up better than I thought he would to that mob today. Dinner won't take long, and I'll run you back to town afterward. As for your clothes, we'll eat right here." Walking to the edge of the pool, he called, "Okay, troops, ten minutes to get into the dressing rooms and put your clothes on."

"Or what, mister?" Dave yelled.

"Or you'll miss hamburgers, double sides of chips, and malted milks." He stood back as Dave led the rush from the pool. As they passed Trent they managed to spray him

112

with water. Pulling out a handkerchief, he mopped his face. "What do you say to that?" he asked Karen.

"I'd rather have a cheeseburger," she told him, and added, "And have them hold the tomatoes."

10

THE TRIP BACK to Hampton was a boisterous one. Trent and the children sang all the way, their voices echoing in the sunset, the low white car rolling smoothly over gentle hills. The trees here lost most of the green in their foliage and blazed like gold and crimson sentinels on either side of the road.

"I've got sixpence, jolly, jolly sixpence," Trent sang in an off-key but determined baritone.

The treble voices of the children lustily picked it up. "I've got sixpence to last me all my life."

"Come on, Karen," Trent urged. "We need a soprano."

"Tuppence to spend," she sang obediently.

"Tuppence to lend," the children chimed in.

"And tuppence to take home to my wife—" Trent leered at Karen—"Poor wife!"

They were still spending tuppences when he pulled the car to a stop in front of the library. Light streamed from the windows of the square building, making the park beside it even darker. The bandstand in the middle was a shadowy shape outlined by the lighter paint on the gingerbread trim. Hopping briskly from his seat, Trent ran around the car to help Karen out. She was already on the sidewalk, pushing down the seat so Jamie could wiggle out. Picking the child up, Trent swung her wildly around and set her on her feet.

"I'll wait for you inside," she told her mother. " 'Night, Dave. 'Night, Betsy." She turned her face up to the man. "Thank you very much for the lovely dinner," she told him politely.

"My pleasure." He watched her running up the steps. "Quite a kid. I'll deliver the other two back to the farm and then go along and see Roy. What about you? Where's this friend live that you're visiting?"

"Dinah lives on Lofton Hill, near the hospital."

He rubbed at the crescent shaped scar on his chin. "Dinah would be Mrs. Gaines. I've memorized the houses from the scale map I did of the town. That would be the big brick house—" He broke off and laughed. "Most of them are big brick houses, aren't they?"

"This one has green trim and a metal peacock on the front lawn that's been there as long as I can remember."

"I don't know how long I'll be, but if you wait for me I'll pick you up."

"It isn't necessary. We can probably get a ride home with Dinah's husband."

He frowned down at her. "Be careful. I don't like the things that have been happening to you."

"Relax." She started up the steps. "Tomatoes never hurt anyone."

He called after her. "Remember, you have two whole days to decide if you'd like me as a daddy for that imp of yours."

Her mouth snapped open and then closed, but she was smiling when she stepped into the library. Jamie was at the desk, talking to Cassie and another woman. The woman beside Cassie wore a gray dress. She had mousy hair pulled back into a knot and huge horn-rimmed glasses perched on the bridge of a long nose. Cassie wore gray too, a soft ash gray silk, but there any resemblance stopped. Against the dark walls and book-lined shelves she was exotic, a bird of paradise that had wandered in by mistake. Gray silk outlined the lush curves of her tall figure, and giant silver hoops dangled from her ears nearly to her shoulders. In the madonna face her sensual mouth was smiling, a dark red blossom against white velvet skin.

She turned the smile on Karen. "I'm so glad you came. After this afternoon I wondered. . . . Well, let's go into my office and have a chat." She indicated the woman with the long nose. "Marge will fill out a card for you."

Jamie asked, "May I get a book?"

"Certainly, my dear. Marge will show you where the children's section is."

"I don't want a child's book. I need a book on names."

"Oh. On names. Well, we have different kinds, but they're in the reference section. You can't take them out. You'll have to use them here. Marge, find out just what Jamie wants and get it, will you, please?" Cassie held out a hand to Karen. "Come in here with me."

Karen followed her through the doorway on the left. Cassie gestured at two chairs in front of a scarred desk. "Try the one with arms, it's a little more comfortable. How I'd like to get my hands on this office and redecorate, but the library board wouldn't approve. Traditional!" She wrinkled her nose. "In other words, shabby and dark."

It was. The walls were dark wood, and the curtains at the window and the material on the chairs were faded and worn. There was a musty smell of old books, dust, and, surprisingly, smoke. On a battered table at the end of the

116

room was an electric kettle, two china mugs, and some jars. Cassie plugged in the kettle.

"Coffee?" she asked. "I'm afraid all I have is instant."

"I wouldn't have thought you'd drink coffee."

"I don't. This is for visitors. I have some juice here, if you'd prefer—"

"Coffee will be fine," Karen told her hastily.

She looked around the office. There were a few touches that spoke of Cassie. On the desk was a lovely pottery bowl with a spray of brightly colored maple leaves arranged in it. There were also a glass ashtray, a small bronze one, a merry-go-round of rubber stamps, a green blotter, and a letter opener shaped like a scimitar. The only pictures in the room were on the wall directly across from the desk. One was a large square photograph in a metal frame, the other a group shot, framed in black wood. The square frame was badly dented, and the glass was cracked and starred.

Cassie set a mug filled with steaming brown liquid in front of Karen and followed her eyes to the pictures.

"Have a look at this." She touched the rectangular one with an oval red nail. "Do you recognize it?"

"Our eleventh grade picture. How did you hold on to it? I lost mine long ago." She looked at the faces. In the front row she saw herself, the sixteen-year-old Karen in a short pleated skirt, moccasins, and bobby sox, her face framed by flaxen hair that was the color and texture of her daughter's hair now. Behind her was Jim Miles, tall, blond, good-looking. Alongside Jim was another husky boy, this one with a swarthy face, wearing a sweater with a football letter on it. Pointing at him, she raised her brows at Cassie.

"Jack Jarvis. You must remember him. He was crazy about you, but Jim Miles cut him out. 'Now he's poor Jack.' "

117

"All because of a vasectomy? I take it his father doesn't approve."

Cassie chuckled. "Doc Jarvis took it as a personal insult. He fully expected about six young ones to carry on the Jarvis dynasty, but Jack could barely support the three he had. Jack's wife, 'Ticia, is just as bad. Between them they make Jack's life a hell on earth." She glanced sideways at Karen. "Spotted me yet?"

Karen had found her but hadn't wanted to mention it. At the far end of the front row was the Cassie she remembered. A limp cotton dress sagged over fleshy shoulders and limp hair hung around a moon-shaped face.

"What a monster I was then. But look at me now!"

Surprised, Karen turned to look at the other woman. Cassie pirouetted with her arms extended from her sides. Karen gazed at her grace, the elegance of her dress, the striking face and long slender hands.

"Would you have believed it?" Cassie asked complacently.

"I didn't recognize you the other night," Karen admitted.

Cassie dropped her arms. "Sit down, Karen, your coffee is getting cold."

She slipped into her own chair behind the desk, opened a drawer, and took out a long jade cigarette holder, a pack of cigarettes, and a slender gold lighter. She held out the pack. "Cigarette?"

Accepting one, Karen leaned forward while Cassie held the flame of the lighter for her. "I didn't think you smoked."

"Not often. Once in a while." Carefully she fitted a gold-tipped cigarette into the beautiful holder. "I've been looking forward to talking to you. I wanted you to know how delighted I was when you came back to town, and how thankful."

"Thankful?"

"You're helping me out of rather an awkward situation. Don't look so shocked. I imagine after that terrible scene at the town hall this afternoon you feel everyone in Hampton is hostile. They aren't, Karen, it's just they're all so uptight, and then those awful Dimwiddie brothers and their eggs and tomatoes . . . anyway, what was I saying?"

"You were telling me about being thankful."

The dark red lips tilted into a smile, one that extended to the dark eyes. "I can explain it in one word—Jim. You can't pretend you haven't heard that Jim and I have an understanding."

Guiltily, Karen remembered Jim's arms around her, his lips warmly pressing her own. "Dinah Gaines said something about it."

"You know all about small towns, especially Hampton. Jim was very kind to me, helped me diet off pounds of blubber. We've gone out a few times, he's come to my parties, and we're in the same clubs. So . . . we're paired off. Even Jim seems to have accepted the idea that we'll marry eventually."

"And you?"

Cassie's eyes slid toward the photograph in the square metal frame. Even the broken glass couldn't hide the small mean eyes of Laura Saunders. The heavy mouth was drawn into a smile that the crack across the glass turned into a leer. Without warning, Cassie seized the bronze ashtray and threw it with deadly accuracy at the photo. It thudded against the frame and fell to the floor.

Karen nearly dropped her cigarette. Leaning over, she stubbed it out in the glass ashtray. She was shocked. Cassie nodded at her.

"I'll bet that's the first time you've seen a person use a picture of her mother for target practice. I hope wherever she is now she can see me! I was kept in prison for over thirty years! And that's my jailor." Putting out her cigarette too, Cassie carefully replaced the fragile holder in the drawer. She took a deep breath. "I have no intention of returning to prison. Not even with a jailor like Jim Miles."

"You don't like Jim?" Karen asked incredulously.

"Of course I like Jim. I like him and admire him and am grateful to him. But he's an old-fashioned man, one who wants a wife, not a career woman."

"You mean the library?"

"Heavens, no! The library means nothing to me. What I want to do is to turn my house into a health club. I'm trying to get one started now in the school gym, but it's not working out too well." Dreamily, her long-lashed eyes looked past Karen's shoulder. "Saunders's Spa. I have plans for it at home. A gym, a sauna, perhaps an indoor pool. There'll be a kitchen with a dietitian and a salon run by a fine beautician. If it works out I'll have a chain of them. Maybe I'll open one in Katoma next." She shook her head and looked at Karen. "Sorry, I get carried away when I talk about it. And your coffee must be icy. Shall I make you a fresh cup?"

"No, this is fine." Lifting the cup, Karen took a sip of tepid coffee. It was horrible. "You don't think Jim would approve of this spa—that is, if you married him?"

"I called him old-fashioned. Perhaps chauvinist would better describe him. That house where Jim and his father live! Mrs. Miles died young, and some people say the old doctor makes a better bachelor than he did a husband. Jim is much like his father. There's no way I would be allowed to redecorate the house during Dr. Miles's lifetime, and he's a healthy old man. Jim would expect me to act as housekeeper, arrange his appointments, and do a little church work. A career, a spa—no. It would be a jail like the one *she* kept me in." Cassie stabbed a finger at the battered picture of Laura Saunders and Karen held her breath, thinking the glass ashtray would follow the flying path of the bronze one. But Cassie dropped her hand, spun the merry-go-round of rubber stamps, gently touched the spray of bright leaves, and said, "So you can see why I was so glad to see you."

"I still fail to see the connection."

"Don't be naive. You and Jim were always meant for each other. The golden girl and the golden boy. It broke his heart when your mother took you away after your father died."

Karen stared at the other woman. "Are you saying you hope I'll marry him?"

"Frankly, yes. Wouldn't you like to?"

"I don't really know. I'm fond of him, but it was a girl-and-boy affair. It's been so long. We're different people."

Cassie smiled warmly at her. "Don't look so worried. You don't have to sacrifice yourself. Just by being in Hampton you're helping to break the pattern. People may stop trying to pair us off, and I'll be free to live my own life. Remember, you've already had what I've always wanted."

"Which is?"

"An exciting career, a life of my own, freedom."

"Freedom can be lonely."

"Nevertheless I'd like a taste of it." Abruptly, Cassie changed the subject. "How did Alfred make out with Jamie yesterday?"

"They got along famously."

Cassie got to her feet. "Good, I'm glad to hear it. He's truly lonely, and he's such a fine old fellow." She picked up a slip of paper. "Which reminds me, he sent in a list of books he wants. I'd better get them gathered up. I'll try to find time tomorrow to take them around to him. Lottie is supposed to pick them up but she always forgets."

Standing up, Karen opened the door. Seated at a table was Jamie, bending her flaxen head over a thick book. She wasn't alone. Amos Lofton was sitting across from her and Bruce Gotham was bending his small form over the table. Marge was standing at Jamie's side, peering down at the book. In the background was the old man with the two canes who had been making his painful way down Main Street the day of their arrival.

"Let me guess," Amos Lofton was saying. "Oliver . . . hmm, would that be Oliver Twist?"

Jamie shook her head and Marge muttered, "There's a big black cat called Oliver in a comic strip."

"No," Amos stated. "I don't believe Jamie would pick an obvious reference like that. Describe the kitten again."

"About this long." Jamie held out her hands. "Long gray fur, and a white spot right under his chin."

"What about Oliver Hardy?" Bruce Gotham asked.

Jamie turned bright eyes up to the little man. "No. Do you give up?"

"We'll have to," Amos said. "We've run out of Olivers."

"Oliver Cromwell!"

"Of course." Amos Lofton nodded at Bruce Gotham. "A fine strong name for a gray kitten. He will have to grow very large to live up to that name, though." Noticing Karen, he got to his feet. "Mrs. Dancer, I've been waiting for you."

What for, Karen wondered, to take up the battle where he had left off at the meeting? But he was smiling pleasantly at her.

"Jamie tells me you're going up to see Dinah Gaines. I live right across from her, so I thought I'd offer you a ride."

122

Karen smiled back. "You're very kind. I didn't know you were still on the hill."

He shepherded Jamie and her mother toward the door. "I gave up my house some time ago. After Mrs. Lofton's death it was much too large and empty. I took rooms on the hill that are quite adequate for my needs." On the steps he pointed out a venerable sedan. "There's my car, ladies. That's right, jump in, Jamie. Now, Mrs. Dancer. Ahem, yes . . . fine."

Getting stiffly in behind the wheel, he started the motor. It had a smooth powerful sound. Twilight had darkened into night, and frosty stars twinkled above the maples. The street was empty of both cars and pedestrians, and dry leaves spun across the blacktop the headlights illuminated.

Lofton spoke across Jamie's head. "I was most—ah, disturbed at the meeting today. The indignities you suffered at the hands of those young lads, high-spirited but most misguided boys. I am hoping you have not decided to side with ANPP." He paused, changed his train of thought, and said softly, "You know, of course, that I am the last Lofton. My two sons died during the Second World War and the name dies with me. I must assure you that during my lifetime I intend to see that Hampton remains as it is, a peaceful oasis in a disturbed world."

"What about after your death?" Karen asked bluntly.

"That is beyond my control." He paused, as though to consider if it *really* would be beyond his control. "But then, my dear Mrs. Dancer, I shan't know anything about it."

"Après moi, le déluge?"

"Exactly. Now, I was going to suggest that if you are desirous of selling your property I would gladly purchase it from you. I cannot, of course, hope to equal the amount ANPP probably offered, but if you need funds—"

123

Karen turned her head toward him sharply. "The money doesn't interest me, Mr. Lofton."

"Forgive me, I was clumsy. And I should have realized that you were in no need of money. John Hampton's estate—well, John was a shrewd businessman."

"I also had a husband, Mr. Lofton. Jamie and I are well taken care of financially."

Amos Lofton pulled the old car smoothly to a stop in front of a big house on the crest of the hill. Light streamed from its windows. The porch light silhouetted the outline of a strutting peacock, its iron tail spread in a frozen pattern of grace.

"I do hope I haven't offended you, Mrs. Dancer."

Karen's cheeks were hot and all she managed as she climbed out of his car was a grunt. Jamie put one hand on the old man's arm and looked up at him. "Thank you for the ride," she said softly. "Do you really like my name?"

"I like it very much. My elder son was named James, and it's a name I'm partial to."

Karen turned back. "I'm sorry if I was abrupt. This whole business has been most upsetting."

"I understand." He patted Jamie's head. "Never shorten your kitten's name. Under no circumstances allow him to be called Ollie."

"I won't," Jamie promised, and followed her mother up the walk to the porch.

Before they reached it, Dinah swung it open. "Karie, how wonderful. After that business this afternoon—"

"Which is over. Let's forget it, shall we?"

"By all means. Come in. Ah, Jamie, here my own children are, waiting to play with you." Shutting the door, Dinah waved toward the three children standing behind her. "This is Wendy. She's the oldest and almost thirteen now. Brian is eleven his next birthday. And here's Arthur, who is exactly your age. Say hello, children."

124

The children said hello. The girl was much like her father, tall and grave. The two boys were more like Dinah, plump, with a tendency to giggle.

"What would you like to play?" Wendy asked Jamie.

"Poker," Arthur said.

Dinah tapped him on the head. "No way, gambler. What about a game of Scrabble?"

"I'd like that," Jamie told her.

"All right, away you go. Upstairs; and remember, Arthur, no betting."

Wendy took Jamie's hand and led the way up the staircase. The boys trailed along behind. Karen heard Arthur say sotto voce to Jamie, "How about a quarter a game?"

Dinah shook her head, her fair curls dancing. "It's hopeless." She sighed. "He'll probably end up in Las Vegas."

Taking Karen's arm, she steered her through an archway into the living room. It was bright and homey and untidy. A hockey stick leaned against one wall with a tennis racket propped beside it. On a long coffee table was a jumble of magazines, newspapers, a dish of candy, and a pile of mending. Frowning down at it, Dinah sighed again and swept the newspapers off on the floor.

"I'm a lousy housekeeper, Karie. Les is a saint, but even he gets tired of this mess. But with the children— well, anyway, I started a fire. Like it?"

Karen held her hands out to the flames on the hearth and sank down in a shabby comfortable chair. "Love it. Feels good on a night like this. Isn't Les home?"

"No. He had to go over to Katoma on business this afternoon and may stay the night." She lowered herself into the chair facing Karen. "Hey, come to think of it, how will you get home? That was Amos Lofton who dropped you off, wasn't it?"

"Uh-huh, but don't fuss, Dinah. Let's relax and wallow in the past. Let's play 'remember when' all evening and forget about meetings, ANPP, children, and going home."

Dinah passed her the candy dish. "Right. For refreshments we're having hot chocolate with marshmallows melting on it, a deep-dish apple pie guaranteed to put pounds on, and—"

"Whoa! Sounds as though you aren't one of Cassie Saunder's health fiends."

"Perish the thought." She patted her round stomach. "Speaking of Cassie, seen Jim around?"

Karen recognized the innocent look on her friend's face. "What are you getting at?"

"Getting at?" Dinah giggled. Deep dimples appeared in both cheeks. "Okay, Fran March phoned this afternoon and told me she has the flu and Jim was around to hold her hand. She said he talked all the time he was there about you and Jamie. Karen this, Karen that."

So, Karen thought, Cassie was getting her wish. Already memories were reviving about Jim and her, and soon tongues would be speculating. Damn all small towns! She decided she would give Dinah something to really mull over.

"Sorry, chum, but I spent the afternoon with the man I'm going to marry."

Dinah jerked upright. "Who?" Her elbow hit the pile of mending and it slid to the floor, but she paid no attention. "You can't mean . . . no, it couldn't be that chap from ANPP. I know he drove you away from the town hall, but—"

"That's the one."

"You must be joking!"

Throwing back her head, Karen laughed. "I am, but

that's how rumors get started. Forget about Jim, and let's get back to school days."

School days lasted until well after midnight, when Karen and Jamie started home. The air was definitely crisp and both of them were wearing sweaters that Dinah had insisted on lending them. Karen stopped Jamie and buttoned hers up to the throat.

"Cold, honey?"

"A little, but wasn't that chocolate and pie delicious?"

Karen took her hand. "Scrumptious. Did you enjoy Scrabble?"

The child put her hand into her pocket and jingled some coins. "I won fifty cents."

"I don't doubt it," Karen told her dryly. "You're an imp."

The word imp reminded her of Cal Trent, and as they cut across the street and turned left on Aspen, she thought about him. Involuntarily she found she was comparing him to Jim Miles. Jamie's thoughts must have been paralleling hers.

"Karen," she asked, "who do you like better, Jim or Cal?"

"I don't really know."

Jamie skipped along, her fine blond brows drawn in a frown. "Jim's much handsomer, but I think I like Cal better." She looked around. The houses were dark and huddled back among darker shrubs and trees. Leaves blew around their feet, their dry rustling the only sound that disturbed the silence. Shivering, Jamie clasped her mother's hand tighter. "It's spooky, isn't it?"

Silently, Karen agreed with her. She found herself wishing they had left earlier, when there were still lights in the windows and perhaps a few people on the streets. She looked down the long street and started to walk faster. It would be even worse when they reached the

127

place where the sidewalk ended and they had to walk down the country road past the farm.

Jamie squeezed her hand. "Look, there's a car coming. Maybe we can get a ride." Her voice quavered. "I'm cold."

Karen looked back over her shoulder. It was an old car, and for an instant she thought it was Ashley's Buick, but as it came closer she could see it was an old Ford painted in green-and-white zebra stripes. She felt an urge to pull Jamie off the sidewalk into the shadows of the maples. Mentally she shook herself. This was ridiculous.

The car put on a burst of speed and drew up level with them. Karen tried to see the driver's face but the headlights blinded her. It pulled into the curb ahead of them, two men climbed out, and her heart sank. She recognized the long lanky figures of the Dimwiddie brothers. One of them pulled the back door open.

"Come on, Hopper," he ordered. "Out you get."

"I don't want to." The voice came from the depths of the car. "I've got to get home."

"Out!" the other Dimwiddie said. "We're gonna have us a little fun."

"Karen!" Jamie cried. "It's those hoodlums!"

Pushing the child behind her, Karen looked wildly around. There was no one else in sight. She glanced back at the Ford. Bob Hopper was getting reluctantly out of the backseat. "Better leave them alone," he said. "Jim Miles was talking to my dad, and Dad said he'd skin me alive if I bothered—"

He stopped abruptly. Tim had slapped him viciously across the mouth. Danny was strutting toward Karen and her daughter. "So, li'l lady, we meet again. Nice and quiet, ain't it? You owe us, lady, you and that brat behind you."

Karen's chin went up and she made her voice icy. "I'd advise you to take your friend's advice."

"Don't need any advice," Tim said, stepping up beside

his brother. "Sure a good-looking chick, ain't she, Danny? Not all that young but still a looker." He put one hand on her arm and slid it up toward her shoulder. "Be nice to us. We can be right agreeable if you don't rile us."

Karen tried to pull her arm away. "Take your hands off me!"

Tim's hand tightened, and his brother grabbed her around the waist and pulled her toward him. Danny's face was within inches of her own and she could smell the sour odor of his breath and see the gleam in his pale eyes. Oh, God! she thought. Tim's hand was moving, sliding down from her shoulder, fumbling at her breast. She started struggling against them, and Jamie darted out from behind her and flailed at Danny's leg.

"Leave my mother alone!" she sobbed.

"Get the kid out of here," Danny said huskily. "Come on, Bob, put the little brat in the car."

"Hey," Bob Hopper yelled. "Knock it off! There's a car coming!"

The boys took their hands off Karen and stepped back. Karen, her breath sobbing in her throat, took Jamie's hand and began to run down the middle of the street toward the approaching lights, dragging the child behind her. She waved her free arm.

"Stop!" she shouted. "Please stop!"

The low white car pulled up and Trent's tall form climbed out. Behind them a motor gunned, but she didn't look around. Trent reached her and she threw herself at him. He put one arm around her and the other around Jamie, who had buried her head against his hip and was making stifled sobbing sounds.

"What's going on?" he demanded. "That car. Did those Dimwiddies—"

"It's all right," Karen panted. "Jamie—she's had a scare."

His arms tightened around them. "I can see that. Thank God I came looking for you! I stopped at Dinah Gaines's and she said you'd just left, so—thank God I found you." He whispered in Karen's ear. "Did they do anything to either of you?"

"They grabbed me." She was choking tears back. "Jamie," she told Trent.

He hugged her tighter and then released her. Detaching Jamie's tight grasp from his leg, he knelt beside her. Jamie burrowed into his arms while Trent stroked her hair and murmured to her. Karen stood beside them, her eyes blurred with unshed tears, her arms folded across her breast, gazing down the dark length of the quiet street. There still wasn't a light in any of the houses. No one seemed to have heard her shouts as she had pulled Jamie down the street or the screech of the Dimwiddies' car as they pulled away. If Trent hadn't come looking for them—she pulled herself up short.

Trent stood up with Jamie in his arms, her legs dangling against his chest, both her arms clutched around his neck. She lifted a tear-blotched face to him. "They were hurting Karen," she sobbed.

He gazed down at her, his hazel eyes grave. "Jamie, do you think if I make a promise to you that I'll keep it?" Her head bobbed up and down against his chin. "I'm making you a promise. Those boys will never bother either your mother or you again. Do you believe that?" Her head bobbed again. "Okay, I'm taking you home. You'll soon be safe in bed."

With one hand he opened the car door, waited until Karen was in the car, and lowered the little girl to her lap. Convulsively Karen's arms tightened around her daughter. She had to force herself to loosen her hold. As Trent got in behind the wheel, Jamie wormed around so she could face him and leaned back in her mother's arms.

130

"Are you going to bash them?" she asked.

He started the car and, without looking at the child, muttered, "You'd better believe it."

"Keep out of it," Karen urged. "I'll ask Ashley or Jim Miles to talk to them. You'll only get into trouble if you do anything."

"Some trouble I don't mind. Now, you sit back and unwind. I'll have you home soon."

He was as good as his word. In a few minutes he pulled his long form out of the car and stared up at the outlines of the house. The only light was in the hall, shining through the colored fanlight over the door. He turned around. "Is there any alcohol in that mausoleum?"

Mausoleum wasn't a bad description, Karen thought. Aloud she said, "The only Hampton I know who has wine around is Uncle Alfred. He likes a nip now and then. I doubt whether Ashley would allow even cooking sherry in the house."

Reaching into the back of the car, Trent pulled out a brown paper bag. "Lucky I come supplied. Rum, and good stuff too. After we get Jamie bedded down I'll fix you a drink. I must admit I make the best hot buttered rum your lips have ever touched."

"All this and modesty too," Karen said, as she took Jamie's hand.

Swinging open the front door, she led the way inside. Trent gazed up the staircase and around the hall. He opened the door of the front parlor and peered in. "Lovely setting for a horror show. Any danger of waking up anyone, or are your relatives not home yet?"

"Mac goes down to her cottage right after dinner, and nothing could wake Ashley and Sybil. They wouldn't hear a bomb exploding, as far away as their bedrooms are."

Jamie was tugging at her mother's sweater. "May I

131

show Oliver to Cal?" She explained to Trent. "That's my kitten's name. I picked it tonight. He's up in my room."

Karen nodded. "All right, but make it fast." As Jamie ran up the stairs she said to Trent, "That rum sounds like a good idea. Come into the kitchen."

He followed her down the long hall to the swinging doors. She fumbled for the switch, and the overhead light came on.

"You sit down," he told her. "I'll take over. Where's the brown sugar and butter?"

"In the cupboard beside the stove."

He reached for the kettle, filled it, and put it on the stove. Karen watched as he moved around. Her hands were pushed deep in the sweater pockets, but even though she clenched them tightly into fists she could feel them shaking. He glanced at her, put down the butter dish, and dug into his pocket. He lighted two cigarettes, stuck one in the corner of his mouth, and handed her the other.

"This will give you something to do with that lower lip of yours."

"Don't make fun of me." Karen realized she was close to tears again and bit at the offending lip.

He patted her head. "I'm not making fun, and don't bite your lip, that won't help. Where are the cinnamon sticks?"

"In the spice rack, if Mac has any."

"Aha, trust Mac. Cinnamon sticks and nice long ones." He put a steaming cup on the table in front of her, stuck a cinnamon stick into the murky fluid, and gave it a brisk stir. "Try that."

She lifted the cup with both hands and took a gulp. It was strong and buttery and good. Trent sat down on a chair alongside, so close his knee was touching hers. "Tell me what marvelous hot rum I make."

"You make marvelous hot rum, and it's so strong I can feel it right down to my toes."

"Good. Drain your cup and I'll refill it."

She had almost drunk it all when the doors swung open and Jamie came in. "I can't find Oliver," she told her mother.

"He was in your room with the door shut when we left this afternoon. Perhaps Mac opened the door and he slipped out. Did you look around?"

"I went through my room and yours, I looked around in the other bedrooms and the bathroom, I called and called, but he didn't come." Picking up her mother's cinnamon stick, she popped it in her mouth and then pulled it out hastily. "Ugh!" She made a face. "Will you help me find Oliver, Cal?"

"Okay, will do. But let's do it my way. Use our heads and save our legs. Is Oliver's mother still around?"

"Right outside. She sleeps under the steps. Shall I get Ruby?"

"Do that." He pointed at Karen's cup. "Drink up."

Jamie came in through the back door, banging it behind her, with the cinnamon-colored cat in her arms. The cat's slanted emerald eyes looked incuriously around the room and then slowly closed.

Standing up, Trent reached for the animal. "This is our bloodhound. Takes a cat to find a cat." He deposited the cat on the floor. "Do your stuff, Ruby."

Ruby sniffed his pant cuff, flexed her claws against the brown linoleum, and moved with stately grace toward the swinging doors. "Follow that cat." Grinning, Trent led the way out of the kitchen. Ruby leisurely padded down the hall, sniffing at the doors opening from it. At the dining room door she stretched up a paw and pushed at it.

"Aha," Trent told the excited child. "She's got the

133

scent." He opened the door. "Where are the ruddy lights?"

"Right here." Karen touched a wall switch, and the chandelier blazed with light. Ruby was standing beside the breakfront buffet, her nose pushed against the crack of the door.

"Room after room," Trent marveled. "What's that one?"

"The dying room," Jamie told him. "Mac showed me where it is, but I've never been inside."

Stepping up behind her daughter, Karen laid both hands on the thin shoulders. Her fingers tightened, and she could feel the child's sharp shoulder blades.

"Ouch, Karen! You're hurting me!"

Trent looked from the child to Karen. "Great name for a room," he told them. "You ladies wait here, and Ruby and I will investigate."

Swinging open the door, he clicked on a light and with the big cat close behind him disappeared into the room. Jamie struggled to follow him but Karen held her tight.

"Let me go," Jamie demanded. "I want to go with Cal and Ruby."

"You heard him, honey; ladies stay here. Oh, there's Cal back again. Any luck?"

Trent had the big cat in his arms. Reaching back, he turned off the light and pulled the door to. "As a bloodhound this cat is a failure. Must have been on the trail of a mouse. I would imagine an old place like this would have a fair share of rodents." He glanced down at Jamie. Karen had released her and she was rubbing her shoulder. Her lower lip stuck out ominously.

"Where *is* Oliver?" she demanded.

"Take Ruby." The man deposited the cat in her arms and swung both of them up. "Could be that Mac left the back door open long enough for the kitten to slip out."

134

"Then let's go outside and look."

"It's after one," Karen said. "The only thing you're looking at is your bed. And Jamie, if the kitten had been out there, wouldn't he have been with Ruby? He's a very small cat."

Jamie pounded a fist against Trent's shoulder. "I want Oliver!" she shrieked. "I want him right now!" The big cat she was clutching uttered a howl and clawed at Trent's chest.

He pulled the claws out of his sweater, grimaced, and asked Jamie in a mild tone, "How would you like to be turned over my knee and get a good walloping?"

To Karen's surprise the ferocious look disappeared from her daughter's face and was replaced by an enchanting smile. She slid the hand she'd been pounding him with around his neck. "Would you really spank me?" she asked demurely.

"Damn right I would."

"I'll go to bed, Cal. Would you carry me up, and can Ruby stay with me tonight?"

"Yes, and yes. Now, Karen, you go out in the kitchen and see if you can rival my hot rum. Use lots of butter. I'll get this imp to bed and be down directly."

Karen waited until she heard Trent going up the staircase. Then she took the few steps necessary to bring her to the door of the dying room. Putting out a hand she turned the white china knob. It felt like a lump of ice. She forced herself to step into the darkness beyond and fumbled on the wall for the switch. A light went on in the middle of the room, a small bulb shaded by a green glass cover.

The green cover made the light dim, but she could make out the bulky form of the chiffonier against the opposite wall. The room looked the same as it had the last time she had seen it—twenty-nine years before. The wall was covered with a dingy paper in wine-and-green

135

stripes. Two straight chairs were pushed against the wall near the door of the closet that had been made into a bathroom. Beside the bed was a table with a dark-shaded lamp on it. On the floor were three small rag rugs, their colors as faded as the wallpaper. Against the wall beside her loomed the large bedstead, the high top and footboard ornamented with carvings depicting tangled oak leaves and acorns. Drawn smoothly over the mattress was a washed-out green cotton spread.

One thing had been added. In the middle of the green spread a tiny heap sprawled. It took a moment for Karen to realize it had once been a gray kitten. The knife that had disemboweled it was neatly aligned beside the body. The blade was covered with blood and other things that left ugly stains on the spread.

Karen clung to the wall, the room describing colored pinwheels before her. She was aware she was whispering a name. At first she thought she was trying to call Cal. It was some time before she realized she was saying "Oliver," over and over again.

TRENT FORCED A cup into Karen's hands and stood frowning down at her colorless face. He had half carried her from the dying room back to the kitchen, and now he was standing at her side, one hand pressing hard on her shoulder.

"Why?" she whispered. "What is happening? Who is doing these . . . these things?"

"Drink," he ordered.

She tried to pull away from him. "I can't. I want to go to bed. I can't take any more."

He forced the hand holding the cup to her mouth. "In a while, not right now. There's no way I'm leaving you in this condition. Why did you go in there?"

"There was something about you when you came out. You were acting. I could tell. I knew you were hiding something from us."

"It looks as though we can read each other almost too well. When you grabbed Jamie and hung on to her, I knew you were scared stiff of that room. That's why I went in alone. Why the fear? At that point you didn't know about the kitten."

"Something happened there years ago, when I was younger than Jamie." Her mind flickered back to that night long before and then back to the present. "The knife on the bed, that came from the drawer over there. Someone came into this house, went up to Jamie's room, took the kitten down—"

"And butchered it. This afternoon, when you told me about the panda and pitchfork and the balloon at the kid's window, I knew something pretty horrible was going on."

He was leaning against the counter, his arms folded across his chest, his face serious. The white scar on his chin was more noticeable than usual.

"What is this all for, Cal?"

"Probably just for the effect it's having on you right now. To scare you green, get you totally demoralized and much too frightened to dare sell your farm to ANPP. I'd say it was a series of warnings." Walking over, he sat down across from her. "What is a dying room?"

She gave a shaky laugh. "What does that have to do with it?"

"Maybe a lot."

"All right. A dying room is a first-floor room with its own stove that once was used for sick people. It was a practical idea. In these big houses before central heating was put in, several generations usually lived under one roof. The women of the house couldn't possibly run up and down stairs all day to care for patients. Fuel could be carried easily to stoves in downstairs sickrooms. Most elderly relatives breathed their last in those rooms, and they got to be known as dying rooms. That's all."

"That isn't all. What happened when you were younger than Jamie?"

"I don't want to talk about it."

"You have a bad habit of bottling things up inside of you."

138

"That's what Mac says."

"Mac's an uncommonly shrewd woman. Now tell me, or I may put *you* over my knee."

She took a deep breath. "I was about seven, and the house at that time was full of relatives. My father's brothers and sisters, my three cousins, and my grandfather, Cyrus Hampton, all lived here. I was fond of my grandfather. He had snow-white hair, and he was so old and frail all he ever did was sit out on the back porch in the sunshine whittling. He made little toys for me, tiny horses and cows, beautiful little wooden dolls. We were very close. And then he had his first stroke. . . ."

Grandfather had been carried down and put in bed in the room opening off the dining room. The house was quiet. Everyone went around on tiptoe. Karen's father, Uncle Alfred, and Cousin Ashley moved the dining room table and chairs into the back parlor so Grandfather wouldn't be disturbed at mealtime. Karen tiptoed up and down the hall, peering through the dining room at the closed door, wishing she could go in and see him. Dr. Miles came every day and would stop to pat her head, and sometimes he would bring her a peppermint stick or a licorice whip. All the aunts, Cousin Sybil, and Mama went back and forth to the room carrying towels, bottles of medicine, basins of water, and bowls of broth.

"Can I see Grandfather?" Karen asked Uncle Alfred, and each time he told her, Not yet.

On the night she had finally been allowed to see him she was playing with her dollhouse in the room that opened off her mother's. Her mother and father were talking, and she stopped playing to listen. Her mother's voice was generally low and gentle. That night she was close to screaming.

"I tell you I won't let you do it, John! I've worked as hard as Sybil and Flo and Celia taking care of him, but this

139

I won't have. She's going to remember him as he was, not as he is now. She's only seven!"

Father's voice was lower, and Karen had to strain to hear him. "He loves her, Mary, and she loves him. It's a tradition in this family. Father took me in to see my grandfather when he was dying. The whole family is down there. Roy's there, and he's only four years older than Karen."

"Roy! That boy hasn't a nerve in his body. But our child has. Karen is highly imaginative and sensitive. An experience like this could do terrible things to her. I won't have it!"

There was a tap at the door, and Karen heard Uncle Alfred's voice. "Better hurry, John. He's not going to last much longer."

"Mary doesn't want Karen to see him," John told his brother.

"Nonsense! Where is the child? Karen!"

Karen jumped up so quickly she dropped a little wooden doll on the roof of her dollhouse. She ran the few feet into her mother's room. Mama reached out for her, but the two tall men stepped between them and Uncle Alfred took her hand. As they left the room the last thing Karen heard was her mother. She sounded as though she was crying. Then her father shut the door.

"Am I going to see Grandfather?" Karen asked.

"Yes, you are, dear. Now be a brave little girl," her father told her.

Karen wondered why she had to be brave, but Uncle Alfred said, "Grandfather is dying, and there are angels hovering over his bed waiting to take him to heaven."

When Uncle Alfred opened the door of the dying room she couldn't see any angels, but all the family was crowded into the small room. Ashley and Uncle George were standing in front of the bed and she couldn't see the patient. In the corner Sybil sat beside Aunt Celia and Uncle Clifford Paul. Aunt Celia was crying and she had her arms around her son, Roy. Roy turned his face toward Karen, crossed his eyes, and opened his mouth in a horrible grimace so his tongue lolled out on his chin. On the other side of the bed the spinster aunts were gathered in a dark-clad weeping huddle.

"Let Karen through," Uncle Alfred ordered.

Ashley and Uncle George moved to one side, and Uncle Alfred led Karen to the bed. She looked down at the face on the pile of pillows and didn't recognize the kind old man who had sat in the sunshine carving toys for her. One side of his face was pulled out of shape, mucus trickled from the corner of his twisted mouth, his left eye was closed, and the other one bulged from its socket. That terrible eye was rolling around as though searching for something. Karen stared at the ceiling. She couldn't see any angels, and she decided that if Grandfather could they must look awful because he looked scared. One of his hands was plucking at the blanket.

"He wants to hold your hand," Uncle Alfred said and put her warm little hand into the old man's. It was bony and as cold as ice and closed around hers in a painful, spasmodic grip. She tried to pull her hand loose and couldn't. This wasn't her grandfather; they were playing a trick on her! The odors of the sickroom closed in on her: medicine, a basin of scummed water, and, although she didn't know it, the smell of death.

Suddenly the old man lurched against the mattress and his spine became rigid, arching his body up like a bow. The eye rolled desperately toward Karen and then stopped rolling and glared right into her own eyes. Death came at that moment, and with it his sphincter muscle relaxed and the foul smell of decay flooded her.

Held a prisoner alongside the dead man by her Uncle

141

Arthur, Karen threw back her head to scream for her mother. Her mouth moved in agony but no sound came out. In a way, her twisted face bore an uncanny resemblance to the one on the bed beside her. . . .

Karen returned from the past, from the dying room, to smell the odor of rum, butter, and cinnamon and to see Trent's horrified eyes staring across the table at her.

"They did that to a little child?" he asked. "My God, that uncle and father of yours should have been horse-whipped!"

The old-fashioned term brought a faint smile to her face. Strangely enough, now it had been said, she felt better, as though a load had dropped from her shoulders. Picking up the cup, she noticed that for the first time in hours her hands were steady. Good therapy, she told herself, and drained the cup.

Trent was frowning down at his hands. He had good hands, she decided, big, blunt-fingered, the nails clipped short, another scar, this one long and jagged, on the back of the right hand. "Tell me, Karen, how many people know about your experience in that room?"

"The whole family, of course. And they'd tell other people. It's a small place, so I suppose everyone in town knew. Roy used to tease me about it, threaten to lock me in there if I didn't do what he wanted."

"Everyone in town, huh? So . . . the kitten is slaughtered in there, right on the same bed. Yes, I think we have a fear campaign going on, aimed at you."

"But hitting at Jamie too. Her panda, her sweater, her window, her kitten."

"What better way to hit at you than through your only child?"

She got to her feet. "What can I tell her tomorrow? I can't let her know."

He reached a long arm for his jacket. "You'll have to let

142

her think the little thing strayed away. I'll wrap it up in the bedspread, put it in my trunk, and dispose of it. I'd better take the knife too." He pulled his jacket on. "Are there any locks on those doors of yours? I should have looked when I put Jamie to bed."

This time her smile was genuine. "Nobody in Hampton would dream of locking a door. As Amos Lofton says, it's a peaceful little oasis in a troubled world."

He laughed. "Sure it is. Does Hampton frown on tools too, or are there some around?"

"There's a toolshed outside with a workbench at the back. Why?"

He opened the back door. "Because I'm not an engineer for nothing. I'm going to put locks on your bedroom door and Jamie's. You go check on her and I'll be up in a few minutes." Before she could answer he banged the door shut.

When Karen went into Jamie's room the child was curled up in a little ball, her arms embracing the big red cat. Switching on a lamp near the door, Karen sank into a rocking chair beside it and waited.

Trent came down the hall so quietly the loose floorboard in front of Jamie's door didn't even squeak under his weight. As he entered the room Karen noticed the way he moved, his slouching walk actually light and rather wary. In one hand he carried a wooden box piled with tools and in the other a tangle of rusty metal.

"Struck it lucky." Putting the toolbox on the floor, he bent to examine the door. "Apparently they believed in fastening outbuildings. I took the bolts off both the barn door and the shed door. Primitive, but they'll serve." He glanced at the bed. "I may wake her up, but I'll be as quiet as I can." He selected a hand drill. "Going to make a mess of this woodwork. Looks like mahogany."

"It is, but it doesn't matter," Karen told him.

As he worked a sleepy voice came from the bed. "What are you doing, Cal?"

"Putting a lock on your door, Jamie. Go back to sleep. I'm nearly finished."

"Good." Rolling over, the child buried her head in the pillow. "This is a horrendous house."

"That about describes it," Trent agreed.

A few minutes later he stood back and surveyed his work. He pulled the metal bolt and then clicked it back in place. "It's a bit stiff and no beauty, but I dabbed some oil on and it'll work. Now we'll get one on your door."

Switching off the light, Karen pulled the blanket up to her daughter's chin and followed him into the other bedroom. Deftly, he positioned the bolt and screwed it into place.

Dropping the screwdriver into the box, he wiped his hands on a piece of waste and then turned back to Karen and pulled an object wrapped in a scrap of plastic from his pocket. "Got a present for you. Do you know how to handle this?"

Karen flinched. He was unwrapping a revolver. He held it out to her and she looked down at it. It was snubnosed, the metal shone blue-black, and the stock was of highly polished wood.

"Police special. Thirty-eight. This little fellow has been my constant companion for a number of years." He said again, "Do you know how to handle a gun?"

"Jeff—my husband—had one in our apartment. I was alone a lot. He insisted I learn to use it but"—she gave a shaky laugh—"I'm afraid I'm no expert, and I loathe guns."

"I'm not crazy about them myself, but at times they can be a comfort. Don't worry about expertise. This is fully loaded and all set to go."

"No, Cal, I don't want it. You should keep it anyway—"

"Its twin is down in my car. It belongs to Vince, but he won't mind my hanging on to it for a few days. Take this one and keep it handy."

She backed away from the gun he was extending to her. "This is ridiculous! I don't *want* a gun."

Stepping closer, he lowered his voice. "Do I have to remind you that someone doesn't like you and Jamie one little bit? That someone started on tires, moved to a panda, and then killed a cat. Always cold steel—an ax, a pitchfork, and now a knife. First rubber and now living flesh. And you're virtually alone in this mausoleum. Those cousins of yours wouldn't know if the roof crashed down on you."

"Are you trying to frighten me?"

"I am, for your own good. Someone was in these rooms tonight. Someone was in Jamie's room." He thrust the gun into her hand. "No more arguing. Stick that under your pillow and get some sleep."

"Are you leaving?"

"Yes, I'm going back to the hotel to sack out. I can use some sleep myself." At the door he turned. "Bolt this after me."

Sliding the bolt into place, Karen pressed her ear against the door panel. There was no sound from the hall; she couldn't hear him making his way along it, going down the stairs. She looked at the gun with distaste, walked over to the dressing table, and opened a drawer. Then she shook her head; Jamie would be bound to find it there. She wrapped it in her shower cap, pulled a chair over to the wardrobe, and, standing on the seat, shoved it to the back of the shelf.

As she got into bed she thought of Trent driving back to his hotel.

Trent was driving in the opposite direction from the road to Katoma and his hotel. He was driving down a deserted Main Street, heading toward Factory Hill. His car rolled past darkened storefronts, then past a large building with high letters on the roof spelling out LOFTON CHINA AND POTTERY. This hill was steeper than the one on the other side of town, and the houses that lined it were not the large prosperous brick homes of the other hill but small clapboard cottages. Most of them were neat and well cared for, and the yards had trim gardens surrounded by picket fences.

Pulling the car over, he got out, patted the bulging pocket of his jacket, and opened the trunk. He pushed a bulky bundle under one arm and moved silently down the sidewalk. The house he was looking for was near the end of the street. He stopped and surveyed it grimly. This one wasn't well cared for; in fact it was a mess. The porch sagged to one side, the gate in the rickety fence was half off its hinges, and there were two derelict cars in the yard, partially stripped down.

The two windows in the front were dark so he circled around to the rear, avoiding a rusty washing machine and a pile of old tires near the back door. Noiselessly he crept up two steps and peered in the lighted window. Behind tattered curtains the kitchen looked even more squalid than the yard did. Pots and pans cluttered the burners of the stove, the sink was overflowing with dirty dishes, and a case of beer sat on the table. He wasted no time on the disorder. All his attention was concentrated on the two figures seated at the table.

Danny Dimwiddie, wearing an undershirt and jockey shorts and holding a large stein, was lounging in a chair tipped back against the wall. His brother, still fully dressed, was drinking his beer straight from the bottle.

146

Trent's hand closed on the doorknob, and in one movement he flung open the door and stepped into the kitchen. Slamming it shut, he leaned against it. Danny's mouth dropped open and Tim jerked around.

"It's that dude from ANPP," Tim blurted. "What you doing here, Trent?"

Danny smashed the front legs of his chair down and lurched to his feet. "You just get out as fast as you come in. This here is our house."

Trent shook his head. "Uh-uh, boys. Came here to have a quiet little talk with you." In one stride he reached the table and, knocking the beer stein to the floor, plunked the bundle down and pulled back the green cotton. With one finger he poked at the handle of the knife. "You left something behind you."

Both boys stared at the table. "What's this bloody mess?" Danny demanded.

"Bloody is the key word, boys. As you should know, this was—until you got a knife into it—a kitten. Jamie Dancer's kitten."

They were both staring at him, and Trent could have sworn the bewilderment in their pale eyes was genuine. "Come on," he probed, "you were driving from the direction of the Hampton house when you stopped to pay a little attention to Mrs. Dancer and her daughter tonight."

"Told you that was this dude's car," Tim told his brother accusingly.

"Button your lip," the other Dimwiddie snarled.

Danny was the brighter of the two, Trent decided, not that he was overly bright either. He spoke directly to him. "Too late for details. Better tell me the truth."

Danny's lips pulled back from his teeth in an ugly sneer. "We don't have to tell you nothin'. Take off before we break you in two."

The boy's hand was inching toward the stained knife

147

on the green spread. Trent pulled his own hand out of his pocket. He held a snub-nosed revolver. Reversing it, he brought the butt down viciously on the boy's hand. Danny uttered a scream that sounded almost like a woman's.

"You've broken my hand, you bloody—"

From the corner of his eye Trent saw the other boy lunging out of his chair. Spinning around, he caught Tim by the front of his shirt and smashed the revolver butt across his face. Tim sagged forward limply, and Trent threw him back onto the chair.

Pushing the gun back into his pocket, he leaned against the cluttered counter. His nose wrinkled at the smell: grease, beer, smoke, and the combined stench of boiled cabbage and fried onions. "Tell me about the cat, Danny."

Danny shook his head in violent denial. He was white to his lips. "Honest, mister, we didn't have nothing to do with that cat. All we was doing was riding around, and we saw the Dancer broad and—"

"Decided on a little rape scene," Trent finished for him.

Danny stared at his brother, at the blood trickling from the corner of Tim's mouth. Angry color flooded back into his face. "I'm gonna have Chief Barnes on you. Coming in here attacking us and threatening us with a gun. You'll be behind bars!"

"While you're at it, better tell the police about Mrs. Dancer."

"Just her word against ours. Barnes will believe us."

"What about Bob Hopper? How long do you think he'll stand up under questioning? No, this is between you two and me." Leaning over, Trent bundled up the bedspread and thrust it under his arm. Bending over the table, he looked first at Danny and then into his brother's terrified eyes. "I'm only saying this once, so listen. If you two ever get within ten yards of Mrs. Dancer again I'm going to beat you to death, one inch at a time. Keep away from her, her daughter, and her house." He glanced around him with disgust. "I'll take the cat with me. I wouldn't even leave a dead animal here."

As the door banged behind Trent, Tim felt gingerly at his mouth. His fingers came away wet with blood. "Think he means it?" he mumbled through swelling lips.

Kicking aside the brown stein, Danny turned the cold water tap on and held his hand under it. "You always were a bloody fool. Sure he means it!"

Tim wiped his fingers across his shirt. He looked down at the bloodstains. "Then I ain't doing nothing else, even for money. It ain't worth having that maniac after us."

"For a change," his brother told him, "you're talking sense."

12

The following morning Karen slept until she was roused by a ray of sun, slanting across the bed and shining on her face. She came awake by degrees, finally lifting her head long enough to make out the tiny gilt numerals on her travel clock. She called to her daughter, but there was no answer from the adjoining room. Slipping her legs out of bed, she stretched and reached for her robe. Then she padded to Jamie's room and looked around the connecting door. On Jamie's bed the covers were thrown back. Under the window was a red litter box, a bowl of water, and a dish of cat food.

Memories of the previous day came flooding back. She wondered what she could tell Jamie about the kitten and then suddenly realized the child might already be outdoors searching for Oliver. Hastily she brushed her hair and pushed her feet into slippers.

When she reached the kitchen, a disgruntled-looking Mac was lifting pancakes from a skillet onto Jamie's plate. "What's got into this youngster today?" she grumbled. "Accusing me of putting that dratted kitten outside—"

"I didn't say that," Jamie protested. "I asked if you could have left the door open."

"Well, I didn't. After all the work I went to, fixing up that box and food. I checked on the kitten before I left and asked Sybil to look in and see if it needed more water." Mac banged the skillet back on the stove. "I'm going to phone down right now and ask if she left the door open."

Behind Jamie's back, Karen caught the old woman's eyes and shook her head warningly. Puzzled, Mac looked from Karen to the child at the table. "Here's some maple syrup for those cakes," she told the little girl. "Bet you don't get that in New York. Sit down, Karie. Want I should make hotcakes for you?"

"Toast and coffee will do," Karen told her.

As Jamie finished her breakfast, the children from the farm pressed their faces against the screen. Jamie looked inquiringly at her mother, and Karen nodded.

"Stay in the yard," she told the children.

When the door banged shut, cutting off Jamie's excited voice asking if they'd seen Oliver, Mac turned away from the stove. "What's going on with that blamed cat?"

After Karen had told her, the old woman sat down heavily. Behind round lenses her eyes were bewildered. "Don't know anymore whether I'm standing on my head or my tail, Karie. Things like that don't happen in Hampton. Who could have done it?"

Shaking her head, Karen reached for the radio on the windowsill and clicked it on. Rock music filled the room and she winced, turned down the volume, and tried another station. A hearty voice promised, "This one will be a real old-timer, folks," and he was correct. A nasal voice began to sing about the dear hearts and gentle people in his home town. Karen fumbled with the switch and turned it off.

"My home town," she muttered morosely. "My home

town has given me nothing but ruined tires, insults, and slaughtered kittens! Someone is trying to terrify me and drive me out so I won't sell my land. I'll tell you one thing, Mac, I'm going to get to the bottom of this and I'm doing it today!''

"Calm down, Karie. Don't take on. Where you going?''

"I don't know. But another thing. If I can't find out who is responsible, I'm going to ram that nuclear plant right down the throats of those dear hearts and gentle people!''

"You always did have a wicked temper.''

Karen flung through the doorway, the swinging doors grating madly. Over her shoulder she yelled, "I don't have Hampton ice water in *my* veins. I have good red Italian blood, and it's boiling!''

I've had it, she told herself furiously. Bolts on her bedroom door and a gun in the wardrobe, while someone laughed slyly at her. One of the faces she knew hiding a smirk while she locked herself in! She marched down the hall and stopped by the marble-topped table where the phone rested. In the mirror over it she caught a glimpse of her flushed face. Dark circles ringed her eyes. Damn it to hell, she muttered, and reached for the phone book.

There were three rings before the receiver was picked up and she heard her uncle's precise tones.

"I'd like to come down,'' she told him.

"By all means. Are you dropping Jennifer off? Perhaps we could have a rematch.''

"I'll bring her with me, but I want to talk to you alone.''

"You sound very serious, my dear. Is it about that abominable business at the meeting yesterday?''

"No. I want to ask your advice.''

There was a pause, and then he said, "This is very

flattering. Old chaps like myself are so often pushed on a shelf they cease to feel they can advise anyone. When will you be here?"

"My tires still aren't fixed so I'll have to walk."

"Make it as soon as you can."

They actually made it in a very short time. As Jamie and her mother walked by the farmhouse, Nat Jenks's battered pickup rattled down the driveway, turned out on the road, and pulled to a stop beside them. Leaning over, he swung the door open. "Going to town, Mrs. Dancer?"

He caught her off balance. She had expected him to avert his head and drive past them.

"Climb in," he said. "Here, Jamie, give me your hand."

Karen boosted the child up and Nat pulled her into the cab. Karen climbed in beside her. Nat piloted the truck down the road, looking straight ahead.

"Don't have much turn for words," he told her, "but I wanted to tell you how bad I feel about them boys throwing tomatoes at you. We all got pretty riled up—" Breaking off, he wrenched his eyes from the road and looked at her. "Meant every word I said there, but—" He broke off again and muttered gruffly, "Pretty nice of you to take the two tykes swimming, after what happened. They had a good time, all they could talk about all evening."

"I'm glad they enjoyed themselves. They're nice children."

For the first time since she had met him, he smiled. It wasn't much of a smile, but his lips did curve up briefly. "Where you heading?"

"Alfred Hampton's. If you could drop us off near the post office it would be fine."

"Drive you to the door," he told her.

He let them off at the Lovatt house and touched the

153

brim of his hat. Before walking up to the front door Karen paused, stared after the truck, and said, "Well!"

"I thought that was Nat Jenks," her uncle called from the doorway. "You got here in good time. I hear Jake Squeers is having trouble getting the proper tires for your car."

"Do you hear everything?"

"Just about, my dear. Hello, Jennifer, how are you today?" Without waiting for an answer he stood back and gestured them in. He was holding something in his hand. Holding it up, he gave the child a frosty smile. "Here is the General. I've been laying out the battle order again." He looked down at the tiny red-coated soldier on the white horse. "Come along into the library."

In the library the long plywood table was set up with rows of tiny soldiers, microscopic wagons, and miniature cannon. Putting the general down gently, Alfred touched Jamie's shoulder. "You can practice with these if you wish. If not, I have battle plans here for the War of 1812. Very interesting and complex. If that fails to hold your interest, there's a thesaurus here that is bound to increase your word power." He closed one gray eye in a wink. "The kitchen is right through that door, and I've put a piece of chocolate cake on the counter for you. The milk is in the refrigerator. Will you be all right while your mother and I talk?"

Jamie squeezed the frail hand resting on her shoulder. "Wonderful, Uncle Alfred."

"You're very good to her," Karen told him as he led the way to the parlor.

Closing the door behind him, he pointed at two chairs near a window. "I have something for us too, a little glass of Amos's port."

She was touched. Between the two chairs was the Queen Anne table. The chessboard had been moved back and two goblets of wine sat on its top. She sipped hers and lit a cigarette.

"What is your problem?" her uncle asked.

"Quite frankly, I'm scared half out of my wits. Ever since Jamie and I came to Hampton there has been a type—a type of terror campaign directed against us. You know about my tires being slashed, but there's more to it than that."

She twisted the stem of the goblet in her hands as she told him what had happened. He listened in silence, drawing his breath in sharply when she told him about the kitten and the knife. When she looked up she saw his fine-boned face, sunlight slanting through the window highlighting his high forehead and cheekbones. His brow was drawn into a frown.

"This is bad, very bad, my dear. I had no idea. . . . But tell me, why did you come to me?"

"For two reasons. This can't continue. So far I've managed to protect Jamie from it, but I don't know what will happen next. You know every person in town, you know their parents and their grandparents. I thought you might be able to guess who would do this sort of thing." She paused and then added, "And you're the only one I trust."

Reaching over, he put his hand over hers. She looked down at the dry skin, the blue knotted veins. "I'm glad you trust me, Karen. I have always felt you hated me because of that thoughtless thing I did when Father died. If I had known—but then I didn't, and it's too late. We can't relive the past, can we?"

"The past is dead, Uncle Alfred, dead and gone. It's the present we must worry about."

He removed his hand, and his voice was brisk again. "I have always fancied myself as a good judge of human nature. Now, the main thing to do is to try to pin down details. One must be meticulous with details." He opened the delicately carved drawer of the table and selected a pad of paper and a ballpoint pen. Balancing the pad on his knee, he said, "First let us work out the time sequence. Precisely what time did this first incident take place—the tire slashing?"

With a rueful smile she realized her uncle was throwing himself into the role of detective with the same enthusiasm he brought to his battle games. But she was committed; she had to go along with him.

"I don't know. Mac left about seven o'clock, and Jamie and I went directly to bed. Ashley and Sybil were out. Sybil was going to choir practice and Ashley had a meeting. They didn't see the damage to my car until the next morning, so it must have happened after they got home. They parked their car right beside mine, so one of them would have noticed."

"Hmm." His brow furrowed. "We can place it fairly closely. Choir practice would be over at nine-thirty sharp. Sybil always has tea and a talk session with her friends afterward in the church kitchen. About an hour. Allow time for Ashley to pick her up and drive home. Eleven. It would have to be after that." He wrote in cramped script on the pad. "Now, the balloon and the panda."

"I can pin that down. Mac saw the sweater and panda just before she went to bed. Ashley and Sybil were home just after eleven. Mac didn't go upstairs until after they did, and she was asleep when Jamie saw the balloon."

"After eleven again, then. Last night?"

"I phoned Sybil just before I came here and pretended the kitten was lost. She told me she had stopped in Jamie's room before she went to bed, around ten-thirty, and it was fine. At least, that's what she said."

He stopped writing and looked sharply at her. "Do you suspect Sybil of this outrage?"

She shrugged. "Sybil has never liked me. You know that. And Ashley and she both feel the house should be theirs."

"It's true it should have been. They would have loved and cherished it. But it was willed to John and he willed it to you. Do you think Sybil would do a thing like this? There is not one person in this town who would stoop to such despicable business."

"It has to be someone in town. There are no strangers here."

"You're forgetting those two men from ANPP."

"One of them was with me last night and the other one—" Karen broke off, trying to picture Vince Halloway sneaking around with a cat in one hand and a knife in the other. "That is ridiculous. What would their motive be?"

He glanced slyly at her. "To make you so furious with Hampton that you agree to their demands to sell your land."

"That motive includes Roy Paul too, and—as he's so fond of saying—his mother was a Hampton. Your sister, in fact."

"Roy, hmm. Now that is a thought. He always has been a nasty piece of goods. Didn't take after his mother at all. Celia was a lovely woman. Never could understand why she married a bounder like Clifford Paul. A deceitful man, devious. But . . . Roy?" He shook his head. "Frankly I don't think he has the intelligence for this."

Karen squirmed in her chair. The sun was shining directly on the back of her neck. "Whoever did it would have to know the house and would have to know Sybil and Ashley's hours and habits. Doesn't that narrow it down?"

His pen was racing over the pad. "What's that? No, it doesn't narrow it down. Almost everyone in town knows the Hampton house inside and out. As for your cousins'

157

hours, you can almost set your clock by their movements. Now, let's think. Each episode occurring after eleven. A night walker. When the streets are empty and there's very little traffic. And all those shadows to duck into, those trees to shelter him. I say *him,* of course, because we must use some term. It could easily be a woman. As I mentioned to you, women can be deadly."

Despite the warmth across her shoulders, Karen shivered. "Don't, Uncle Alfred."

Startled at her tone, he glanced up. His eyes traveled over her hair and her face and then down to her throat. "I never realized it before, Karen, but there is a strong resemblance between you and Maybelle. Sitting there with the sun shining on your hair . . . it's almost uncanny. Superficial, of course; her hair was much lighter."

Intrigued, Karen asked, "Who is Maybelle?"

His eyes dropped back to the pad on his knee. "A girl I once knew," he said shortly.

Karen scented a romance. It had to be an old one, she thought. Lavender and old lace, a girl he had known years before. The only woman in his life she had ever heard about was the sour-faced Lottie.

Her uncle seemed to have forgotten she was there. He was staring down at the pad, but she was certain he didn't see it. "Uncle," she said tentatively.

His head jerked up. "What's that? Oh, yes, I was saying it had to be a night walker. We must definitely get to the bottom of this. Unsavory. We can't have Jennifer exposed to it." He added hastily, "Or you either, my dear." He glanced at the tall clock in the corner. Under the glass panel a pendulum was swinging back and forth. "Lottie will be here in a few minutes to make my lunch. As soon as she leaves I will make a few phone calls and see what I can find out. If necessary I will ring you later." Putting the pen and pad in the drawer, he closed it.

He got stiffly to his feet and, opening the door, called down the hall. When Karen reached the front door, he was patting Jamie on the head. "Did you eat the cake? Yes, I can see you did." He pulled a handkerchief out of his pocket and carefully wiped crumbs off the child's chin. Then he took her mother's hand in a warm, reassuring grip. "Did you know, Karen, that we had an ancestor who acquitted himself illustriously in the War of 1812? An earlier Alfred. Major Alfred Hampton." He looked down at the child. "Hamptons have always been valorous, my dear Jennifer."

"Am I val-or-ous?" she asked.

"I think so, I think you are indeed." He squeezed Karen's hand. "Leave everything in my hands and don't worry, don't worry any further."

After they left the Lovatt house, Karen stopped at the post office to buy some stamps, and when they came out of the building Jim Miles was standing there beside a late-model car. He waved at them, smiling, as they joined him. "I saw you and waited to give you a ride home. That is, if you're going home."

"We're going home," Karen told him, and stood back to let Jamie slip into the car first. "I'm glad to get a ride, Jim. If Jake Squeer doesn't come up with tires soon my feet will be worn out."

"Walking is excellent for you," he said with a grin. "And that's the doctor speaking. On the other hand, it must be annoying. And you, Jamie, how are you enjoying your visit?"

"Some of it has been fun, some hasn't."

"That's an honest answer. I was wondering if you'd like to go to Sunday school this coming weekend. Cassie Saunders teaches a class for your age group."

Karen thought wildly of Jamie loose in the First Anglican Church, perhaps organizing a sit-in. She opened her mouth but Jamie spoke first.

"I'm considering converting to Buddhism."

He wrenched his eyes away from the road. "What?"

"She doesn't know what that means," Karen said quickly. "It's only another word she's picked up."

"Peace of mind through meditation," Jamie murmured dreamily. "The ideal state of nirvana."

The truck directly ahead of them slammed on its brakes and Jim nearly rammed it. He wiped his brow. "A heathen, Karen! Haven't you seen to her religious training?"

"Watch the road, Jim, and pay no attention to her. She's pulling your leg."

"I am not," Jamie said indignantly. "I'm thinking of converting—"

"That's enough." Karen hastily changed the subject. "How's the doctor business?"

He turned north on Cypress. "As a matter of fact, it's blooming. Old Mrs. Jarvis is having her gallbladder removed, and I had a couple of patients bright and early this morning who might interest you. The Dimwiddie brothers."

Drawing her breath in sharply, Jamie straightened in her seat. Karen sent her a warning look. "What's wrong with the Dimwiddie brothers?"

"Looks like someone put them through a meat grinder. Tim has two puffy lips and will have to have dental work on his front teeth, and Danny has two bones broken in his right hand. They said they were in a fight, which is nothing new. What is unusual is that they're generally on the handing-out rather than the receiving end."

Jamie smiled radiantly. "Good!"

He gave her a reproving look. "What a strange reaction from a little girl. I do think, Jamie, you should be taken in hand."

"Would you spank me?"

"Me? No way. I believe in reasoning with children, not in physical punishment. Children are small adults, and they can be reached by common sense and reasoning."

Jim enlarged on his theory of peaceful coexistence with small adults all the way through town, down the stretch of country road to the brick house set back in its canopy of flaming maples. Karen found herself becoming bored and kicked her daughter repeatedly, every time she saw her lips opening.

As he got out of the car and hurried around to open the door for them, Jamie muttered in her mother's ear, "Cal smashed them good, didn't he?"

Karen glared down at her. "You've got a wonderful start on being a serene Buddhist. Besides, we don't know for certain that Cal did it. They *could* have been in a fight."

Giving her a look of derision, Jamie ran to welcome her two friends, who were waiting for her. Both Davy and Betsy had bright scarves wound around their heads and each wore one large hoop earring. Dave waved a wooden sword at Jamie. "Paw made these for us! Made you one, too. Wanta play pirate?"

"I'll be captain and make you and Betsy walk the plank!" Jamie yelled, and the three of them disappeared around the grape arbor.

Mac met them in the hall and beamed at Jim Miles. "Good to see you. Shouldn't make such a stranger of yourself. Can you stay for lunch? We're having chicken an' dumplings. Chocolate pie for dessert."

"Sounds tempting, Mac, but not today. I only have a few minutes free. I wanted to talk with Karen."

"No problem." Banging open the front parlor door, Mac waved them into it. "No hurry for lunch. It'll keep.

161

Take your time." As she closed the door the eyelid of one round eye lowered in a wink at Karen.

Karen wandered restlessly around the room. She picked up Ashley's humidor from the table beside his favorite chair and then put it down again.

"Karen," Jim said.

As she turned, her first thought was that he looked as much at home in the room as Sybil and Ashley did. He was a handsome man, she mused, and age would not make many changes. When his hair grayed it would be as thick and smooth as it was now, and his tall well-proportioned body would have the same dignity. Idly she picked up one of Ashley's pipes. Taking it from her hand, Jim replaced it in the pipe rack. He put a hand on her wrist. "Don't fidget," he said, and with no change of voice asked, "Will you marry me?"

She glanced at the hand on her wrist. It was well cared for, the fingers long and tapering, the nails beautifully kept. No scars on Jim's hands, she thought absently. Her eyes went from his hand to his face. "I was thinking of saying something trite, like 'How sudden!,' but it really isn't. I've been widowed for eight years. Why haven't you phoned or written or come to see me in all that time?"

"I don't know. I thought about it often, but there never seemed to be an opportunity. My practice kept me pinned down."

"There was still the mail and the telephone. Why *now*, Jim, after all these years?"

His eyes looked warmly into hers and his hand tightened. "It was seeing you again. Seeing you that day walking down Main Street. Time just rolled back and I knew I still loved you, that I'd always loved you."

Dropping her arm away from his hand she wandered back to the table again. Beside the humidor was a china ornament shaped like an eighteenth-century gentlewoman. The puffs of hair were arranged high on the tiny head, and a delicate hand held a fan in front of the lower part of the face. Cornflower blue eyes smiled over the fan, echoing the color of the tiered skirt. Karen picked it up.

"And if we did marry, Jim, would you return to New York with me?"

He looked shocked. "I'm a doctor."

"There are doctors in New York too."

"I'm needed in Hampton."

"Where your father was a doctor, and your grandfather was a doctor, and—"

"Be careful, you might drop it." He took the miniature from her hand and carefully replaced it. "It's Lofton china and an excellent piece, very old. What is the matter with you, Karen?"

Disregarding his question, she asked another of her own. "What would you expect of me as a wife? Would you agree to my continuing with my own work?"

His mouth firmed. "Of course not. Managing the house and with Jamie to raise . . . of course not. I want a wife, not an exhausted career woman. Is your work that important to you?"

"I don't know. But I do know one thing. I think you are confusing me with the girl who left Hampton. I'm not the same person."

"I love *you! You* as you are this moment." He reached out and pulled her close to him.

His arms were warm and strong around her. She felt his lips touch her hair, her brow. Tilting her chin back he kissed her gently on the mouth. Against her breast she could feel the hard contours of his chest, the muffled beat of his heart.

"You love me too," he whispered.

She leaned back in the circle of his arms and gazed up at him. "Yes, I do. But is it the memory I love, the boy I

163

used to know and lost, or the man with me now? I'm confused, Jim, badly confused."

His arms fell away and he took a step backward. "You need time. I'm afraid I sprang this on you too suddenly. Take your time, Karen. I can wait."

Waiting you're good at, she thought, and immediately felt a pang of remorse. She was identifying Jim with Hampton and taking out her accumulated grievances on him. And he didn't deserve it. He was attractive, talented, honest. He wanted to marry her.

She opened her mouth to tell him she would seriously consider his proposal and found entirely different words coming from it. "Where do you stand on this issue with ANPP?"

He blinked. "What's that got to do with—" Breaking off, he rubbed a hand across his hair. "You deserve the truth. Hampton is no place for a plant of this type. I strongly oppose it."

"You are an intelligent man, Jim, and an educated one. Don't you think the plant is necessary?"

"It may or may not be necessary; there are two sides to that. But even if it is—"

"They should find another place for it. Somewhere more suitable."

"Exactly." Pushing back an immaculate cuff he checked his watch. "I must run. I have to check on Mrs. Jarvis." He brushed his lips across her cheek. "Think about it, darling."

"I will," she told him. "I will think about it."

Karen was absentminded all the time she was eating lunch with Mac and the children. She paid no attention either to the children's chatter or to Mac's occasional remark. Mac, strangely enough, didn't chide her. Shaking her head at Karen's virtually untouched plate, she sighed

164

and scraped the cooling chicken, dumplings, and gravy into the garbage container.

Karen pushed back her chair. "I think I'll write some letters, Mac."

"Use the library. Ashley's got all the writing stuff in the middle drawer. Mind you don't muss the drawers up. He's fussy as an old maid."

Karen wrote for nearly an hour at her cousin's desk. She wrote a short note to her boss at the advertising agency, another to the superintendent of her apartment building, and a long letter to her closest friend in New York. She saw Shirley's lean face before her eyes as she wrote. Shirley might be short on looks but she was long on personality and had a mind like a honed blade.

Two proposals in two days, she wrote her friend gaily. *One serious and the other a joke. One from a handsome man and the other from an animated scarecrow. And I find I wish the scarecrow had been the serious one.* She stopped, looked at what she had written, and thought, Now that's a Freudian slip if I ever saw one. How could she compare Cal Trent to Jim? Cassie had been quite right about Jim: He wanted a full-time wife. A wife's career had no place in Jim's life. So what about her work? How important was it to her? Granted she enjoyed it, but was she using it as a substitute? Was she a liberated woman or just one waiting around for a dominant male? And what's with all this soul searching? she asked herself impatiently.

She picked up her pen again. Outside the door she heard the phone ringing and Mac's heavy footsteps sounded along the hall. A few minutes later, Mac stuck her head around the door.

"Alfred Hampton for you. Don't bother getting up. He told me to tell you to come down and see him." She added, "Now."

"I'm almost finished here, Mac." Fishing in her pocket, Karen found the book of stamps she had bought that morning. "I want to get these in the mail."

"Better take time to run up and do something about your face, Karie. Noticed at lunch your lipstick was all smudged." Mac fired a parting shot. "Almost as though somebody had been smooching with you."

Grinning, Karen reached for an envelope. After she'd addressed her letters and sealed and stamped the envelopes, she took Mac's advice and freshened her face. She took her time walking into town. Probably Uncle Alfred wanted to make more notes on times and details. She could picture him leaning over his meticulous pages. Hampton's own Sherlock Holmes.

As she passed the library she met Bruce Gotham. Under his arm he held two books, and when he saw her his face brightened.

"Hi, Karen, nice to see you again so soon. That's sure a bright little girl you got. Where is she today, home tending Oliver?"

His words brought everything flooding back: the dying room, the kitten on the green spread, the knife beside it. Despite the warmth she shivered. "I'm afraid Jamie has lost her cat, Bruce."

"Say, that's a shame." He scratched his bald pate. "My daughter's cat just had a batch of kittens. Cute little things. Want I should get one for Jamie?"

"No, but thanks for the thought. If she insists on having another one I'll get it for her when we go back to New York."

"Got time to have coffee with me?"

She smiled down at him. "Not now, Bruce. May I have a rain check? Uncle Alfred's waiting for me, and I'd better hurry."

He nodded and she walked swiftly down Main Street,

turned at Hopper's Drugstore, and hurried toward the post office. As she neared the building she slowed long enough to push the envelopes through the letter slot. By the time she reached the stoop of the Lovatt house she was panting.

She half expected her uncle to be watching for her and to swing the door open. When he didn't, she knocked briskly. There was no answer. She knocked again.

From behind her a voice called, "Hey, Karen."

Swinging around she saw Cassie Saunders coming up the walk. The tall woman was wearing a crimson sweater. Under a slim skirt her long legs flashed in a loose, athletic stride. In her arms was a pile of books.

"There's no answer, Cassie. I wonder where Uncle Alfred can be."

"He must be in. Lottie would skin him alive if he dared to go out. Maybe he didn't hear you." Cassie pounded on the door. "That's odd. We'd better check."

Turning the knob, she opened the door. Karen was on her heels as she entered the hall. It was dark, so dark she could hardly make out the outlines of the staircase.

"My God!" Cassie threw out an arm and stopped her. The books fell out of her arms, and she knelt on the floor.

"Uncle Alfred!" Karen screamed.

Alfred Hampton looked small and crumpled on the old Turkey carpet at the foot of the stairs. He lay face down, one arm twisted under him, the other thrown out at an unnatural angle. The fingers of the extended arm were clenched into a fist. From it protruded the helmet and shoulders of a toy soldier. Alfred's General Wolfe had fought his last battle.

13

IN THE CHAIR behind Alfred Hampton's desk, Theo Barnes shifted his heavy body and the springs groaned a protest. The sun had worked its way around the house and now shone through the foliage of the maple outside the library window. Splinters of light fell yellowly across the long table and the rows of tiny soldiers. Barnes moved his eyes from their silent ranks to the soldier on the white horse placed on the desktop squarely in front of him.

"Well, I guess that's about everything," he told the two women facing him. He sighed heavily. "Lottie's going to take it hard. Waited all her life to get her hands on Alfred and then loses him. Only fifteen years they been married, eh, Cassie?"

"More like eighteen."

"That's right. Millie and me and our son went to their wedding. Now Millie's gone and boy's gone and so is Alfred."

"You still have your grandson," Cassie consoled him.

"Don't remind me of Junior!" His eyes swung to the other woman. "Haven't met Junior yet, have you, Karen?"

She shook her head. She wasn't thinking of Junior. She was thinking that Theo Barnes hadn't changed any more than the town had. His navy blue uniform was wrinkled, the elbows and seat as shiny as they had been when she was a child. His cap sat beside his elbow, and its brim had left a deep line across his brow. A grizzled rim of close-cropped hair surrounded a high bald dome, and the face under it was as fat and red as it had been twenty years before. He still had an asthmatic wheeze.

He sighed again. "Haven't missed much not meeting the lad. Watches too much television and gets his job as constable mixed up with acting like a Wild West marshal. That getup he insists on wearing. Know what he asked me to call him? Tex! Told him as long as I was still kicking he'd stay Theo Barnes Junior." He peered hopefully at Cassie. "Sure don't relish having to tell Lottie."

"If you want I'll do it," she volunteered.

"Appreciate it. A woman is better at that sort of thing than a blunt old codger like me."

Uncrossing her long legs, Cassie stood up. "I'd better go down to her shop. I feel very bad myself. The town is not going to be the same without Alfred." She added violently, "Why couldn't he have kept off those stairs? Lottie warned him and warned him!"

"Gotta remember that Lottie was the one who bundled him up those stairs every day like a little boy to have his nap. Can't treat a man like a baby. Alfred Hampton was a man."

Picking up the books she had dropped, Cassie touched Karen's shoulder and opened the door. Karen made a move to get out of her chair.

"Close that door behind you, Cassie," he called. "You stay put a minute, Karen. I'll give you a ride home. You're not fit to walk all the way out to the farm." As the door shut, he nodded toward it. "Fine woman, Cassie Saunders, she'll handle Lottie. Now, I know you feel bad but there's a couple of things I want to ask you." He picked up the little soldier and ran a blunt finger over the red tunic.

Karen was twisting her handkerchief in her fingers. "I still can't understand why that was in his hand."

"Seems clear enough. Alfred was always playing with these things. Must have decided to go upstairs and carried it along with him."

"They're antiques and he prized them, Theo. When I was here this morning he was holding that one when he came to the door. But before we went into the parlor to talk, he brought it in here and put it in its exact place on the table. He was a meticulous man."

"Regular fussbudget. Ashley Hampton's just like him. But Alfred was getting on, and people do tend to get absentminded. Getting that way myself." His tiny eyes under tufted white brows settled on her face. "Hate to keep you here. Your eyes look like a couple of holes burnt in a sheet. But you had a talk with Alfred this morning, and now you're back this afternoon. Had to walk all the way in. What was it about?"

She smoothed the handkerchief out over her knees. "Does it matter now?"

"Just curious. Don't like loose ends." He paused and then asked, "Have anything to do with your tires being slashed?"

Startled, she glanced up at him. He might be getting absentminded but his eyes were shrewd. "Part of it."

"Better tell me the rest."

She told him. When she reached the events of the preceding evening she hesitated. Should she tell him only about the kitten or should she tell him also about the Dimwiddies? She decided against too much honesty. From the description of the boys' injuries she might get

170

Cal Trent into trouble. He heard her out, his eyebrows drawn together over the bridge of his fleshy nose.

"What'd you want from Alfred?"

"Some help. I thought he might be able to figure out who is doing it."

"Why didn't you come to me?"

That was a hard question to answer. She was wondering why herself. "Alfred was family. I suppose I didn't think it important enough to bother the police with."

"That's the trouble with most people. Go anywhere but to the law. This is my town and I've policed it for forty years. Anything goes on here, I want to know about it!" Breaking off, he patted his chest and wheezed heavily. "Shouldn't ought to get het up. Makes my blood pressure turn handsprings. Well, what about it, could Alfred help?"

"He didn't say much. He took notes and was particular about the time these things took place. Finally, we pinned down the fact that all three of them must have happened after eleven at night. He said something about a night walker."

"Alfred was a night walker himself. Lottie kept him cooped up all day, but he snuck out many a night. Good walker, Alfred, used to meet him all over town while I was making my rounds—before Ashley put Junior on as my constable, that was. Junior takes night duties now." He pointed at the end of the desk. "Mind handing me that phone? Don't like to move around more'n I have to."

Leaning over, Karen put the phone into his hands. He dialed, wheezed a bit, and then said, "Junior, this is the Chief. And stop calling me Grandpaw during working hours. Listen, I want you to pick up those Dimwiddie brothers. . . . Yeah, Dimwiddie. . . . Just a minute, I'm not done. Better get Bob Hopper and Chuck Paul too. . . . I know Bob's dad is sick." Barnes wiped his brow off on the back of his sleeve and directed an exasperated look at Karen. "Holy Jehoshaphat, will you listen instead of yammering? Get Sarah from the grocery store to take over the drugstore for a couple of hours. . . . Yeah, you got that? . . . Yes, in my office, you dummy, where did you think?" Crashing the phone down, he lumbered to his feet. "Come on, Karen, we're going to get to the bottom of this."

She stood up. "What does it have to do with those boys?"

Opening the door, he stood back and waited for her. "Don't know rightly, but we'll see. Jim Miles told me about that mix-up in the drugstore, and I heard those Dimwiddies were sure enough anxious to pelt you with tomatoes at the town hall. Well, let's go talk to them."

The last people she wanted to see were the Dimwiddies, but Barnes herded her into his office on the lower floor of the town hall, sat her down in a shabby armchair at one side of his desk, and sank into a creaking swivel chair behind it. The office looked as worn and untidy as he did. The walls were painted a bilious green, the floor was covered with faded linoleum, and white paint was flaking off the radiator. Barnes settled back comfortably, his eyes half closed, his hands folded peacefully over his paunch. She half expected him to snore, but when the door opened his eyes snapped open.

"Sure took your time," he grumbled at the apparition leading the four boys in. "This lad's my constable, Karen. Looks a little like Wild Bill Hickok, don't he?"

Barnes wasn't far off. The tall scrawny young man was wearing a police uniform but he had added a white Stetson and was balanced on the high heels of a pair of gaudy cowboy boots. She soon found out that he had also cultivated a drawl. "Rounded the varmints up, Grand-

172

paw—" He caught his grandfather's bulging eyes and said hastily, "I mean, Chief."

"Okay, Junior, now get out and practice your fast draw or something."

"Can I stay and help you grill them?"

Barnes merely cocked a big thumb at the door, and the boy beat a hasty retreat. The old man turned to the four boys standing in a huddle by the door. "Sit down, lads. Want to ask a few questions."

One by one they took their places on the four straight chairs lined up in front of his desk. The Dimwiddies hurriedly selected the two farthest from Karen. Tim's face was swollen and bruised, from his beard to the bridge of his nose, and Danny's right hand was in a cast. Chuck Paul lounged beside Danny, and Bob Hopper perched on the edge of the end chair.

Barnes seemed to be in no hurry to begin. He sat back, his fingers laced across his paunch. Karen glanced sideways at him. He was staring directly at Bob Hopper's pimply face. The boy moved uneasily and blurted, "I was with them, Chief, but I didn't have a thing to do with it. I told them to cut it out—"

"Shut up," Danny growled.

"Better do that yourself," Barnes snapped. "Not another word out of you. Now, Bob, you were saying?"

The boy's eyes slid from Danny's set face back to Barnes. "I told them to let up on Mrs. Dancer and the kid. Danny hit me." He moved one finger along his lips. "I just happened to be with them. They saw her and the kid walking along Arbutus, and Tim says, 'Let's have some fun.' So Danny stops the car and gets out and they give her a bad time." Color swept up into his face. "I don't know what they'd have pulled if that other car hadn't come along."

"When'd this happen, Bob?"

"Last night. But you know. She must have told you."

"Matter of fact, this is the first I've heard about it." His cold eyes moved toward Karen. "Left anything else out?" She shook her head and he asked, "You have anything to do with slashing Mrs. Dancer's tires, Bob?"

The boy's head shook violently. "I heard about it, but I was at home that night. You can ask Dad, he'll tell you—"

"Okay." Barnes jerked his head at the door. "You better get back to the store. Tell Sarah thanks for me."

Jumping up, the boy left the room as fast as his legs would carry him. As he opened the door, Junior stuck his head into the room. "Got a guy out here who wants to come—hey, you, stop that pushing!"

Junior was thrust aside as Trent shouldered past him. He cast one cold look at the three boys in front of the desk, nodded to Barnes, and moved over beside Karen.

"Mr. Trent, is it?" The old policeman peered up at him. "What you doing here?"

"I heard about your uncle," Trent said to Karen. To Barnes he said, "I'm taking her home."

"Not yet, you aren't. But you can wait here till she's done, if you want." Trent leaned against the wall behind Karen's chair and Barnes turned back to the boys. "Seems to me you lads are taking quite an interest in Mrs. Dancer here."

Chuck Paul leaned forward. "I had nothing to do with all this, Chief. Why did you drag me in?"

"Hear that, Tim?" Barnes asked in a friendly tone. "Young Chuck had nothing to do with it. Looks like you and Danny are going to take all the blame. Better tell me about Mrs. Dancer's tires, lad."

Tim's swollen mouth moved grotesquely. His eyes flickered from Trent's face to Chuck Paul. Chuck turned his head away.

"Okay," Tim mumbled. "I'm not taking this alone. Chuck's the one who put us up to it—"

Danny swung on him. "Will you shut your mouth, you damn fool?"

Barnes's hands dropped away from his stomach. With surprising speed he was out of his chair and around the desk. Grabbing a fold of Danny's shirt, he hauled him clear of his chair. "Told *you* once to keep your mouth shut. But if you want to talk so bad, go ahead. Hard to understand your brother through that mashed mouth anyway." He loosened his hold, and the boy thudded back on his chair. Stalking around the desk, Barnes dropped into his swivel chair. In a milder tone, he said, "Give."

Danny stared sullenly at him. "And if I don't?"

"Looks like you got one mighty sore hand. Want another?"

Danny shrugged. "Tim's right. Before Mrs. Dancer got here, Chuck showed us a snap he had. She was pretty young in it, but we had no trouble recognizing her. So we gave her a bad time in the drugstore and threw tomatoes at the meeting. We—"

"Whoa! Let's start from the beginning. What'd he want you to do!"

"Hassle her. Get her all riled up and mad at the town and everybody in it."

"Money change hands?"

"Sure. Chuck gave us a hundred bucks between us."

Barnes whistled softly through his teeth. "A lot of money for a little hassling."

Danny's grin pulled his lips wolfishly back from stained teeth. "We thought so, but what the hell; we could use it. Tim and me sneaked out to the Hampton house that night and waited till we saw the lights go out and then we went into the garage and did her tires."

Barnes grunted, pulled open a drawer, and thumped a

175

pad of paper and pen on his desk. "Okay, how about the next night?"

Danny's low brow furrowed. "What next night? We saw her and the kid *last* night, but—" Catching Trent's eye, he broke off abruptly.

Swinging around, the policeman stared at Trent. "I'd swear these boys are plumb scared of you." Trent gazed back stolidly and Barnes continued. "Before you gave Mrs. Dancer and her little girl a hard time last night did you drop in to her house and kill a kitten?"

"No way! Look, Bob Hopper was with us all evening. He'll tell you we were nowhere near that house."

"How about the night before? That'd be Tuesday. Up to any hassling that night?"

"Honest to God, Chief, all we did was ruin the tires."

Barnes leaned back again, rested his head against the chair, and looked at the ceiling. The only sound in the room was his wheezing. "Can you two prove where you were Tuesday night?"

Danny turned toward his brother and they exchanged looks. "Better tell him," Tim mumbled painfully.

"We were playing poker. Bob Hopper was in on the game."

"Usually takes four. Who was the other one?"

"Uh . . . well, it was Junior."

"Junior?" Barnes came bolt upright. "Did you say *Junior?* He was supposed to be on duty, checking the stores out and making the rounds. Junior," he roared, "get in here!"

A white Stetson poked around the door. "Want me, Grandpaw?"

"Stop calling me that and take that stupid hat off!" Patting his chest, Barnes forced his voice down to a rumble. "Now tell me, where were you and what were you doing Tuesday night? Don't be scared, tell the truth."

176

A prominent Adam's apple bobbed up and down in Junior's scrawny neck. "We had a few hands of poker, Bob and Tim and Danny and me."

"How long did those few hands take, son?"

"Uh . . . from about seven till three."

Barnes lunged to his feet. "Get out of here, you . . . you dimwit, 'fore I forget you're blood kin!" He braced both hands on the desktop. "That blame idiot's going to be the death of me! Holy Jehoshaphat, how does Ashley think I can teach him policing when he couldn't even learn to be a mechanic?" He waved at the Dimwiddies and they sprang to their feet. Barnes half turned toward Karen. "You want to prefer charges about your tires?"

"No," she told him.

"You're getting off lucky this time," Barnes told the boys. "Want you to go home and get packed and clear out of here for a time. Go over and visit them cousins of yours in Katoma; make your visit last about a month. One more thing. If someone hadn't already rearranged your face"— he pointed a big finger at Tim—"and broke your hand for you"—the same finger jabbed at Danny—"I'd do it myself. Nobody hassles women and young ones in my town. When you do get back here you better keep your noses clean. I'll have my eyes peeled, and if you so much as spit on the sidewalk I'll run you out of town permanent like. Understand?"

They evidently understood and wasted no time in putting the door between them and the irate police chief. Karen marveled at the old man. Age didn't appear to have taken his razor sharpness from him. She noticed a white-faced Chuck Paul edging toward the door. His sneer was gone and he looked much younger.

"Get back here," Barnes ordered. "Didn't tell you to go."

"You've got nothing on me," Chuck said earnestly. "I

can prove where I've been every minute since Cousin Karen came to town."

"Siddown!" Barnes waited until the boy obeyed and then sank back into his big chair. Mopping at the sweat beading his bald head, he peered at the sodden tissue and threw it toward an overflowing wastepaper basket. It missed. "Gotta calm down," he muttered. "No sense in getting all het up."

Karen bent and put the tissue on top of the litter in the basket. "May we leave now?"

"Sorry," the old man said gently. "Shame to put you through this today, but I don't like what's been happening to you and that child of yours. Never heard anything like it all the time I've been chief here. Don't like it one little bit." He swung his head around. "Who give you the money, Chuck? Was it your mother or your dad?"

Chuck's lips set in a firm line. "Why don't you ask why I wanted it done?"

"No sense in plowing a field more'n once, lad. Reason's as plain as the nose on your face. Get your cousin here all fussed up and mad at Hampton and what's she going to do? Sell her land just to spite the town. Who's going to gain? Your family. Nice fat commission for your dad, more money than he's made for years. I know for a fact his realty business is shaky, and the mortgage on your house is worth more'n the house is." He pulled at his lower lip. "Can't force a son to speak against his own parents, but I guess I don't have to. Roy Paul . . . no. He's hungry for the money, but he wouldn't do this to Karen. But Vi? She always has been a schemer. I remember when she was a gal and had a crush on this young preacher. He couldn't see her, so she let on he'd made improper advances. Poor devil was run out of town. Uh-huh, could be the sort of thing Vi would do. Don't have to say anything,

178

Chuck. Just get out of here and tell your mother no more, hear?"

The boy left the room slowly, his feet dragging, and Barnes swiveled around so he faced Karen. "We know part of it but not all. That leaves us with who's doing the rest, and the rest is the rotten part. I'll think on it and keep my eyes open. Karen, you look out for yourself." He shook his head and glared up at Trent. "Well, what are you waiting for? Girl's fagged out, best get her home. Take care of her, she's had a rough time."

Putting his hand under her elbow, Trent helped her to her feet. She found she was leaning against him. He tucked her hand under his arm and led her toward the door. The old man's voice stopped them.

"Gotta admit you got Hampton blood, Karen. Most females had the time you've had would be plumb crushed."

"The Hampton's have always been valorous. Uncle Alfred told Jamie that just this morning," she said—and unexpectedly dissolved in tears.

"Don't take on. Women crying always get me all het up." He peered up at the man supporting her. "Off the record, Trent, what'd you use on the Dimwiddies, your fists?"

Trent grinned at him. "What if I told you a gun butt?"

Barnes chuckled. "Wouldn't want to hear that. Wouldn't want to hear that a'tall."

14

SWINGING THE WHITE car into traffic, Trent glanced sideways at Karen. She had stopped crying and wiped her eyes and was staring straight ahead.

"Let's get out of this town for a little while. How about a drive before I take you home?"

"Please. But don't go too far out. I should really be getting back. I have to tell Jamie."

"She got pretty fond of the old gentleman, didn't she?"

They were passing Amos Lofton's factory. Karen darted a glance at it and then looked at the rows of cottages lining the sides of the hill. She pointed out a small white house with blue shutters. "That's where Mac lives. Yes, it's not going to be easy to tell Jamie that Uncle Alfred is dead. Funny, I can hardly believe it myself. I know he was old but he was so . . . so vitally alive."

They had reached the crest of Factory Hill, and Trent swung the car off the blacktop of the main road left onto a narrow graveled track. The tires kicked up a cloud of dust behind them and maples crowded up to the snake fences on either side. They drove past a cluster of barns and silos and then an old farmhouse with a gabled roof and a deep cool-looking veranda.

"Nice peaceful country," he mused. "Pastoral. But it hasn't been particularly peaceful for either you or Jamie. I was wondering, Why not cut your holiday short? How about me driving you to Toronto to get a flight back to New York? Or if you don't want to go back there yet, what about a few days on the West Coast?"

"There's nothing I'd like better, Cal, but we have to stay until after the funeral. If your offer is still open then, I might take you up on it."

"Will there be a coroner's inquest?"

"I suppose so, but it will only be a formality."

"No possibility of foul play?"

She glanced at his profile. "Of course not. Chief Barnes showed me the gouges in the wallpaper and the mark on the rail where his body hit. He must have slipped on one of the treads or had a fainting spell. Why did you say that?"

"Seems queer, just as he was trying to help you uncover the identity of X."

"X?"

"We've got to call your tormentor something. Like Barnes, I figured the Dimwiddies were X, but it's evident now that two groups are operating—or, I should say, *were* operating. Barnes has put the Dimwiddies out of business."

"With your help. I can't imagine your actually using a gun butt on those boys. I hate violence."

"Don't care much for it myself, but talking to the Dimwiddies was a waste of time."

She frowned, her light brows drawing together over large brown eyes. "You said group."

"X doesn't have to be one person. Could be two or even more."

She glanced out the window. "We'd better start back now."

He slowed the car, turned into a driveway leading to a barn, and reversed. A shaggy white-and-brown dog raced toward them. He barked, threw himself at the car, and then, his duty done, stood back calmly and watched as they turned back toward town. Karen rolled down her window and lifted her heavy hair off the nape of her neck. A light breeze, perfumed with the smells of country and fall, stirred the hair at her temples and cooled her neck. Somewhere leaves were burning, and the tart smell drifted into the car.

Trent drove in silence until they turned from Lofton Hill onto Arbutus. Then he said slowly, "This is a bad time to mention it, but Vince asked me to find out if you've come to any decision on your land. He certainly doesn't want to push, but the head office is pressuring him."

"This morning I was so furious that if I'd had an agreement of sale in front of me I think I would have signed it. Now . . . I just don't know. But I'll have an answer for him soon. After Uncle Alfred's funeral I'll tell him."

They were approaching the farmhouse, and Maudie Jenks was sitting on the porch steps with a pot on her lap and what looked like a bucket of peas beside her. She smiled and waved. Karen waved back. Swinging the car into the next driveway, Trent pulled to a stop behind her cousin's Buick.

"It looks like Ashley and his sister are home," she told him.

He grinned. "I was going to come in and say hello to Mac and Jamie, but I guess I'd better not. The way his honor the mayor feels about me, it might be a little awkward for all concerned." Stretching a long arm across her, he opened her door. As he drew his arm back, his hand brushed her knees.

"One more item, Karen. I've heard rumors about you and the young doctor. Any truth to them?"

"That depends on what you heard. Who is the rumor monger?"

"Roy Paul. He's keeping an anxious eye on you. The rumor—wedding bells may be going to ring." His voice was light but his hazel eyes were hard and cold.

Shrugging, she got out of the car. "Hampton is like any other small town. Rumors are always flying."

"And that's a neat way of avoiding a direct answer. I'm warning you, the doc's in for heavy competition. Can't have my girl throwing herself away on a stuffed shirt like him."

"Will you stop joking?" she snapped.

"Joking? I was never more serious in my life."

Shaking her head, she walked around the house to enter by the back door. Jamie came dashing out of the barn, waving a wooden sword and pointing at her head. Around her flaxen hair she had tied a vivid crimson and yellow scarf. From the lobes of one ear a long glittering earring dangled.

"I'm Blackbeard," she called. "I borrowed a scarf and one of your earrings."

"So I see—my best scarf," Karen called back, and opened the screen door.

Mac was at the sink scrubbing carrots and Ashley Hampton sat dejectedly at the table, his dark suit and tie in harmony with his haggard face. On either side of the swinging doors sat a pile of luggage. Near Ashley's feet were a toilet case, an overnight bag, and a large tan leather suitcase. On the other side were a battered Gladstone and a rattan sewing basket, several pieces of bright material and the handles of cutting shears protruding from it.

As punctilious as ever, Ashley came to his feet and held a chair for Karen. As she sat down he sank back on his own chair and passed one hand wearily across his brow. "A sad day, Karen, a sad day for all of us."

She noticed his resemblance to Alfred Hampton. When his hair whitened it would be even stronger. "How is Lottie?"

"In pieces." He pointed at the heap of luggage near him. "Sybil and I are going down to stay with her for a few days. I'll have to make the funeral arrangements, and I'm the executor of his estate. He was the last of our fathers' generation, Karen. Now there's only three of us left: Sybil, you, and me."

"You're forgetting Roy and his son. And there's Jamie too."

He sighed. "The name will die with me. No more Hamptons . . . no more Lovatts. Amos is the last of the Loftons. Perhaps Roy is right, the town is dying."

Her heart went out to him, and she reached over and touched his hand. He looked up at her and blinked. "I'm being selfish. We must think about you and Jamie. You can't stay on here alone. Your car is still out of operation, and—"

"We'll be fine, Ashley."

"No, no, Karen, it won't do. When I mentioned to Theo Barnes that Sybil and I were moving in with Lottie he insisted I have you come too. She has lots of room. You and Jamie come with us."

A voice from the door said sharply, "You'd better consult Lottie before you're too free with invitations."

Sybil stood in the doorway, a jacket over one arm, her fine face blotched and swollen. As she regarded Karen bitterly from red-rimmed eyes, Karen remembered the hatred Sybil had always had for her mother and herself.

"Sybil!" her brother said.

184

"She might just as well know. Lottie blames her for Uncle Alfred's death."

"I don't understand," Karen said.

Sybil took a couple of steps toward the other woman. "When Lottie came home at noon to make Uncle Alfred's lunch, she said you had him all upset. He wouldn't eat a bite. Lottie figures as soon as she left the house he tried to come downstairs and tripped and fell. She says she warned you not to make him nervous. He was a frail old man, and—"

"That's enough!" Ashley ordered. He turned back to Karen. "Lottie has no idea what she's saying right now, and you must forgive Sybil too. She's not herself." He rubbed his brow again. "But I guess it doesn't seem a good idea to take you into Lottie's house. Maybe you could stay with Dinah and Les Gaines."

"Maybe Karie could stay right here!" Mac swung away from the sink, dropping the knife she had been using. She pointed at the Gladstone bag and the sewing basket. "As soon as you phoned about going to Lottie's, I had one of my neighbors get my duds together and bring them up. Karie won't be alone. I'm staying right here with her." The old woman darted a look of pure hostility at Sybil and turned back to her work.

Ashley seemed relieved, but before he could speak, there was the clatter of high heels on the porch and the screen door banged open. Mac glanced over her shoulder and muttered something. Karen recognized the big beefy figure in the doorway. Leticia Jarvis's hair was still falling over her face, and the face was just as ruddy and ill tempered as it had been in the town hall the previous afternoon.

"Hi," the woman said. "I knocked on the front door, but I guess you folks didn't hear. Terrible thing about Alfred. I told Doc I'd better come straight out and see how I

185

can help. You look pretty poorly, Sybil, and you too, Ashley."

Sybil's face crumpled and she started to cry. Leticia strode over to her and enveloped her in beefy arms. "Cry it out, lambie," she told Sybil, and glared at Karen over the smooth chestnut head.

Karen started to smile at her, decided a smile was out of place, and said, "Hello, Leticia."

"Hello yourself," the big woman snapped.

Ashley said quickly, "You must remember Karen, 'Ticia, you two went to school together."

"How could I forget Karen Hampton, with Jack always talking about her? Sure, I remember." Leticia's expression didn't reveal that it was a particularly pleasant memory. "Satisfied?" she snarled.

Slowly, Karen pulled herself up to face the woman. "What are you talking about?"

"As though you don't know. Ever since you come back to town, things have been going from bad to worse. Everybody in town knows you come between Cassie and Jim, and now Alfred—well, it's more'n a body can stand. I just told Doc, Doc I said, someone's got to tell that tramp. Not just Jim Miles, either. Folks have seen you riding around in that foreign car with that troublemaker from ANPP. Always thought you were too good for us common folks, didn't you? I just told Doc—"

Ashley lifted a trembling hand. " 'Ticia, please!"

At the same moment Mac threw down the carrot she was holding and advanced like a tiger on the bigger woman. "You get out of my kitchen, 'Ticia Jarvis! You got a big mouth and a foul one. Karie don't have to listen to this at all!"

Leticia stood her ground. "You're getting too big for your boots too, Mollie MacLean! This here ain't your kitchen. It's Sybil's."

Karen had had more than enough. "You're mistaken. This happens to be *my* kitchen and *my* house, and Mac's right. You're not welcome. Please leave!"

"Hoity-toity! Ain't we something! 'Please leave,' she says. Sure I'll go." Leticia bent her frowsy head over Sybil's. "Come on, lambie, we're not welcome here. I'll drive you down to Lottie's."

Pulling the weeping woman with her, Leticia banged through the swinging doors and strode down the hall.

As he spoke, Ashley's face was colorless. "You mustn't pay any attention to that woman. She's a . . . she's a virago."

"That about describes her." Karen managed a faint smile. "Fishwife fits too. She hasn't changed at all. Don't look so worried, Ashley, you go along to Lottie. We'll be fine."

Gathering up the two larger cases, he stuck the toilet case under one arm and then paused. "If you need anything don't hesitate to call me. Oh, I've been wondering—have you told Jamie yet?"

"I haven't had a chance, and I'm not looking forward to it, but she has to know." At the end of the hall she pulled the front door open for him. A dusty sedan was pulling away from the house, and she recognized the back of Leticia's head and her heavy shoulders. At her side Sybil looked small and forlorn.

After saying goodbye to Ashley, Karen shut the door and stood in the colored pools of light thrown through the fanlight onto the carpet. She gazed down at her white sandals, one now tinted blue, the other the color of blood. She was badly shaken and her hands were trembling. She heard Mac's heavy tread and then a warm arm slid around her waist.

"Don't fret, Karen, 'Ticia has always been wild jealous of you. Forget it and come out and I'll make a pot of coffee." She urged Karen toward the kitchen. "How are we going to tell that youngster?"

Karen gently detached herself from the older woman's grasp. "I don't want her to hear from someone else, Mac. Would you send Betsy and Dave home and tell Jamie I want her upstairs? Waiting won't make it easier."

Karen was braced for difficulties but she wasn't prepared for her daughter's reaction. Jamie perched on her mother's bed, and as Karen explained about her uncle's death the fresh color seeped from the child's cheeks, leaving them as pale and the little face as pinched as it had been when they'd arrived.

"I'm losing everything," she said stonily. "First Caesar, then Oliver, now Uncle Alfred." She added miserably, "I never even had the chance to let his general win the battle."

Watching her just as miserably, Karen thought over the child's words. Losing everything . . . the empty, empty feeling she knew only too well. Cry, she begged her daughter silently, please cry, get it all out.

Mac had opened the bedroom door in time to hear the child's words. "Stuff 'n' nonsense, Jamie! You still got your momma and me, Betsy and Dave, and there's Jim and Cal. Toys and cats can be replaced. As for your uncle, he was an old man, child, old people die." Standing over the bed, she looked sadly down at the small frozen figure. "Just like your momma, bottling it all up. You let old Mac hold you."

Jamie averted her face. "No. Leave me alone."

Bending over, the old woman scooped her up and settled heavily in the armchair. Jamie's fist beat a tattoo on the fleshy shoulder, but Mac held her firmly. After a time the hand stilled and Jamie buried her face against the woman's breast. Catching Karen's eyes, Mac jerked her head toward the door. As Karen left the room, she could hear the soft croon of the old woman's voice.

Hardly aware of what she was doing, she wandered down the stairs, switched the light on in the hall, and made her way out to the kitchen. It was growing dark, and she paused to turn on the overhead light and then sat thinking, losing track of the time. Finally, she rose, picked up Mac's battered Gladstone and the sewing basket, and retraced her steps. As she reached the top of the stairs, Mac came out of the bedroom, gently pulled the door to, and put a warning finger to her lips.

"How is she?" Karen whispered.

"Cried her eyes out and dozed off in my arms. I bedded her down in your room. Poor little mite! What's that you got, Karie? Here, I'll take my bag and put it in my room, but you better take that basket back down to the kitchen. I'm piecing a quilt and might's well keep it downstairs to work on in my spare time." Taking the Gladstone, she tiptoed into her own bedroom.

Karen paused at the head of the staircase and glanced down. She realized it was exactly like the one in her uncle's house. Along the outside ran a polished banister, along the inside flowered wallpaper came right down to the treads. Shifting the basket from one hand to the other, she grasped the banister. She was partway down when she stopped dead in her tracks. "Mac!" she called.

Mac appeared at the top of the stairs. "Ssh! You're gonna wake Jamie."

Karen lowered her voice. "Look, I'm holding your basket in my left hand!"

"Well, good for you. Now, do you think you can get it down the rest of the way?" Mac plodded down behind her. "Have you taken leave of your senses?"

"I've just found them." Pausing under the fanlight, Karen stared into the owlish eyes of the older woman.

189

"All afternoon I've been thinking I *did* get Uncle Alfred too excited . . . that Lottie might be right. Now—" Breaking off, she looked down at the phone.

Mac shook a baffled head. "I'd better get some food ready. You're lightheaded, Karie." She disappeared into the kitchen.

Karen reached for the phone but before she touched it it rang, the shrill peal making her jump. It was Jim Miles. His voice echoed warmly in her ear. "I heard about Alfred Hampton and I was wondering if I should come up. Or could I pick you up and take you out for dinner?"

"Thanks, Jim, but not tonight. We've just told Jamie and she's in bad shape. I think I'd better stay with her."

"I don't wonder. It was a terrible shock for everyone. Maybe I could take you out tomorrow night. Are you nervous there alone? Ashley—"

"Mac's staying here. We're fine. Actually, neither Ashley nor Sybil were around enough to make much difference."

"Well . . . I'll stop by tomorrow morning. Good night, Karen."

Replacing the receiver she tapped it with her nails and then, opening a drawer, she pulled out the directory. "Mac," she called, "what's the name of that new motor hotel near Katoma? It has an Indian name. Erie? Mohawk?"

"Algonquin," the old woman called back.

She ran her finger down the page, closed the book, and dialed. No, Mr. Trent wasn't in his room. Mr. Halloway? One moment, ma'am.

"Mr. Halloway, this is Karen Dancer. Do you know where Cal is?"

Even on the phone his voice had a rich timber. "He's right here, Mrs. Dancer. One moment, please."

"Cal, could you come to the house?"

"Is there anything wrong?"

"I'd like to talk to you."

"Be right there."

The line went dead and she put the receiver down. As she nibbled at her dinner, she wondered why she hadn't let Jim Miles come, why she had phoned Cal instead. Mac decided sleep was more important than supper for Jamie and went upstairs to bed. When Cal tapped on the front door, Karen was washing the few dishes.

He was still wearing the suede jacket and denim pants, but he had changed his sweater for an open-neck shirt. His hair was even more untidy than usual and he needed a shave. She was never so glad to see anyone in her life. He glanced from her soapy hands to her excited face. Catching up a corner of her apron, she hastily dried her hands.

He grinned. "Did you invite me over to help with the dishes?"

Grasping his arm, she turned him toward the staircase. "Look, Cal, this is a twin to the staircase in the Lovatt house. Only one banister."

"Okay. So?"

Her fingers dug into his arm and she pulled him into the front parlor. He sank into Ashley's favorite seat and waved her toward the high-backed chair opposite him. "Calm down. I can see something's got you plumb het up, as our friend the Chief would say. Sit down and let's hear about it."

Trent didn't look at home in the room. Among the heavy Victorian furniture and the clutter of bric-a-brac, he seemed an alien, and the expression in his eyes didn't echo the smile on his lips.

Karen took a deep breath. "I was carrying Mac's sewing basket down for her, and when I reached the top of the staircase I automatically changed hands so I could hold on to the banister. Those stairs are steep; no one in their right

191

mind goes down without holding on. Certainly not Uncle Alfred. Cal, I took the banister in my *right* hand."

"So?"

"When we found him he was clutching a toy soldier in his hand . . . his *right* hand."

"So . . . he wasn't coming down the stairs. But couldn't he have been going up them?"

Momentarily, she was deflated and then her mouth set. "Theo Barnes was convinced he fell down them. He was on his face, and the marks . . . no, it doesn't fit. And it doesn't fit that he was holding that toy soldier. He would have put it back with the rest of them in the library. He was a man of strong and definite habits." She stared over his shoulder.

"Tell me what you're seeing."

"I see him in the hall. He's just come from the library, and he's holding the general in his hand. Someone is with him and he becomes frightened. He's cut off from the front door and from going back toward the kitchen, and the only place he can go is up the stairs. He hurries up with someone following him. He's an old man and can't really move quickly, so there's no rush for the person behind him. At the top, the other person catches up, swings him around, and—" Breaking off, she buried her face in her hands.

"What you're seeing is murder. I had a hunch myself, but there's no motive. Admittedly, your uncle might have figured out who X is, but what has X done? A couple of rather nasty things, but certainly nothing that could be termed criminal. Nothing drastic enough to commit murder to conceal."

Raising her head, she shook the fall of dark blond hair away from her face. "This X you talk about wouldn't even have to worry much about public opinion. Not many people in Hampton would be disturbed by someone trying to frighten me out of siding with ANPP." She saw again the hostility in Leticia's and Sybil's faces. "In fact, many of the people here would think X is a hero. Cal, do you think I should call Theo Barnes?"

"The Chief? I don't know, I really don't. He'll ask the same question. Why?" Trent gazed around. "Where is everyone tonight?"

"Mac's up with Jamie. We told her about Uncle Alfred, and she's heartbroken."

"What about your cousins?"

"They're staying with Lottie Hampton. Ashley is going to take care of the funeral arrangements."

He jerked forward. "You and Mac are alone here?"

"I hardly knew they were around anyway."

"At least someone else was in the house." He stood up. "Show me around this mausoleum, will you?"

She led the way into the hall. "I'll give you the guided tour." She pulled a door open. "The library. This next door is to the back parlor, and across from it is the dining room. You were in there the other night."

"One moment." Striding across the dining room, he circled the table and opened the door beside the buffet. He clicked on the light and glanced around the small room. "Okay, lead on."

In the kitchen she pointed. "That's the door to the cellar. The stairway leads up to the second floor. The pantry's over there."

He had the door to the cellar open and was peering down into its black depths. Then he spun around and stared up the narrow steps. "How many bedrooms?"

"Nine, and two baths."

"Attics?"

"Acres of them."

"Any inside bolts on the doors or windows?"

"As far as I know, none."

193

He leaned against the counter. "My God! Wide open to anyone with a skeleton key who wants to sneak in and dozens of places to hide in, and you three here by yourselves. I suppose the nearest house is that farmhouse where Nat Jenks lives." Taking a couple of steps, he put his hands on her shoulders. "I think I'd better stay here tonight. I'll drive back and pick up some shaving gear and a change of clothes."

"No way, Cal. I'm afraid Mac would have a fit. In Hampton it just isn't done."

"Then pack a bag, some clothes for you and Jamie. We'll drop Mac off at her house and I'll check you into the hotel until after the funeral."

Her jaw set. "We'll be perfectly all right. Mac is as good as a company of marines and she's right across the hall from us."

Removing his hands, he balled one into a fist and smashed it into the palm of his other hand. "Anyone ever tell you you've got the instincts of a mule? You win for tonight, but tomorrow you're going to have to make other arrangements. I'll be by in the morning. You decide where you want to go. This is the last night you spend in this house. Understand?"

"My, but you're masterful. Very well. I'll phone Dinah in the morning, but tonight, at the risk of sounding rude, I'm exhausted. I'd better get to bed. Thank you, Cal, for coming running when I called."

Thrusting both hands into his pockets, he walked toward the front door. As he swung it open, he turned, gazed around the hall, and told her firmly, "Mac or no Mac, you keep those two bedroom doors bolted and have that gun handy. I'll be here as soon as I can in the morning."

Karen remembered that Jim Miles had promised to see her in the morning too, but she was too tired to worry about it. Upstairs, in the middle of her bed, Jamie was curled up, sleeping soundly, her eyelids red and swollen. Gently, Karen rolled her over and slipped in beside her. She was stretching out a hand to turn off the lamp when she remembered her promise to Trent. Easing herself out of bed, she shot the bolt on her door and then went into Jamie's room. A puff of cinnamon fur nestled on the pillow. Ruby opened green eyes, peered sleepily up at her, and then closed her eyes. Karen bolted that door too, picked up the cat, and returned to her own room. She put Ruby down beside the sleeping child and watched the animal cuddle up beside Jamie. With a sigh she switched off the light and soon was sleeping as soundly as the child by her side.

Much later the cat stirred restlessly and lifted her head. Her gleaming eyes shifted around the dark room and stopped to stare fixedly at the door panel. The knob was turning. The cat held her head erect, her ears tense and listening. No sound came from the hall. The board that squeaked outside of Jamie's room was silent but the knob of her door gently turned too.

Later still a wind blew in from the northeast, ripping foliage from the trees surrounding the house and sending leaves hurtling with a dry crackle against the windows. Almost lost in the howl of the wind was a muted buzzing. Again the cat jerked her head up, but soon she lost interest, yawned widely, and settled back comfortably against the child's stomach. Both Karen and Jamie slept deeply, the sleep of exhaustion. In time the buzzing stopped and only the sound of the wind could be heard, creaking branches and moaning under the eaves of the old house under the maples.

15

DESPITE HIGH WINDS in the night, Friday morning was fresh and bright. Karen looked over the scarlet geraniums on the windowsill at a patch of blue sky.

"I still say it looks like a fine day," she told Mac.

Mac massaged an elbow. "And I still say when my elbow aches like blazes it will rain 'fore sundown." Opening the fridge, she took out a dish of butter and a quart of milk. "Want to help me beat this batter up?" she asked Jamie.

Shaking her head, the little girl turned a page in the comic book in front of her. She was too quiet and withdrawn, Karen thought, regarding her with ill-concealed anxiety. She tried to draw her out. "If Mac's right, honey, you'll get your wish and be able to play in the attic."

"I don't want to play in the attic."

Mac stirred the batter in the large green bowl. "Dave and Betsy will probably be over to play with you later."

"They're going to Katoma with their mother," Jamie said listlessly.

Over her bent head, Mac and Karen exchanged

glances. Mac opened her mouth and then closed it as the screen door opened. "Land sakes, you're out early, Jim. How about breakfast? It's nearly ready."

Jim Miles looked as fresh as the morning in a well-cut tweed suit. Dropping his bag on the floor, he ruffled Jamie's hair and beamed at her mother. "Nothing would suit me better, Mac. You make the best hotcakes in town."

"And that's the truth," she told him complacently. "Sit down and I'll put on an extra plate. You want sausages or ham?"

"Both." He turned his attention to Karen. "You're looking great this morning. Offhand, I'd say you had a good night."

"I slept better last night than I have since we arrived. I was completely exhausted. But tell me, how is Mrs. Jarvis and her gallbladder?"

He told them not only about Mrs. Jarvis's gallbladder but also about some of the rest of his patients. With orange juice they had the details about a fall one of Ed Cross's sons had the day before; over hotcakes, sausage, and ham, he explained about Dinah Gaines's younger boy, Arthur, and his case of flu. He had just reached coffee and the mild stroke old Mr. Evans had suffered the previous night when the screen door creaked open.

Jamie came suddenly to life. "Cal!" she cried, and rushed to meet him.

He swung her up into his arms and she hugged him. Mac looked from him to Jim Miles and muttered something under her breath. Karen could feel color sweeping from her throat up into her cheeks.

"You two have met?" she asked.

Jim bobbed his head and Trent grinned at him. "We have. Making house calls early today, doctor?"

"Not at all. Couldn't resist Mac's hotcakes," Jim said, and added, "Or seeing Karen and Jamie."

Trent deposited Jamie back on her chair and sat down. He waved away hotcakes but accepted a cup of coffee. "Jim doesn't believe in spanking children," Jamie confided. "He reasons with them and calls them small adults. I'm a small adult, Cal."

"You're an imp."

"What would you say if I told you I'm thinking of converting to Buddhism?"

"I've considered it a few times myself." He winked at Karen. "Might quell some of my more bloodthirsty impulses."

Neatly folding his napkin, Jim aligned it with his plate. "I feel it's a mistake to jest with children on matters of religion, Trent."

"I'm not jesting. I'm serious. You see, I have these impulses to commit mayhem, and peace through nirvana sounds like a good idea."

The other man stood up. "I really must be going, Karen. Will I see you tonight?"

"I don't know, Jim. My plans are rather indefinite."

Opening the door, he stepped out on the porch. "I'll phone you later, then."

"Wait up," Mac said, picking up his bag. "You're forgetting something."

He nodded at her, divided a smile between Jamie and Karen, and made a stiff inclination of his head to Trent.

Leaning back in his chair, Trent said innocently, "I do hope the doctor didn't leave on my account."

Mac started to clear the table. "You know blame well he did. Nirvana!" She patted Jamie's shoulder. "I'm going to bake up some bread. Want to help?"

A spark of interest was in Jamie's voice. "Can I make a loaf for Cal all by myself?"

"You can, but first we'll do up these dishes. Now, no

complaints. Karie, you and Cal clear out of here. Why don't you go outside?"

"Fine idea, Mac." Reaching over, Trent captured Karen's hand and pulled her to her feet. "We'll go for a walk. Do you good."

"All I've done for the last four days is walk."

They paused in front of the garage and Trent pointed to the drifts of colored leaves on the driveway. "Some wind in the night. Look at those."

They wandered down to the road and of one accord turned away from Hampton and strolled along on the shoulder of the blacktop. Although the sun was shining, dark clouds were piling up in the west and there was a stiff breeze. Karen's hair blew forward around her face. She searched in her pockets for cigarettes but Trent anticipated her and pulled out his own pack. Lighting two, he handed one to her.

"Quiet night?" he asked.

"Jamie and I slept like logs."

"That's more than I did. Frankly, I was worried. I finally gave up trying to sleep and drove back here about three and checked around."

"That was foolish, Cal. We were perfectly all right."

"There didn't seem to be anything out of the way, but the toolshed door was wide open and banging in the wind."

"You took the bolt off. Probably it was ajar and the wind caught it."

"Uh-huh." He kicked a rock and watched it bounce into the ditch. "Have you made up your mind where you're going to stay?"

"Jim said Dinah's Arthur is sick so I can't go there. I've decided to stay on here. The funeral will be in a couple of days, and it seems silly—"

"What about your uncle? Was that silly too?"

She gazed around. Four Jersey cows and several calves were grazing in the field they were passing. In the distance a thread of smoke drifted from the chimney of a farmhouse. A truck loaded with bales of hay rumbled past them, and the small boy in the cab leaned out and waved. She could smell smoke, the sweet odor of hay, and the fainter scent of fall flowers.

She waved a hand. "I think I built something gruesome up out of an accident. Look around. Does this look like a place where a harmless old man could be killed in cold blood?" When he didn't answer, she continued, "I'm staying on in my house, Cal."

His chin was set and the scar on it stood out whitely. "I think you're a damn fool! If I can't budge you I'm going down and talk to Barnes. He seems to be a pretty smart old boy."

"Maybe the smart old boy can give you a logical reason why Uncle Alfred might have been killed."

"Maybe he can, but I've got an idea on that myself. It came to me in the midnight hours when I couldn't sleep."

Abruptly, she wheeled and started to walk back. He spun on his heel and caught up with her.

"What's wrong with you this morning, Karen?"

She was frowning. "I just can't accept what I've been thinking. I know these people. Some of them are rather disgusting—Leticia Jarvis and the Dimwiddies—but the majority are kind and gentle small-town folk. People who call each other by first names and are right there in times of sickness or trouble. Certainly they don't want their town changed, certainly they're hostile about ANPP, but there are people like Ashley and Amos Lofton and Bruce Gotham—nice people. There are men like Nat Jenks, angry one day and giving a ride to the people who angered him the next." She paused for breath and said gravely,

200

"You're a stranger here, Cal, and I'm a nervous wreck. Our imaginations are running away with both of us."

Her frown was mirrored on his face. "You won't want to hear this, but I'm going to tell you anyway. What if Alfred Hampton wasn't murdered because of what *has* happened? What if he was shoved downstairs because of what *is going* to happen?"

She slowed her step. "You mean—"

"I mean that possibly Alfred interrupted some well-laid plans. If he threatened to expose them—well, they could have panicked and killed him. And just who is the target?"

"I refuse to listen to this!"

"You're going to listen. There's something ugly going on here. I can smell it. Anyone in town could be plotting at this very minute. If you don't care about your own safety, think of your daughter."

"I *am* thinking about her, but I can't believe what you're saying."

He went on relentlessly. "It could be one of your nice people—Lofton, Ashley, Gotham. It could be Ed Cross or Doc Jarvis. It might be Leticia or Sybil. It could even be Lottie—"

"She adored Alfred!"

"It could be Nat Jenks. Now, he can be ugly. It might be Cassie Saunders—"

"She has no reason."

"Jim Miles is a good enough reason. Roy Paul tells me they were going to be married before you turned up." He paused, but she pressed her lips tightly together and said nothing. "And there's your cousin Roy, and Vi the schemer, there's her charming son Chuck and Jim Miles—"

"He's a doctor."

"So was Dr. Cream and the doctors in the Nazi concentration camps. History tells us Jack the Ripper probably was a medical man. Jim Miles is narrow-minded, almost a fanatic. The perfect type to go around the bend and do something violent."

Her voice was as cold as her expression. "Jim was with me every minute the night the panda was put in the barn and the balloon was used to frighten Jamie."

"As I mentioned yesterday, it could be two people. Jim could have been with you while a confederate did the dirty work."

They turned up the driveway and Karen kicked violently at a pile of leaves. "You're unbelievable!"

"I'm a realist, not a dreamer like a certain Karen Dancer I happen to know. Did you ever consider it might be Mac?"

She swung to face him, her eyes blazing. "You go too far! Mac is like a second mother to me."

"Who could have a better opportunity? Roy tells me Mac hates the idea of the nuclear plant as much as anyone else in town does." His face relaxed and he reached for her hand. "I'm not serious about Mac, but I was about everyone else."

She wrenched her hand away. "There are two others you didn't mention—you and Vince Halloway!"

Without looking back, she ran around the grape arbor and flung herself down on one of the chairs under the umbrella. More slowly, Trent followed and sat down on the grass. Pulling off his jacket, he tossed it at a chair.

Karen averted her face and they sat in silence. Pulling a blade of grass from the lawn, he chewed the end of it. "Would you like me to leave?" he asked.

She shrugged and started to answer, but at that moment Mac came out on the porch and shook out a throw rug.

"How's Jamie coming with the bread?" Karen called.

"Like all youngsters, got started and then lost interest. Betsy and Dave came over after all because Maudie decided not to go to Katoma. Betsy said her dad is bringing my eggs, so you won't have to make the trip. Wish he'd hurry, I need them for lunch." She squinted across the yard. "What's the matter with you two? Got faces like thunderclouds."

Instead of answering the question, Karen asked another of her own. "Where are the children?"

"Don't know. Might be playing in the barn. I'll have a look."

Karen got up and, without glancing at Trent, followed the older woman. Lazily, Trent pulled himself up and watched them. Mac swung open the barn door and called Jamie's name. "Not in there. Better try the shed, Karie."

Karen walked over to the shed and swung the door open. She disappeared inside. "No sign of them in here either," she called. There was a thud. "Ouch! Who left that saw there? I tripped over it."

Strolling over, Trent peered into the dim interior. "A power saw. Who uses that?"

"Ashley does, once in a blue moon. Not very good with his hands, though," Mac told him. "Funny, he usually takes good care of everything. That saw hangs on a peg back there. First time I've seen it laying on the floor like that."

Picking it up, Karen put it on the workbench. "He should be more careful. If one of the children got it started they could hurt themselves."

Trent put a hand on the older woman's arm. "Where would they be? Could they have gone over to the farm?"

Mac shook her head. "Not without asking. Jamie tried it the other day and I told her I'd tan her britches if she did it again. Maybe they're playing on the swings. Let's have a look."

The two women headed toward the barn, and Trent trailed along behind them. As they rounded the corner of the barn, Betsy whirled, clapping a guilty hand to her mouth.

"I told Jamie and Dave they was gonna get it. You gonna whip Jamie, Mrs. Dancer?"

"I'm going to do just that," Karen said grimly.

Jamie was on the forbidden swing, her legs pumping madly, her long hair flying out behind her. Dave, his freckled face red and perspiring, was pushing her with all his strength. The child was swinging in dizzy arcs over the ravine.

Trent shouldered in front of Karen and walked toward the huge maple. His eyes wandered from the thick red-and-gold foliage to the bole of the tree. "Sure is a big one. Must measure more than five feet around the trunk. What's that on the ground? Looks like sawdust. Now, where in the devil—"

His eyes moved from the roots of the old maple to the limb where the chains of the big swing were fastened. He seemed to be listening.

Then Karen heard it too—a dull, ripping sound. Puzzled, she followed his eyes. Suddenly he shouted, "Dave, get out of there! You too, Karen, stay clear. That branch is breaking off!"

Karen was rooted to the ground but Mac dashed in with surprising speed, grabbed the boy by the back of his shirt, and hauled him out. Her free arm caught Karen and dragged her back with them.

"Jamie!" Karen screamed.

The child turned her head and her puzzled eyes looked toward her mother. She was still wildly swinging back and forth over the ravine. Trent came off the ground like a big cat, trying to catch a chain. His first and second tried were short. The limb was bending, and the swing canted to one side.

"Hold tight, Jamie!" he shouted.

He sprang at the chain again and this time got it. Pulling back with all his weight, he managed to slow the tipping seat. As soon as the child was within reach he grabbed for her. She was clinging to the chains with her small hands and he had to tear them loose. Then she was in his arms and he was backing away from the edge of the ravine. For a moment it looked as though they would make it and then the branch gave one last agonized groan and splintered off the main trunk. Trent, the child clasped to his chest, tried to get clear. He glanced up and dropped to the ground, rolling toward the edge of the ravine. The huge branch, with its weight of gloriously colored leaves, came crashing down and engulfed them.

The last thing Karen saw before the leaves hid them from view was Trent and her daughter, sliding together down the steep gravel slope toward the water and the rocks far below.

16

AT ONE TIME the waiting room at Hampton Hospital had been the main drawing room of the Lofton house. In it generations of Loftons had entertained both the local elite and out-of-town visitors with grace and a certain amount of elegance. When Amos Lofton had deeded his home to the town, changes had to be made to the entire structure. The former drawing room was now floored in long-wearing tiles of black and white. On this checkerboard pattern, functional furniture was arranged. Chrome-framed chairs and banquettes covered in a plastic that attempted to emulate leather were flanked by plastic-topped tables heaped with outdated magazines and scattered with heavy glass ashtrays.

Traces of the room's original beauty still lingered. A bay window of gracious proportions dominated the front wall. Long windows at one side came nearly to the floor and soared upward toward a ceiling molded and corniced on which delicately tinted garlands framed a sky-blue background emblazoned with nymphs and plump cupids. A symmetrical archway led to a huge hall, again floored in black and white, on which rested a black metal admitting desk.

The distinctive odors of a hospital filled the room— antiseptic smells mixed with the odor of stale food and a more pungent one of fresh floor wax.

Karen, seated on one of the banquettes facing the bay window, was oblivious to the odors, the room, and the other people in it. Her nylons were torn and muddy, one of her sandals was missing a heel, and the hem of her skirt was sodden. A gash extended from the knuckles of her right hand to her wrist. Vaguely she knew that Mac, still wearing an apron, was hunched on her right and Dinah Gaines, in a long coat, was on her other side. Karen stared straight ahead. She seemed to be gazing fixedly at the group of men standing near the window: Ashley Hampton, wetter and muddier than Karen was, talking in low tones to an impeccably dressed Amos Lofton while Ed Cross and Bruce Gotham listened. Seated near the men were a number of women. Sybil watched her brother anxiously while Cassie Saunders, in a purple wool suit and dramatic amethyst necklace, talked in low tones to Leticia Jarvis and a wan-faced Lottie Hampton. In one corner Nat Jenks perched on the edge of a chair, his soggy overalls and flannel shirt partially hidden under a gray hospital blanket. On another banquette, apart from the others and studiously ignored by them, was the Paul family. Roy, seated between his empty-faced wife and scowling son, had his eyes fixed on Karen's face.

All of them had approached and tried to talk to Karen. Earlier Leticia had stood in front of her, shifted awkwardly from one foot to the other, and blurted out, "I'm sorry about the kid, Karen, and sorry because of yesterday. I had no business to talk to you that way."

Karen had heard all the words but hadn't comprehended any of them. Her mind was concentrated in

207

another part of the hospital, down the long corridor in the room where Jim Miles was closeted with Jamie and Cal Trent. When they had been carried in she had tried to follow them, but Jim had nodded to Mac and the old woman had led Karen to the waiting room.

Her memories of the earlier hours of the morning were blurred, lost in shock. From the moment she had watched Trent with Jamie in his arms rolling into the ravine she could remember only fragments. Nat Jenks must have arrived about the time the huge branch had torn loose and fallen across the ravine, because a basket of brown eggs had rolled wildly around her feet while the farmer scrambled down the gravel slope to the creek.

Mac had yelled something about Jim Miles and was no longer there. Karen found herself clawing her way down the gravel toward Nat. Then Ashley Hampton had plunged past her into the creek and the two men pulled Trent and Jamie out of the water. She saw blood streaming down Trent's face and Jamie's frighteningly still body. There had been blood on Jamie too; where had it been? It must have been her leg, because Karen sat on the grass beside her daughter pressing a handkerchief to her knee while Nat Jenks backed his truck around the barn toward them. Someone was arranging blankets in the truck bed. Mac had the blankets, and then the men had lifted the two quiet bodies onto them.

Then came a period she had lost. Next she was driving Trent's car, Mac beside her, following the pickup bumping along toward the hospital. Jim Miles was in the back of the pickup, his bag open, and Ashley was handing him things from it. After that had been the waiting room and people coming in: Cassie holding her hand and murmuring comforting words, Sybil's shadowed eyes, Lottie telling her something, and Nat Jenks sitting quietly in the corner, water dripping from his clothes onto the polished black and white of the floor.

There was a change now and Karen stirred. After a moment she realized that the murmur of conversation was stilled and everyone was turning toward the archway. It was a nurse, the older one who appeared to be in charge. Jim had called her Nurse Murphy. Under a white cap was a broad placid Irish face that matched her name. She bustled toward Karen, her skirts rustling starchily, and bent over her.

"Jamie?" Karen asked. Her mouth was dry and the word came out as a croak.

"The doctor's still with her. I was wondering, would you like a sedative or—"

"No," Mac broke in, "I don't hold with that sort of stuff. Bring her milk, hot milk, do her more good."

Nurse Murphy nodded and swished back across the gleaming floor. The voices began to murmur again, and then someone else was in the archway. Theo Barnes, his cap worn dead straight across tufted white brows, glanced in, waved at Ashley Hampton, who was calling to him, shook his big head, and continued down the corridor.

Dinah leaned over and whispered something to Mac, but Karen wasn't listening. Now the faces of the men and women were coming into focus. What had Trent said shortly before the swing broke? One of them, one of the people in this room, was X, and she turned her head away from him, became angry, refused to listen. Now he might be dying and Jamie—

"Jim!" Dinah cried.

Karen sprang to her feet. Jim Miles was striding toward her, a white jacket over his tweed suit, his face expressionless. Disregarding everyone else, he put an arm around her waist.

"Jamie?" she whispered. "Is she . . . ?"

"She's going to be all right. Both of them are going to be all right."

The room darkened around her and she sagged forward. Jim was holding her head down between her knees and Theo Barnes, who had come back, was saying gruffly, "Better give her a drink. Don't you keep any liquor here?"

Liquid gurgled and a glass was pressed into her hands. Obediently she raised it and drained it. It burned her throat but she felt warmer and her mouth wasn't as dry.

"How bad are they?" she managed to say.

"Jamie got off more lightly. Trent's body must have cushioned the fall. She has a six-inch cut under her right knee and a contusion on the back of her head, and she's a mass of bruises. She's in shock, of course."

"And Cal?"

"Well enough that he tried to get off the table while I was examining him," the doctor said dryly. "I had to get a hypo into him fast. Actually, he's a mess, but luckily none of the injuries in themselves are too severe. As I said, he took the brunt of the fall. He has a bad welt on the side of his head, possibly concussed, and a deep cut across his left cheek. Six of his ribs are broken, and his right ankle is badly sprained. He's also a mass of bruises."

"Thank God that's all," Mac breathed.

"Can I move Jamie?" Karen asked.

"Of course not. Both of them are heavily sedated and I intend to keep them that way. There is still a possibility of internal injuries, not a great one but always there. They'll have to be under observation for at least twenty-four hours, and Trent shouldn't be out of bed for a week. What do you mean, move her?"

"I want to take her away from this town. Anywhere. By ambulance, if necessary."

"I can understand how you feel, Karen, but it's a poor idea right at present. In fact, I won't consent—"

"Is she alone? Did you leave her alone, Jim?"

He rose and walked around the desk. "Get a grip on yourself, Karen. There're nurses with her and with Trent. In a little while you'll be able to see them, but right now Chief Barnes wants a few words with you."

"In private," Barnes said. "Come with me, Karen."

"I'm coming too," Mac said.

"No, Mollie, you're not." Theo Barnes was firm.

Mac grumbled a little but she stayed behind.

Barnes led Karen down the corridor and into a small office. Shutting the door behind them, he circled the desk and lowered his bulk on the chair behind it. He took his cap off, peered into it, and wiped the sweat band off on his sleeve.

"Sit down, Karen," he said. Shrewd little eyes examined the woman opposite him.

Karen realized there was something she must tell him, and she tried to remember what it was.

Barnes spoke first. "You in any shape to talk?"

She was. It occurred to her she was in fairly good shape. Her hands were steady, and there was no telltale trembling of her mouth.

Reaching for the bottle Jim had left on the desk, Barnes poured a couple of ounces in Karen's glass and located another glass in the cupboard behind him. He filled it half full, winked, and took a swallow. "There's some don't hold with an officer on duty having a nip, but I'm not one of them." To prove his point, he polished off the remainder of his drink.

Karen sipped at hers. "That branch had been cut partway through, hadn't it?"

"Just come from your place. Junior and I had a look around. You're right. That branch was cut nearly through,

211

and if Jamie hadn't been a lightweight it would have broken off with the first few shoves. It was a death trap." He tilted the bottle over his glass. "Ashley's saw was used. Must have been done sometime in the night, because he claims the saw was in its usual place yesterday."

"The swing was used three days ago, Theo. By me. It was all right then."

"Uh-huh. Wind in the night would have covered the sound of the saw. Checked the house over, too, and found bits of dried leaves and caked dirt along the outer side of the stair treads. Right where a person would walk if they was sneaking around trying to be quiet. Got a hunch the sawer was in your house last night." He took a drink and looked over the rim of the glass. "Saw the bolts on the bedroom doors. Have them pulled last night?" When she nodded, he said gravely, "Figure you saved your life by locking yourself in. The swing trap must have been the second idea of killing you."

"Me?"

He made an impatient gesture. "Everybody in town knows who uses that big swing at the Hampton house. They know you're a good mother and wouldn't figure on the little girl being on it. So . . . it was set up for you."

Karen thumped her glass down. "But it could have been anyone in the swing—Betsy or Dave Jenks, for instance. And it was Jamie who was hurt."

"Plumb loco, isn't it? Which leads to the thought that the person behind this *is* plumb loco. Kill crazy. Set a trap that might kill a kid just in hopes of killing you. And you would have died, too. Only thing that saved your daughter was that young fellow Trent. Thought fast and acted faster. If he'd tried to run away from the ravine, the full weight of the branch would have crushed both of them. Nat Jenks deserves a lot of credit too, and so does Ashley. Good thing Ashley stopped by to see you right then. Took both of them to get Trent and your girl out of the creek before they drowned. No, I figure it was you who was supposed to die."

"The nuclear plant?"

The bald head jerked in a nod. "No one in town wants it, but someone's gone clean crazy. If you were killed, your daughter would inherit, wouldn't she? And what about the property then? She's a minor; who's your executor?"

"Ashley Hampton. I considered Uncle Alfred but he seemed too old to care for Karen."

"Ashley would never let the property be sold."

Karen leaned across the desk. "There's something else I just remembered. Uncle Alfred—"

"I know." He chuckled at the astonishment on her face. "Not such an old fool as I look, eh? Knew yesterday when I saw the toy soldier in his hand that someone pushed him down those stairs. Old folks sometimes do get forgetful, but not Alfred. Smartest man in town, regardless of age. Way I see it, he must have made a pretty good guess about who had been pulling those mean tricks on you. I knew it yesterday but there was no real proof, and I couldn't figure out why he was killed. Well, now we know." Pausing, he drained his glass. "Think back, Karen. Did he say anything at all that might give us a clue?"

Her brow furrowed with concentration. "All he did was figure out the time sequence. And he talked about a night walker. He said he was going to make some phone calls and told me not to worry. That's all."

"I figure when he was talking to you he knew who it was. All that walking he did at night . . . used to hike out toward the farm, just to look at the old house. Either he met someone or seen someone around there. Probably didn't think anything about it until you told him what had

213

been going on. Then he must have phoned the person he'd seen and they come around."

"But wouldn't one of his neighbors have seen that person going into the Lovatt house? It was early afternoon."

"The alley behind the Lovatt house comes out on the other side of the post office. Lots of people coming and going around there. Just slip down the alley and in the back door. Alfred never was one for kitchens; figured they was just places to cook food in. He'd lead the visitor toward the parlor, still holding that toy soldier. By the time he realizes he's got a loony on his hands it'd be too late. He must have been cornered in the front hall and cut off from the door. So he hiked up the stairs with the loony after him. Wouldn't take much strength to handle Alfred. He was so weak and light a child could have shoved him down." Barnes snapped his fingers. "The only person who knew would be dead and it would look like an accident. Then the loony was free to go after you."

Karen shifted on her chair. "If you think this person is deranged, can't you tell who it must be? You know everyone in town."

Picking up his cap again, he examined the inside of it as though looking for an answer there. When he spoke his voice was slow and serious. "Can live cheek by jowl with someone for years and not know what's going on inside of them. Only murder we ever had in Hampton was years ago. A shoemaker killed his wife. We all thought they were a devoted couple. Wasn't until after the woman was dead that we found her husband's diary and learned he'd been planning to kill her for years, mentioned every weapon you can think of. He was wild jealous and her with a face like a potato, but he imagined she was cheating on him with every man in town—including the preacher and me. One day he picks up an ax and chops her head

214

half off. Right out of his mind for years and not one of us suspected. Quiet little fellow. No, Karen, it could be anyone. Thing to do is figure out who."

Her mouth set in a narrow line. "You can do the figuring. As soon as I can move Jamie, we're leaving."

"Don't blame you a'tall. But till Jim releases her, where will you stay? Dinah Gaines is eager to have you visit with Les and her. Be a good idea."

Karen opened her mouth to agree and heard herself saying, "I'm going back to the house."

"Not sensible, but Hamptons have always been a stubborn lot." He got heavily to his feet. "Can't have Mollie and you alone. I'll send Junior with you. I'm not taking any chances. Been cussing myself for not having him there last night. Not that he's overly bright, but he's willing, a dead shot, and better'n nothing. Just a minute."

Banging the door open, he bellowed down the corridor. His grandson, wearing the Stetson at a jaunty angle, appeared in the doorway.

"Got a job for you, son. No goofing off either 'cause this ain't trying shop doors. It's homicide."

"Homicide!"

"Keep your mouth shut and listen. I want you to take care of Mrs. Dancer here. Stick closer'n a burr to her. Where she goes, you go. Got that?"

"I got it, Grandpaw—er, Chief. Stick right to her. Yes, sir, I'll do that. Homicide, huh?"

Jim appeared at the boy's side. "Karen, you can see Jamie now."

Eagerly she followed him down the corridor. It ran the length of the house. Several doors opened from it and at the end was an old French door, the tiny squares of glass set in polished wood. Through it could be seen the rear garden, the corner of a gazebo, several maples, and some

215

lilac bushes. It was untended, the grass growing long and rank, leaves blowing across it.

Jim opened a door to the right of the French door and beckoned to her. On the high bed Jamie's small form hardly made a mound in the bedclothes. Her hair lay in flaxen arabesques on the pillow, framing a pale face. Long lashes rested silkily on the colorless cheeks and one hand lay on the spread, the fingers bruised and scraped. Bending over, Karen gently touched the child's cheek and smoothed the thick hair from her brow.

The nurse beside the bed watched Karen with sympathetic eyes. "This is Nurse Baker," Jim whispered to Karen.

"Will you be staying with Jamie?" Karen asked.

"Until I go off duty at five," the nurse told her.

Jim moved closer to the two women. "I've arranged for Julie Loren to take night duty. She'll be in about four-thirty. Under no circumstances leave the child alone."

Nurse Baker raised sandy brows. "I thought Julie was off, getting ready for her wedding."

"It's next week, but when I explained to her how short-handed we are she agreed to help out for a couple of days." Turning back to Karen, he patted her shoulder. "Jamie looks pretty washed out, but she's resting comfortably and she's going to be fine. Now, the doctor has orders for you. You go home and get those damp clothes off. Hey, you have a cut on your hand—"

"It's only a scratch. I'll dab something on it."

"Right. As I was saying, have a hot bath and get some rest. Will you do that?"

Nodding, she bent over the child again and kissed her gently. Jamie sighed in her sleep, and her head moved on the pillow. Karen tiptoed from the room to find Junior stationed outside the door. His grandfather was clicking the French door open and shut.

Swinging around, Barnes said to Jim, "Get this dang-blamed thing locked, and keep a close watch on that little girl. I don't want anyone but the nurse in her room. Got that?"

"I've given everyone orders," Jim said stiffly. "I'll have Nurse Murphy lock that door and Jamie's window as well. What about Karen? I can't lock her up."

"She won't be alone. Junior here is going to look after her. Aren't you, son?"

"Bet your life I am, Chief."

Barnes looked grimly at him. "It's *Karen's* life we're betting. Remember that."

Jim was staring at the old policeman, but before he could speak Karen touched his sleeve. "Could I see Cal?"

"Of course." He opened the door of the next room. A young nurse with auburn hair was bending over the bed. She stepped back and Karen gazed down at Trent. Bandages were wound around his head turban style, tilting down over his left eye. His face was badly bruised and the left cheek had a bandage running from his eye to his mouth. One eye was a deep purple color.

She gasped.

"He looks worse than he actually is," Jim said quickly. He has a strong constitution, and in a few days most of these abrasions will be on the mend."

"When will he be conscious?"

"I'm keeping both of them sedated until morning. They need the rest. Perhaps by noon he'll be lucid."

He touched her arm and they returned to the corridor. Junior was now leaning against the wall beside Trent's door, watching them intently. Barnes was bending over the reception desk, talking earnestly to Nurse Murphy.

"Karen," the doctor said softly, "what does Trent actually mean to you?"

"What do you mean?"

217

"Don't be evasive. I saw the expression on your face in there."

"He saved Jamie's life."

"That wasn't gratitude looking out of your eyes." He hesitated and then asked, "Are you in love with him?"

"Please, Jim, I don't know how I feel about anything right now."

"I think you owe me an answer."

She was saved from replying by Barnes, who was waddling down the corridor toward them. "Come along, Karen. Junior can take Trent's car and get you and Mollie MacLean home. And I want a word with you, Jim."

Leaving the doctor, Karen walked down the hall with Junior close on her heels. She found herself wishing it was Trent behind her. For some reason she felt very much alone.

EASING HER BULK into a chair near the window of the kitchen, Mac sighed heavily and rubbed her elbow. "Don't know when I've felt so beat." She glanced at the rain pouring down the pane and added with a certain amount of gloomy satisfaction, "Leastways my elbow was right as usual. Look at that storm."

The young constable, his white Stetson still worn at a jaunty angle, peered out the window. "Looks like a humdinger. Look at the way those trees are bobbing." He cleared his throat, the Adam's apple moving up and down. "Must admit I'm a mite hungry. Missed my lunch in all the excitement."

"Didn't we all." The old woman levered herself out of the chair. "Guess I'd better throw some supper together."

Karen stubbed out her cigarette. "You go rest, Mac. I'll make sandwiches and coffee."

Mac eyed her up and down. "If Jim Miles didn't have sense enough to tell you, I will. You go up and get out of those clothes and do something about that hand. Could get infected. That's an order, Karie."

Karen made a mock salute. "Aye, aye, sir. Going right now."

Jumping up, Junior settled his hat more firmly and trailed Karen across the room.

"Hey," Mac said. "Where do you think you're going?"

He drew himself to his full height. "Chief said to stick to Mrs. Dancer like a burr. Where she goes, I go."

"Into the tub?" Mac asked.

He blushed but kept going. As Karen reached the top of the stairs he caught up with her and laid a restraining hand on her arm. "Stay back. I'd better have a look-see."

She stood in the doorway of her room while he switched on all the lamps and looked around. This included the wardrobe, behind a tall chair, and a brief foray into Jamie's room. Karen leaned against the doorjamb and sighed. "How about under the bed?" she called.

"Clean forgot." He got down on his knees. "Okay, all clear."

Moving around the room under his alert gaze, she gathered up undergarments from a drawer, took a denim slack suit from the wardrobe, and picked up her makeup kit. She started down the hall toward the bathroom with the young man trotting along behind.

"Always had a hankering to live in one of these big houses," he confided. "Grandpaw and Mom and Dad used to have one, but Grandpaw give it up when they died. He took rooms over Evans Hardware, and that's where I was raised. Can't even remember the house."

As she reached the bathroom, he clapped a hand on her shoulder. "Stand back." He pushed his jacket clear of the big leather holster on his hip. "Might be an ambush."

Incredulously, she watched while he scouted the bathroom, opened the door of the linen closet, and peered in. When he shoved back the glass door on the tub she could no longer keep quiet. "An ambush in a *tub?*"

"Never know. The swing was booby-trapped, weren't it?"

"It was. You certainly take your work seriously."

"Got to. Chief's orders. You can go ahead now."

"As soon as you're on the other side of that door, I will."

He blushed again and retreated. As she shut the door she could see him pulling a straight chair over in front of it. This was beginning to look like a long night. Recklessly she poured twice the usual amount of bath salts into the steaming water and slipped into the tub. Putting back her head, she relaxed. As soon as her eyes closed she saw Jamie's white face. Pushing the picture from her mind she examined other faces. Which face concealed her uncle's murderer? Was it Amos Lofton, ready to fight to his "dying breath"; Sybil and her long-stored bitterness; Ashley, who was determined never to allow Hampton to change? Could it be Leticia Jarvis or Ed Cross? She thought of Nat Jenks and discarded the face with the pulled-down mouth immediately. Without him both Jamie and Cal would be dead, and if he had set the trap for Jamie or her he would have kept his own children home.

While she was thinking, Karen told herself, she had better decide a few other things. This wavering she had done lately, what was at the root of it? Ordinarily she made fast decisions and stuck to them, but since she had come back to Hampton she hadn't been able to make her mind up about anything. By now she should have her answer for Vince and ANPP but she was still torn two ways, one moment wavering toward the town and its desire to resist the plant, the next admitting that the plant would be a good thing for the town. When Jim had asked her feelings about Cal Trent she should have given him an answer, but how could she tell Jim she felt a stronger emotion for the engineer she had known for only a few

221

days than she did for him? And what was that emotion, was it love or was it a desire for his protection? Last of all, why had she suddenly told Theo Barnes she was returning to this house that held only terror for her when she really wanted to be with Dinah and her family?

Impatiently, she sat up and pulled the plug out. Above the gurgle of water Junior's voice drifted through the door. "Nearly done, Mrs. Dancer? I'm getting mighty hungry."

"Only a few minutes more," she called back.

She started to dress, pulling on denim pants and a white turtleneck sweater. Brushing out her hair, she applied a little makeup and touched her lips with color. Then she pushed up her sleeve and dabbed antiseptic on the long shallow scratch. She took a last look in the mirror, pulled on the loose denim jacket with outsized pockets, and opened the door. Junior jumped up, his high heels clicking against the floor.

He was staring down the hall. "Where's that door go?"

"To the other wing, and then there's another door and another wing."

She followed his eyes. The hall was dark and lined with closed doors. The whole house was so still she could hear the rain beating against the bathroom window behind her and the wind thudding against the brick walls.

"Guess I don't like these big houses so much after all, Mrs. Dancer. Keep feeling something is around a corner, behind one of those doors. There's a . . . a listening feeling."

She tried to laugh. "You're supposed to be protecting me, Junior, not making me nervous. Let's go down, I want to phone the hospital."

In the lower hall he waited near the swinging doors while she made the call. The cheerful voice at the hospital identified itself as Nurse Murphy.

222

"This is Karen Dancer. I'd like to speak with Dr. Miles, please."

"Sorry, Mrs. Dancer, the doctor isn't here now. Just a minute and I'll check and see if he left word where he can be reached." The line hummed for a moment and then the nurse said, "He didn't leave a message. Odd, he generally does. I suppose you're wondering about your daughter and Mr. Trent. They're both resting comfortably."

"Could you . . . would you mind checking on Jamie? I'm a bit worried about her."

Nurse Murphy gave a good-natured chuckle. "Nurse Loren's with her and will stay until Nurse Baker relieves her at six in the morning. But if you'll hold for a minute I'll look in on her and on Mr. Trent." The line hummed for a longer time. In the background Karen could hear brisk footsteps echoing and then the rattle of the receiver as it was picked up. "Both fine, Mrs. Dancer. Nurse Loren's sitting right beside your little girl."

"Thank you. Would you mind if I phoned back later?"

"Of course not. I go off duty in ten minutes—at six— but Nurse Lambert will be on the desk and she can help you." Her voice changed slightly. "Don't worry. Chief Barnes spoke to all of us, and Nurse Loren won't leave the room."

Thanking her again, Karen hung up. Mac turned from the stove as they entered the kitchen and raised her brows. "They're both fine," Karen told her.

"It's a miracle. I would have sworn they were goners. Sit down, Karie, and you too, Junior. Don't let this food get cold."

Taking his place quickly, Junior looked appreciatively at the table. A crock of steaming baked beans was flanked by a platter heaped with pink slices of ham and a bowl of tossed salad.

"Wow," he said. "You sure got this ready in a hurry."

"All I had to do was put it on the table." Mac pointed at a basket near the back door. "Maudie Jenks cooked it up and brought it over. There's blueberry pie for dessert. Like blueberry pie, Junior?"

"My favorite," he said as he heaped his plate.

Mac touched the brim of his hat. "Don't you ever take that thing off?"

"No more'n I have to. Helps me think."

Mac grinned and winked at Karen. "Better leave it on, then. Imagine what he'd be like without his thinking cap."

The boy gave her an aggrieved look. "You got no call to talk about me that way, Mrs. MacLean. Chief sent me here to protect you."

"He's right," Karen said gravely.

"Must admit I'll sleep sounder tonight knowing you're in the house," Mac told him.

The boy ate prodigiously, and Karen and Mac automatically. After the second slice of his favorite pie, he tipped back his chair, hooked his heels over the rung, and patted his stomach. "Maudie's a prime cook. Was wondering if you two ladies care for a game of cards? Just to pass the time and take your minds off your troubles."

"What kind of cards?" Karen asked.

"Blackjack, with small stakes. Just a friendly game."

"Fine with me," Karen told him.

"What about you, Mrs. MacLean? Ever play blackjack?"

"Now, what would an old woman like me know about blackjack? But I'll try a few hands."

Digging in his tunic pocket he produced a deck of battered cards. "Better get your money out, ladies."

The two women went for their purses and returned with handfuls of coins. Junior flipped three cards face down out and sat back. Mac took a peek at hers.

"Hit me, Junior."

He dealt her a card face up. It was the jack of spades. She flipped over an ace. "Blackjack. Pay me, Junior, and I get the deal."

"You sure you never played this game before?"

Reaching for the cards, she riffled them with a practiced hand. "Might have played a few hands years ago, but that was beginner's luck, son."

Her beginner's luck lasted for more than two hours. Twice Karen left for more money. Finally she threw down her cards and said, "Deal me out, Mac, this is too high-powered for me."

"How about you, Junior, you chickening out too?"

He was searching through his pockets. "You've plumb cleaned me out, Mrs. MacLean." He looked at her hopefully. "What about an IOU?"

"Us beginners never take credit. But I hear something jingling in your pants."

He pulled out a ring of keys and handed them to Karen. "Clean forgot to give you the keys to Mr. Trent's car. Sure is a nice one he's got there. Real hot."

Sticking them in the pocket of her jacket, Karen pushed back her chair and stood up. "I'd better phone and check on Jamie. What was the name of that night nurse? Oh, yes, Lambert."

Mac glanced up from the coins she was neatly stacking. "Oh-oh!"

Karen tripped over the older woman's work basket. It fell over and gay squares of material and the pair of shears slipped out on the floor. She knelt to replace them.

"Watch them shears, Karie. I keep them well honed."

Handing her the basket, Karen asked, "What was the oh-oh about?"

"Gertie Lambert. You may find her a mite different from Hannah Murphy. Real lemon. Got eyes like shoe buttons, chin like an ax blade, and a disposition to match."

As soon as she heard the voice on the phone, Karen knew that as usual Mac was right. Nurse Murphy's voice had been warm and hearty and good-natured. This woman's was cold, high-pitched, and edged with irritation.

"All I can tell you is what Nurse Murphy reported earlier, Mrs. Dancer. Both patients are sedated and resting comfortably."

For a moment Karen thought she was hanging up and said quickly, "I'd like to speak to Dr. Miles, please."

"Dr. Miles is not here and I don't know where he can be reached. If you'd like a number for Dr. Morris—"

"No. May I leave a message for Dr. Miles? Please tell him I'd like to talk to him and I would appreciate it if he would call. It doesn't matter what time he comes in."

There was a pause and then the woman said tartly, "I'll leave a message. Good night."

Karen felt her face flushing. "I'd also like you to check on my daughter."

"Now look here, Mrs. Dancer, I know mothers get edgy about their youngsters, but this is the second time you've called tonight. There're only three nurses on duty—Nurse Loren is with your daughter, Nurse Moffat is on duty in the upper ward, and I'm alone down here. I haven't time to run my feet off—"

"Now *you* look here! My daughter was nearly killed today. Chief Barnes left special instructions for her safety. You go to her room and report back to me immediately!"

Something crashed in her ear and she thought this time the woman had hung up, but then she realized the nurse must have dropped the receiver on the counter because she could still hear the hum of the line and the sound of heels beating an angry tattoo on the floor.

Despite her protestation about being busy, this nurse kept Karen waiting twice as long as Nurse Murphy had. Finally the receiver was picked up. "Nurse Loren is in attendance and reports your daughter is fine," she snapped. "Anything else?"

Karen told her there wasn't and didn't bother offering thanks. Barely restraining herself from banging the receiver down, she forced herself to replace it gently.

Mac and Junior had been silently watching her. "Bad news?" Mac asked anxiously.

"The only bad news is that ruddy nurse. She must have a disposition like a crocodile. But Jamie is all right."

"Well, that's the main thing, isn't it. You going to bed now?"

Karen stifled a yawn. "I think I'd better, and I'd advise you to have an early night too."

"Going to work on my quilt for an hour or so. Calms my nerves." Mac swung toward the young man. "What room you using, young fellow?"

"Mrs. Dancer's, of course," he blurted and then, seeing the expression on the old woman's face, added hastily, "Chief's orders, Mrs. MacLean."

Karen interposed. "Junior can sleep in Jamie's bed."

He shook his head stubbornly. "I'm staying right where I can see you."

Mac shrugged. "Guess I can't argue with Theo Barnes, but you'll have to sit up all night. There's a big chair you can use, but you won't be comfortable—"

"Doesn't matter. I won't be closing my eyes. No, sirree. Chief told me—"

Karen smiled. "Come along then, Junior."

As she started up the stairs, Mac called, "I'll bring you up a hot drink. Help you to relax."

Junior touched the old woman's arm. "I'm right partial to hot chocolate myself."

She gave him a good-natured shove. "Okay, Junior, a hot drink for you too. Away you go and do your policing."

As Junior followed Karen into her room he looked around uneasily. "This house is giving me the willies. While you were on the phone I could have sworn I heard something downstairs."

Taking a couple of blankets from the lower drawer of the chiffonier, she handed him one. "Where?"

"Don't know exactly, but I was standing a few feet away from them swinging doors."

She pulled a pillow from her bed and threw it into the armchair by the window. "You were close to both the dining room and the library. Shouldn't you go down and have a look?"

He was arranging his makeshift bed. Tugging a small table and a lamp over, he positioned them beside the chair. "If you come down with me. I'm not letting you out of my sight." He plumped up a pillow. "Probably just a board creaking. This old house is full of sounds on a night like this."

He paused and they both listened. She could hear the moan of the wind, the slashing of rain against the window, and muffled creaks from the hall. Holding the curtain back she stared down at the back garden. All she could make out were the dark bulks of the barn and the shed and the circular shape of the umbrella table.

Junior seated himself comfortably and draped the blanket over his knees. "Got anything to read, Mrs. Dancer?"

She reached for a couple of novels on her bedside table and tossed them over. He looked at them and handed them back. "You got any comic books?"

"Jamie has," she told him, and walked into Jamie's room. On the narrow bed her daughter's fluffy blue robe and yellow pajamas were neatly folded, and her fur slippers sat beside the bed. Karen touched the child's brush and mirror, the heart-shaped box Jamie had saved from St. Valentine's Day, and her full-skirted dresser doll. Curled up on the bed was the red cat. Sitting down beside her, she patted the long soft fur. Ruby lifted her head, purred, and rubbed her moist nose against the caressing hand. Karen saw again the white face and bright hair streaming across the pillow, the bruised and scraped hand lying inertly against the hospital spread, and she felt a slow, hot surge of rage.

"Mrs. Dancer," a voice said from the doorway.

"Sorry, Junior, I was thinking."

"I know. But she's okay and so are you."

Pulling herself together, she picked up the cat, which snuggled into her arms and purred louder. "The comic books are over there. Take as many as you want."

By the time Junior had made his selection, Mac was in the other bedroom carrying a tray with two steaming mugs and a generous slice of pie on it. Setting it down on the table Junior had moved, she turned to Karen. "You aren't ready for bed."

"I'm just going to slip my shoes off. If Jim phones I want to be able to run down and answer the phone. Oh, by the way, when you come up leave the hall light on." She thought of what the constable had said earlier. "Junior thinks he heard something downstairs. We'd better check on it."

Mac raised expressive brows. "If there was anything down there, wouldn't I know? Junior is hearing things. Now, drink up that chocolate 'fore it cools." Leaning over, she kissed Karen's cheek. "Sleep well, child."

"I'm going to bolt these doors, Mrs. MacLean. If you want in, knock twice," Junior told her.

"Think I need a password?" Mac asked caustically, and shut the door in his face. She heard him pull the bolt

229

to and waited until she heard the bolt on Jamie's door click into place also. Then she shook her head and made her way wearily down the stairs.

She headed down the hall toward the kitchen. The dining room door was open, and light from the chandelier over the long polished table cast an oblong of light across the carpeting of the hall. She peered into the room. A light was on in the room beyond, and a tall dark-clad figure was standing in the doorway beside the buffet.

"What are you doing in here?" the old woman demanded. "And you've got my sewing basket with you. Should of left it in the kitchen. I'll just have to tote it back again."

The figure in the doorway asked a whispered question, and Mac replied impatiently.

"No, I didn't let on to either Karie or Junior you were here. You asked me not to. Now, what's got you so upset? Is it Jamie? Has she taken a turn for the worse?"

Her visitor beckoned, and Mac walked slowly across the dining room. "You want to talk in there? Make it quick. My feet are aching like boils tonight. All right, I'm coming."

As the figure stood to one side so the old woman could pass, the light gleaming from the chandelier caught the bright scraps of cotton in the basket and splintered into icy brilliance on the handles of the big shears.

Behind Mac the door of the dying room swung to with a soft thud.

18

THE BLANKET WAS too warm against her legs and the cat pressed closely against her side. Twitching the blanket away, Karen eased over on the bed, lit a cigarette, and watched the blue smoke spiraling toward the ceiling. She cast an amused glance at the constable. He sprawled in the armchair, his Stetson tilted over his face, a comic book dangling from one limp hand. On the table beside him was the dish the pie had been on and two empty mugs. Junior had gulped his own chocolate and cast a covetous look at her untouched cup, so she had smiled and nodded. He had made as short work of her drink as he had of his own and minutes later had fallen into what appeared to be a sound sleep. Some watchdog, she told herself.

She was tired but she didn't feel sleepy, and she kept listening to hear the peal of the phone or Mac's footsteps on the stairs. She glanced at her watch. Time was passing so slowly.

Junior grunted and moved, and his arm hung farther over the arm of his chair. Frowning, she slid off the bed. He certainly didn't look comfortable. She walked over to him, picked up his arm, detached the comic book, and put his hand in his lap. He didn't stir. She listened to his breathing, slow and shallow, and then pushed back his hat so she could see his face. Leaning over, she shook his shoulder. His head lolled to one side. Grasping both his shoulders firmly, she shook him roughly. His head fell forward on his chest. She stood back, her uneasiness becoming something stronger. He wasn't sleeping normally. Picking up one of the mugs she inhaled. Nothing she could distinguish. Dregs of chocolate clung to the sides and bottoms but she could see nothing else in the mug.

She tapped her finger against her teeth, her mind going at a furious pace. He was definitely drugged. Could Mac have put some sort of sleeping medicine in the chocolate so they would get a good rest? There was probably something of the sort in the house—Ashley's or Sybil's—but Mac . . . no, Mac had always hated drugs. Her only remedy for sleeplessness was hot milk. But the chocolate must have been drugged. If Mac hadn't done it . . . The noises that Junior had claimed to have heard downstairs?

Karen glanced at the bolted door and then back at the limp figure in the chair. At that instant she knew why she had come back to this house instead of going to Dinah's. Somewhere at the back of her mind she must have been expecting X to try again. By the time she left the hospital X would have known that as soon as Jamie could be moved they were leaving Hampton. And deep within her she wanted to see X, to see the face of the person who had killed her uncle and nearly killed her daughter and Cal Trent. She sensed that person was downstairs, down in the high, shadowy rooms with Mac.

Wheeling around, she pulled a straight chair over to the wardrobe, climbed up on the seat, and thrust a hand to the back of the shelf. Her fingers touched rubber and she pulled out the bundle, flipped out the gun, and opened the cartridge chamber. She looked at the circle of gleaming shells and closed it up again.

Clutching the gun, she unbolted the door and crept along the hall, cautiously skirting the telltale board in front of Jamie's room. She went softly down the stairs, keeping close to the outside edge of the treads.

In the lower hall a light was burning, and she could see the fanlight over the door, the marble-topped table where the telephone rested, and a corner of dun-colored carpeting. She moved quietly along the hall. All the doors were closed, but when she swung back the kitchen doors the overhead light was gleaming from the center of the ceiling. On the counter was a pan crusted with the skin of the heated milk, an open tin of cocoa, and a bowl of sugar. On the table was part of the quilt Mac was working on, a spool of thread beside it, the needle stuck in the cloth where she had taken the last tiny stitch. Karen's hand tightened convulsively around the butt of the gun.

The sewing basket was missing. Could Mac have left her work and gone quietly to bed? No! Never in her life had Mac left soiled dishes behind her. And would she have taken the sewing basket and left the work she was doing on the table?

As Karen turned back to the hall she felt her heart thudding against her ribs. Could Mac be X? Could the words Cal had spoken in jest be the truth? Violently, she repudiated her own thought. Mac would never do anything to harm either her or Jamie. If Mac was still in this house she was in danger too.

Flinging open the library door, she switched on a lamp and glanced around the room. She opened the dining room door. The room was dark, the teardrop prisms of the chandelier catching light from the hall. She was backing out of the room when she stopped abruptly. Under the door next to the buffet was a thin line of light. Lifting the gun, she walked toward it. The china knob turned under her hand and the door of the dying room swung open.

She jumped back and then realized that the strained white face that had startled her was her own, mirrored in the oval frame over the chiffonier. Beside the bed the dark-shaded lamp was burning. On one of the faded rag rugs was the sewing basket, but the shears were missing. The headboard of the bed, ornamented with its pattern of oak leaves and acorns, stood out against the striped wallpaper. The mattress was bare, and on its tufted white-and-blue cotton ticking Mac lay on her back. Her hands were folded against her waist, her legs were stretched out, and her skirt was neatly pulled down into place. She still wore a starched apron, and from its bosom the handles of the shears protruded. The white of the bosom was now crimson, dyed by blood seeping out around the shears.

"Mac," Karen whispered. She bent over the still form, her free hand frantically searching for signs of life, her mind telling her it was hopeless. Behind the round lenses of her glasses, Mac's eyes stared sightlessly at the ceiling. Her work-worn hand under Karen's fingers was still warm.

She hadn't been dead long, Karen thought, perhaps only minutes. The tide of rage and hatred she had been fighting off overwhelmed her. Without fear or caution she ran from the dying room and raced across the dining room to the hall. There she stopped by the phone and lifted the receiver. The line was dead. She pulled at the cord and the end of it was in her hand, cut through. Clinging to the top of the table she listened. Around her the house stretched in silence, broken only by the sound of the wind against the oaken panel of the door. Some instinct, long buried, told her she was alone in the house, with only Mac's body in the dying room and the unconscious policeman in the room above her.

234

Fighting down the tide of rage, she tried to think. Where was the sense in the whole thing? A drug had been used on Junior Barnes and her but it was only a sleeping drug; it hadn't been meant to kill, only to keep them unconscious and helpless. Mac had been killed, quickly and brutally, to silence her. Why hadn't X waited for her to come down or tried to get into the bedroom? She could have slept safely for hours behind closed doors, until daylight and perhaps the arrival of Theo Barnes.

If she was the killer's target, where was the sense? She went back over the series of incidents, beginning with the panda and the balloon, then the kitten, the swing, Uncle Alfred, and now Mac. Theo Barnes was right, X was insane, but even with insanity there had to be a plan, a purpose. Suddenly she dropped the useless phone, pushed the revolver into her pocket, and pulled out the car keys.

Jamie. Jamie's toy and sweater, Jamie's effigy in the barn, Jamie's beloved kitten. The swing. The killer must have known the fascination that swing would have for a little girl. Karen had never been intended to die, Jamie had! From the beginning, from the moment they had driven into Hampton, Jamie had been the target. The killer was going after her daughter!

Karen ran across the hall, wrenched open the door, and raced down the steps. Trent's car was parked on the driveway in front of the garage. As she ran toward it she didn't feel the wind sweeping her clothes against her body or the icy rain beating against her hair and face.

I'm coming, baby, she sobbed under her breath, I'm coming!

Rain was beating against the window of the hospital room. Julie Loren could see the garden, framed in crisp white curtains, the maple limbs thrashing in the wind and

235

their leaves swirling across the long grass. Turning away from the bleak scene, she looked down at her small patient. Julie was fond of children—she and Freddy were planning on at least three—and she hoped one would be a girl. Leaning over the bed, she straightened the spread and laid a gentle hand over the small scraped one on the white spread. Chief Barnes had spoken to her seriously about the child's safety, but she still was unable to believe that anyone could deliberately attempt to hurt this child. It had to be an accident, she decided; no one in Hampton would ever do a thing like that.

Picking up her magazine, she bent her dark head over it. Temporarily she forgot about Jamie. Should she have her hair cut for the wedding or not? The picture she was looking at brought the original argument with her fiancé to mind again. Freddy could be stubborn and he liked her hair long but she had told him she was tired of it, tired of bundling it up in a net while she was working. This girl in the picture had a modified shag, and her face was the same shape as her own. She looked at the picture one way and then another. Yes, her mind was made up. Regardless of what Freddy thought, she would have her hair cut tomorrow.

She leaped to her feet, her heart beating wildly, the magazine slipping to the floor. Something beside wind and rain was at the window. She could make out the outlines of a head, of a raised hand knocking softly at the glass. For a moment, remembering Chief Barnes's words, she was terrified. And then as she stepped closer she smiled and emitted a breath of relief. The hand was moving toward the left, pointing at the French door at the end of the corridor. Taking a quick glance at her patient, Julie opened the door and stepped into the hall. Behind the glass panes of the door she could see a tall dark-clad figure. The big key was still in the lock where Nurse Murphy had left it. For a moment she hesitated, Chief Barnes had said not to open that door for anyone. She chuckled. Poor old fellow, he couldn't possibly have meant to include *this* person.

The lock was stiff and she had trouble getting the key to turn. Then it clicked and she swung the door open.

"What on earth are you coming to this door for?" she asked gaily. "And what are you dressed up for, a masquerade? Come in, you must be soaked through."

The tall figure asked a whispered question.

"She's upstairs giving Mrs. Moffat a hand in the ward," Julie replied. "You know old Lambert, grumbling under her breath just because she has to do a little work. Shut that door and lock it, will you?"

Without waiting, Julie Loren turned her back and took a couple of steps toward the child's room. The door was still open because she could feel a draft against her back. Then a hand crushed her lips and something sharp and agonizingly painful was driven into her back. Behind the gloved hand her mouth fell open, and above it her eyes bulged and then rolled up. She sagged forward and the tall figure dragged her body across the black-and-white tile of the corridor floor into the room where the child slept.

Dropping the nurse facedown on the floor, the figure bent over her, pulled the knife from her back and wiped it methodically on the girl's uniform, and then swiftly and purposely approached the bed.

Karen turned the white car off Arbutus Street onto Lofton Hill. She could see the iron peacock on Dinah Gaines's lawn and then the lights of the hospital. Pulling the car to a screeching halt, she ran across the wet grass, slipped, and nearly went sprawling. Catching herself she swung open the front door and dashed into the entrance hall.

A nurse was bustling down the stairs, a tall gaunt

237

woman with beady black eyes and a sharp chin. "No more visitors," she snapped, and Karen recognized the voice of Nurse Lambert.

"My daughter," Karen panted.

Glaring at her, the woman moved to block her way. "You must be Mrs. Dancer. I simply can't have these disruptions! It's well past visiting hours—"

Desperately Karen tried to shove the taller, heavier woman aside. Nurse Lambert stood her ground. Tugging the gun from her pocket, Karen pointed it at the nurse.

"Get out of my way!" she grated. "My daughter is in danger."

"You're *mad!*" The nurse moved quickly aside and shouted up the staircase. "Moffat! Get down here. We got a mental case running loose!"

Karen raced down the corridor. She could hear the woman pounding after her. Jamie's door was closed but the French door at the end of the corridor was ajar. Karen's foot skidded and she looked down. There were blotches of blood on the white tiles.

"My God," she groaned, and threw open the door of her daughter's room.

She nearly fell over the body of the young nurse. Blood had welled from the wound in the girl's back, soaking the back of her uniform and dripping onto the floor. Karen clung to the doorjamb, her eyes on the empty bed, the smell of fresh blood in her nostrils.

Nurse Lambert peered over her shoulder. "Good Lord! That's young Julie! And where's the child?"

Circling the girl's body, Karen stared down at the bed. Anxiously, her eyes ran over the sheets and blankets. There were no bloodstains. She looked closer. The white spread that had covered the blankets was missing. Striding to the window, she looked out at the desolate garden. Could X have taken Jamie out there to kill her? She shook her head. If death was what X wanted, Jamie would have been knifed in her bed, just as the young nurse had been killed. So . . . Jamie was still alive. But where had she been taken?

She heard someone enter the room and swung around. Nurse Moffat was short and stout. Her eyes were wide and the color was draining from her ruddy features. Both nurses bent over the figure on the floor.

"Is there any way to get a car behind this building?" Karen asked.

Nurse Moffat stared with dilated eyes at the gun still clasped in Karen's hand. Karen shoved it back in her pocket. "Answer me, damn you!"

"There's a lane," the fat nurse whispered. "Right behind the garden. It runs down to Arbutus Street."

The tall nurse got to her feet. "I'll phone Chief Barnes."

She left the room and Karen, closing her eyes, clung to the side of the bed. Where was Jamie? Where had she been taken and why? She forced herself to think back over the evening, searching for an answer. An attempt had been made to drug her, and X would have no way of knowing it had failed. The killer would still believe she slept behind bolted doors in the bedroom. Mac in the dying room, the kitten in the dying room . . . the light left on in the dying room. Everyone in town knew how she feared that room. Her eyes snapped open and she ran down the corridor.

Nurse Lambert was at the desk, replacing the receiver. "I got him, Mrs. Dancer. Chief Barnes will be right here. He said to tell you—"

"Never mind. Listen. When he gets here tell him Mollie MacLean has been murdered too. Tell him to come to the Hampton house. I'm going there, and if my child has

239

been—" Breaking off, she pulled the door open. "Tell him to hurry!"

Without waiting to see if the woman understood, she ran down the steps toward the car.

19

IN THE DYING room, the lamp still burned and silhouetted the tall figure tugging at the body on the bed.

Mollie MacLean was heavy, and she was stiffening up. Too bad to have to take the time to move her, but the setting was important; it had to be just like the imagined one. And there was time, enough time for everything. Junior Barnes and Karen Hampton had enough sleeping drug in them to keep them under until morning. It had been simple enough to do when Mollie's back was turned: two steps, slip it into the chocolate, and Mollie none the wiser.

Finally the body rolled off the side of the bed with a thud. Now, to pull the old woman's back against the wall and prop her up with her face to the door. Yes . . . the legs were getting stiff, better pull them out straight. There, that looked fine. X stepped back for the effect. Now . . . the child.

Stepping into the dining room, X lifted the little girl, still swathed in the cocoon of hospital spread. Dumping the child on the mattress, X carefully pulled back the spread and smoothed it out around her. Some fine hair had fallen forward over the child's face. A gloved hand swept it back into a frame for the face. The girl moved her head and moaned in her sleep. How much she looked like her mother had looked in grade school! The same amber eyes, hair, an identical walk. If she had lived she would have looked like Karen Hampton had in high school: the prettiest girl in town, the most popular girl in town. First I dreamed of killing *her*, X gloated, but then I realized she must live . . . she must live to see what lies behind that door in the morning. The expression on Karen's face when she opens that door and sees Mollie and her beloved little daughter. Karen will have to live with this; for the rest of her life she will see these faces, and she will suffer.

Everything was working out as planned. The only people who could have pointed a finger were dead—that meddling old fool of an Alfred, Mollie MacLean, Julie Loren. Too bad in a way they had to die, but necessary. This way no one would ever know. Theo Barnes would fumble around, but he would never guess. And Karen! Karen would leave Hampton behind her forever, but with her she'd take this memory, this gruesome memory of the dying room she'd always feared. And what would Karen do for revenge? She would sell her property, the plant would be built, and then the plan would be complete.

X's hand touched the knife in the sheath attached to the wide belt. It slipped out easily. Nice and sharp, it had entered Julie's back as though slipping into butter. For Jamie there would be no quick merciful death. The child would look like the kitten had—a bundle of flesh and blood on the clean white bedspread.

The gloved hand moved with deliberation, describing an arc over the sleeping child. I'll pretend it *is* Karen, X thought—and then lifted a startled face. In the doorway a woman stood, her dark blond hair plastered to the fine

242

lines of her head. *Karen.* It couldn't be. She was upstairs, upstairs sleeping a drugged sleep behind barred doors.

"Drop that knife!" Karen's eyes were steady on the familiar face. "Drop it right now, or I'll kill you."

"No!"

The knife swept downward and Karen pulled the trigger, aiming well to the left of the killer. The bullet smashed past the other woman's shoulder and hit the mirror. The glass in the oval frame splintered. The gloved hand froze in midair. Karen shifted the gun to the right, intending to fire another warning shot. Either the shoulder or the wall, just so the knife was clear of Jamie.

It would still have been all right if the other woman hadn't panicked and moved sharply to the right. Mac's rigid legs were directly in her way and the woman tripped over them. She lurched right into the path of the bullet. For a moment she stood erect, her eyes widening, one hand wavering toward her breast. Then she crumpled and fell slowly to the floor.

Circling the bed, Karen stared down. The woman's head, covered by a black knitted cap, rested on Mac's lap. In the middle of the windbreaker was a small seared hole. Karen didn't have to check for a pulse. Dark eyes stared as sightless up at her as Mac's had a short time before. A shard of mirror dropped from the frame to the floor with a tiny tinkle. Karen stared down at the shattered pieces of glass and from distant schooldays a line of a poem came back to her.

"The mirror cracked from side to side," she whispered.

Bending over the dead woman, Karen eased the cap off. Lustrous hair fell back from a deep widow's peak. Death had erased the madness and hate that had twisted Cassie Saunders's oval face almost past recognition. Again she was beautiful—fine-featured with milky skin and a sensual curve of full red lips.

From the same poem more words came unbidden. She didn't know she said them aloud. "He said, 'She has a lovely face,' " she whispered; " 'God in his mercy lend her grace.' "

The gun dropped from her nerveless fingers, and behind her she heard Jamie stir and moan. Picking her daughter up, she walked slowly from the room, making her stumbling way through the dining room, along the hall, toward the front door.

"You'll never see this house again," she promised the sleeping child.

Dimly, she heard men's voices and then the oak door was flung open. Men crowded into the hall behind Theo Barnes. Karen held the child out to him, and he took Jamie from her arms. She swayed, looked at her daughter in the old man's arms, and thought, She's safe. I saved her.

"The Lady of Shalott," she told him, and then the hall darkened around her.

She fell forward and arms caught her. The darkness was complete, merciful darkness that for a time would shield her from the dying room and the dead women in it.

20

OCTOBER WINDS HAD wrenched most of the flaming leaves from the maples, and the few that still tenaciously clung to the branches were dry and brown. The warmth of late September had fled with the leaves, and Hampton shivered under frosty nights and bright but cold days.

On the lower floor of the town hall, ancient radiators clanked and groaned in unsuccessful efforts to heat the drafty building. In Chief Barnes's office the white-painted radiator wheezed even louder than the old man himself, but the room was still clammy. Under his tunic he was wearing a heavy hand-knitted sweater. Five of the six people in the office were bundled in coats.

Karen, wrapped in a long wool cape, was seated in the armchair beside his desk. Next to her Trent, wearing denims and his suede jacket, lounged, a cane propped against the wall at his side. The bandages had been removed from his head and face, and except for a fresh scar down his left cheek he looked much the same as he had the first day she had met him.

The four straight chairs in front of Barnes's desk were

occupied by Sybil and Ashley Hampton, Jim Miles, and Dinah Gaines. Dinah flashed an encouraging smile at Karen, and she forced herself to smile back.

Barnes stopped fiddling with the sheets of typewritten paper scattered over the green blotter in front of him, cleared his throat, and said, "Now you folks all know why you're here. Karen and Jamie are leaving Hampton later today, and though I know none of us are exactly anxious to talk more about this we got to"—he turned his head toward Karen—"it's been pretty tough getting to the bottom of this whole affair. We know who did it, but we have to guess why. But I've been talking to all of you separately and have a better understanding of Cassie Saunders. I learned a bit from Ashley; more from Sybil, who's been closer to Cassie for the last couple of years than any other woman in town; certain facts from Dinah, who remembers Cassie when she was a young gal. Jim Miles here has filled in other things, and now we got to put them all together."

Pushing back in his chair, he laced his fingers across his paunch. "With Cassie dead we're going to have to guess some but here goes. Appears according to Dinah that Cassie—well, Dinah, you better tell it yourself."

Dinah spoke directly to Karen. "You didn't pay much attention to Cassie in school, did you?"

"I can barely remember her."

"Few people can. She just sort of faded into the background. Cassie was a pathetic girl, tied to her mother so she couldn't join in anything the rest of us did, and even if she hadn't been held down she wouldn't have been accepted. Her appearance, her weight, those clothes—well, she was always the butt of cruel jokes. I don't have to spell her early life out to you. But underneath there was another Cassie, one with strong emotions, a proud, passionate person. She hated strongly—her mother—and loved just as violently—Jim. When we were in grade school she watched Jim for a while and then followed him around like a puppy. By the time we got to high school she'd been hurt and teased so much about this that she'd learned to conceal it, to watch Jim from a distance. All she ever wanted in this entire world was Jim—"

"No," Karen interrupted. "You're mistaken, Dinah. Perhaps when she was a young girl this was so, but Cassie herself told me what she really wanted was to be a liberated woman—to run her health spa—and said she was happy when I came back because Jim and the town might stop coupling them and start on me. That's what she said, and I would swear she was sincere."

Barnes barked a laugh. "Gotta remember that Cassie was president of the Drama Club and a fine actress. Best one we had in town."

Sybil leaned forward. "We all knew how badly she wanted Jim. After Laura's death Cassie dieted, bought new clothes, and went right after him."

"All right, folks," Barnes said. "We know she had Karen fooled, and we know what sent her over the brink. A combination of love and hate and jealousy. She must have hated Karen for years."

"She did," Dinah said firmly. "Karen was everything she wasn't, and the only one who never knew how Cassie felt was Karen herself. She didn't seem to know Cassie existed. And that made it worse."

Jim Miles shook his head. "Make that two people. I realized Cassie was attracted to me, but I had no idea how she really felt about Karen."

Barnes sent him a penetrating glance from under tufted brows. "If Karen hadn't come back to town, would you have married Cassie Saunders? Know I'm prying but I'd kinda like to know."

The other man's brow furrowed. "I can't really say I

would. She turned into a beautiful woman and I suppose my ego was inflated when she showed she was interested in me but . . ." His voice trailed off and he stared at Barnes. "There was Laura, you know."

"Uh-huh. Can't say I blame you. Anyway, we got the motive. I guess Cassie started this whole business just with the idea of frightening Karen and driving her out of town. Either that or she figured if she got Karen mad enough she'd sell and Jim would never want to see her again. Cassie was a smart woman and knew how much Jim hated ANPP. She could see how Karen felt about her daughter, so Cassie started out by pulling that nasty trick with the balloon—"

"Why?" Karen asked bluntly. "At that point all that had happened was that Jim escorted me to her party. There wasn't any provocation for it then."

The policeman gestured at Dinah. She said slowly, "The night of the party I went out to the kitchen just after you and Jim left. Cassie was standing by the door with a man's topcoat draped over her arm. I said it looked like Jim's and she told me it was and she was afraid he'd catch cold without it. She said she was going to his house and leave it for him. Les called me and I went back into the living room, but when we were leaving I got my coat from the closet in the hall and Jim's coat was hanging there. I pointed it out to Cassie, and she said she had changed her mind and he could pick it up the next day."

"Let's assume that Cassie did run up the block to the Miles house," Barnes said. "Neither Jim nor his dad ever draw the curtains on that big window they had put in. Gone by at night any number of times myself and seen everything going on in their living room. Could Cassie have looked in and seen anything the night of the party that might have got her all fired up?"

Jim dropped his eyes and Karen, acutely conscious of

Trent beside her, said, "I tripped on a corner of a rug and Jim caught me." She remembered Jim's arms around her, his lips pressing her own. That was what Cassie must have seen.

"So that explains what set her off," Barnes muttered. "All the hate and envy she'd felt about you when you were a young gal must have boiled up stronger than ever. She must have figured you were going to take Jim away from her, so she goes back to the party wild with rage, and later—"

"That balloon," Sybil said tonelessly. "We were having a children's party at the church, and Cassie was painting some balloons for it."

The policeman nodded. "Uh-huh. She knows the Hampton house as well as her own. She knows about the long clothes pole and where Jamie is sleeping, so she paints a scary face on a balloon and goes up to frighten the little girl. When she gets there she finds the panda and sweater and doll on the outside table—" Breaking off, he looked at Sybil. "You were her pipeline into that house, weren't you?"

She flushed. "I had no idea what she was planning. She was my best friend and she was always so sympathetic, so willing to listen to my troubles. Certainly I talked to her. I told her all about Karen and Jamie. About the child being spoiled rotten, still dragging that panda around, and then her mother breaking down and letting her have a kitten right in the house, right in her bedroom." She turned indignant eyes on her brother. "Ashley, you know very well we always had barn cats but we *never* allowed cats in the—"

"Sybil," he muttered, "can't you see yet what you did? You told a madwoman exactly how to hurt the child and Karen."

His sister's head drooped and her smooth chestnut

hair glinted. "I'm sorry, so sorry. But I didn't know. I swear I didn't know."

For a few minutes Barnes sat quietly and wheezed. Trent fished in his pocket, found and lit cigarettes, and handed one to Karen. He gave her the smile that made his whole face charming.

"Better tell us about the swing," Barnes prompted.

Sybil didn't lift her head and her voice was muffled. "Karen didn't know it, but Mac was having the devil's own time keeping Jamie off that swing. She had to pull her off a number of times. I told Cassie all about it."

Barnes looked with cold dislike at her, and then his eyes moved to Jim Miles. "You're a doctor. When do you figure she went overboard?"

"We all know now that Cassie was never normal. Laura Saunders was definitely a mental case, and she gave poor Cassie a life that was unbelievable. But Cassie, after Laura's death, built a picture in all our minds of a wonderful, warm, generous woman. Those tricks she started with—the balloon and the panda—were sadistic, but my guess would be that she lost her mental balance entirely only when she killed the kitten. She must have decided she wanted Karen to suffer more agony than just death. Cassie wanted her alive, with Jamie dead and Mac dead, and both of them in that room. All of us knew how Karen felt about the dying room." He sighed. "Hindsight is a wonderful thing."

Barnes sighed too. "Yeah, it sure is. Live cheek by jowl with a woman and you never know what she really is. So . . . we know the motive and we know how she did it. We also know that Karen Dancer shot to save her daughter's life and didn't intend to kill Cassie at all. It was an accident, and that's the way it's gonna go on the record." He waved a big hand. "Know this hasn't been a mite pleasant but it's over. You can go now." As they got to

250

their feet, he reached over and touched Karen's arm. "Except you. Want to tell you something."

Trent was the last one to leave the office. He had trouble pulling himself to his feet. Karen watched him prop himself on the cane.

"Is your ankle still painful?" she asked.

"More of a nuisance than anything else. How's Jamie making out with Dinah's kids?"

"Wonderfully, and she's well, very well. Thank God she was unconscious throughout that whole night. She woke up in the morning and couldn't figure out why we were at the Gaineses'."

He patted her shoulder, nodded at Barnes, and hobbled to the door. As he shut it, Karen turned to the policeman. "What do you want to tell me?"

Opening a drawer, he took out a bottle of rye and two plastic cups. He poured a couple of ounces in each one and slid a cup down the desk to her. "Noticed nobody asked anything about Alfred Hampton?"

"I imagine they all know Cassie killed him but don't want to talk about it. As you said, she probably came down the lane behind the Lovatt house and found out Uncle Alfred knew too much to let him live. He must have seen her at night around my house, so she decided to kill him and make his death look accidental."

"That was about it. She must have waited until she heard you knock on the front door, then ran up the alley and round the post office and came right up behind you. Those books she was bringing him made a blame good excuse."

"I just thought of something else. When Cassie and I went into the hall it was so dark after coming in out of the sunlight that I couldn't see a thing, but she flung her arm out and stopped me."

"The way I figure it Cassie knew what was on that

251

floor, and if she hadn't left that soldier in his hand no one would ever have guessed. Smart woman, but in Alfred Hampton she met her match. He was plenty bright too."

Karen moved restlessly. Even in the heavy cape she felt chilled. "Is there anything else?"

He was looking into his cup as though searching for an answer. "There was, but she's dead now. Guess it don't make a mite of difference. As young Jim said, hindsight is wonderful. But something else been nagging at me. When you give me Jamie that night, just before you passed out, you said something about the Lady of Shalott. Had Marge down at the library look the poem up for me and I read it, but I still can't figure out what you meant."

Her fair brows drew together. "At that time I was half out of my mind myself. When I saw the cracked mirror I thought of that poem, and then I looked at Cassie. She was so beautiful, and her world was a fantasy one too. A world where she could have anything she wanted, where she was all-powerful, and then she met the real world and it killed her."

"Yeah, I kinda see what you mean." Getting heavily to his feet, he came around the desk and held out a big hand. She put hers into it and he pressed it warmly. "Well, I guess this is goodbye. Wish things could have worked out different for you, Karen. Wish this old fool of a cop could of figured Cassie out. Too dang-blamed old for a cop now, I suppose."

"You're the best and sharpest cop I've ever met, Theo Barnes. Good luck with making Junior one like you."

"That I'll need." He swung open the door. "Speak of the devil! What you want, son?"

Junior Barnes turned warm, admiring eyes on Karen. "That fellow from ANPP wants to see you, Mrs. Dancer. He's waiting in my office."

Eagerly she followed him, feeling her heart thumping.

It must be Cal. But when she entered the cubicle Vince Halloway was waiting.

"Sorry to bother you, Mrs. Dancer, especially at this time, but I understand you're leaving town today."

She remained standing. "You want my answer and it's long overdue. The answer is no." He opened his mouth and she held up a hand. "I know how you feel, but let me explain. If this had been the only site you could use I would have said yes—"

"Cal told you."

"He did. I know it probably sounds foolish, but I simply can't do this to Hampton. I'm sorry."

He smiled ruefully. "I'm sorry too. The other site will prove more expensive for my company, but it's your decision. However, this town will have to wake up eventually and find they're in the twentieth century. You are only delaying that awakening."

"I know that as well as you do, but someone else will have to throw the bucket of cold water—not me." Dreamily, she gazed past his shoulder. "Isn't it rather nice to come to a place that still has a life most of us only can dream about? A place where people live much as their grandparents did and manage to shut a rather ugly reality out?"

"You're extremely charitable, considering what they did to you."

She lifted her eyes to his face. "The town didn't do that. One woman did, and she was insane."

They shook hands, and Karen made her way slowly down the hall to the wide portico. Leaning against one of the Grecian pillars was Jim Miles, the collar of his overcoat turned up around his neck, the sunlight burnishing his fair hair. He straightened.

"I thought I'd wait and offer you a ride up to Dinah's. In spite of the sun it's cold today."

253

"Dinah wanted me to drive up with her, but I want to take a last look at the town."

He took one of her hands in both of his. Both their hands were icy. "Even if Cassie . . . it wouldn't have worked out for us, would it?"

"No, Jim, it wouldn't. You have your life, I have mine. All we have in common are memories of the past. We couldn't live on memories forever."

"I'll never stop loving that sixteen-year-old girl." Releasing her hand, he brushed cold lips across her cheek. "But there's my work, and right now I'm overdue to check in at the hospital. Let's not say goodbye. We'll meet again."

She watched him pick up his bag and stride down the steps and along the ramp. They wouldn't meet again—she sensed Jim knew that as well as she did—but Cassie had said one true thing. Jim had his work. He probably did have the makings of a bachelor.

She was about to follow him down the steps when she heard her name called. She wheeled around.

"Karen," Ashley called again. "Good. I was hoping to catch you."

"I was going to phone you later anyway. This week I had Les Gaines draw up a couple of deeds for me. Will you tell Nat Jenks and Maudie that they're not hard-luck people anymore? I've deeded the farm to them."

He frowned. "That's very generous."

"Nat earned it; he saved Jamie's life. And you helped him. The Hampton house and a couple of acres are yours. Les will give you the papers."

His frown was replaced with a delighted smile. "That's wonderful! I can't believe it. Sybil and I have always wanted the house. There'll be no more Hamptons, but after our deaths we want the town to have it as a museum."

"It will make a good one."

He looked down at her. "You aren't planning on coming back here again, are you."

"No."

"This is your home, Karen."

She thought of the only two people who could have made it a home—her uncle and Mac. "No, it's only a place I once spent a few years in. I don't know where my home is; perhaps someday I'll find it. But it isn't in Hampton. Goodbye, Ashley."

His eyes followed her as she walked down the steps. A gust of wind caught her cape and swirled it around her. Shaking his head, he turned back to the town hall.

As Karen walked down toward Main Street, one part of her mind was saying goodbye and the other was wondering where Cal Trent had gone. She'd seen him only a few times since he had been hurt in the ravine, and each time either Dinah or Les had been there too. She'd read nothing in his eyes and, as she told herself repeatedly, that was because nothing was there. Momentarily he had been intrigued by a woman in trouble, he was fond of Jamie, and he had tried to help them. He had even carried on a mild flirtation with her, but he had never even tried to kiss her. No, Cal Trent and his long white car were probably long gone from Hampton. She felt the sting of tears in her eyes and thought miserably that he could at least have taken a minute to say goodbye. She tried to shrug: After all, she'd lost nothing; she still had Jamie and her job.

Reaching the corner of Main, she turned by the clothing store and as she neared the poolroom she saw Chuck Paul lounging in the doorway. She averted her eyes and glimpsed Bob Hopper's pimply face peering between two displays in the window of the drugstore.

Behind her a horn honked, but she didn't look

255

around. Then a car pulled up level with her and Trent reached over and swung open the door.

"Taxi, lady?"

"I thought you had left," she said as she got in, and nearly added, me.

"I was hanging around patiently waiting for you to say your goodbyes. They were goodbyes, weren't they?"

"They were goodbyes."

He switched off the ignition. "Good as any other place for a private chat."

She glanced out of her window and felt her lips twitching. Ed Cross was passing the car. He slowed as though he was going to stop, and then he lifted his hat and hurried on. Jessie was leaning over the window display at the Casbah idly dusting one of the decrepit palms, her eyes fixed on them.

"You certainly pick your places for privacy," she told him.

He grinned. "Last chance for a juicy tidbit about Karen Dancer and that bloke from ANPP. Vince just told me about your land. Now, what about Jamie? Have you told her about Mac yet—not the way she died, but the fact that she is dead?"

"No, I've been avoiding her questions about Mac. I'm not going to tell her."

"This is one you can't dodge. She has to know sooner or later. Better now; it's only fair to her and to Mac." Lighting two cigarettes, he handed her one. "One good thing is her age. I'll help you tell her, and then we'll distract her."

"How?"

"Simple." He cast a sidelong look at her. "We'll ask the imp if she wants to be flower girl or maid of honor at our wedding."

Karen choked on the smoke. Exhaling, she said weakly, "Are you proposing?"

"No way. Think I'd give you a chance to turn me down the way you did the young doctor?"

She could feel tears prickling her eyes again. "Aren't you going to tell me you love me?"

With precision he butted his cigarette in the ashtray, leaned over and took hers, and did the same thing. Then he slid an arm around her shoulders and pulled her close. "I think I can do better than that. I'll show you."

An old man was hobbling down Main Street on two canes. Stopping by the Casbah, he stared into the car. His face broke into a wide, toothless smile and he lifted one cane and waved it at them. Trent waved negligently back with his free arm and then wrapped its long length around her. He lowered his head and his lips touched hers. Quite a while later, she murmured against his shoulder. "I thought you had left," and this time added, "me."

His cheek moved against her shining hair. "You're stuck with me. I'm never going to leave you."

Epilogue

THE WINDOW WAS now a square of sunlight, the pale lemon yellow of early morning. Karen Trent looked around her spacious kitchen with pleasure. She had found the home she'd mentioned to Ashley Hampton in Cal's Spanish house on Vancouver Island, where waves from the Strait of Georgia broke upon a beach a short distance from its door, where August roses bloomed profusely around the fountain in the middle of a courtyard. Eyeing the masses of red and pink bush roses and the pale oranges and deep yellows of the climbers, Karen wondered how nightmares could pursue her here.

Turning away from the window she gazed fondly around her kitchen, at the dark beamed ceiling, the stuccoed walls, the rows of copper pots and pans hanging above the brick hearth. Then she saw her husband, standing silently in the doorway, his eyes fixed on her face.

"You're up early," she told him. "I'd better get breakfast started."

He hugged her and planted a resounding kiss on her cheek. "You're up early yourself. In fact I heard you sneaking out of bed around three. Don't bother about breakfast yet. I looked in on Jamie, and she's sound asleep."

"Well . . . coffee, anyway."

"Don't fuss, Karen, sit down. I want to talk to you. Had another nightmare, didn't you?"

She sank down on a chair. "The first one in over a month. They're farther apart."

"Not far enough." Leaning over, he tenderly patted the slight rounding of her stomach. "Not far enough for this son of mine—"

"It might be a daughter."

"Whichever. But I already have a daughter and I'm worried about her, too."

There was a scratching at the outside door. Karen opened it and a rangy red setter bounded in, jumped up enthusiastically, licked her hand, and then trotted over to lay his slender muzzle on Trent's knee.

"You're in good spirits, boy," Trent told the dog, rubbing his ears.

Karen was staring at her husband. "What do you mean? Why are you worried about Jamie?"

"Just what I said. I love everything about you, darling, but one thing I must admit is you're not all that observant. Haven't you seen what these nightmares are doing to Jamie?"

"She doesn't even know about them."

"She'd have to be deaf not to. You're quite vocal at times. And it's not helping her get over Hampton either."

"All she remembers about Hampton is that Mac and Uncle Alfred died, she had an accident, we went to stay with Dinah, and then you and I were married."

"You really *aren't* observant, are you? Ever notice she can't stand the color pink anymore and once it was her favorite? Did you notice when we took her into a pet shop

259

she wouldn't even look at kittens, she insisted on a puppy? Jamie is extremely intelligent, and she knows much more about Hampton than you guess."

"But how? I shielded her—"

"The Gaines kids could have let something slip." His heavy brows drew together. "And sedatives are a funny thing, you kind of fade in and out of sleep."

Karen's hands tightened into fists. "Are you suggesting she remembers something about Cassie taking her from the hospital and what happened afterward?"

"Tell me, when did she start calling you Mother?"

"When we were staying with Dinah."

"Exactly, Karen, exactly."

She bent her head and her voice was muffled. "She's never called me Karen since the morning after . . . the morning she woke up at Dinah's."

"So . . . somehow or other that night she dropped the chummy Karen and started to call you Mother. I think that night changed her. I think she knows you fought like a lioness for her life."

Karen's shining hair fell forward, hiding her face. "I've done the best I can. Dr. Lehmar has done all he can. It will take time, Cal. A person can't kill another human being and forget about it in less than a year."

"I had a chat with the doctor myself. We all realize what causes this dreaming, and it's guilt. But not guilt because of Cassie's death. You know you had to do it to defend Jamie, and you know you only meant to stop her, not kill her. Your guilt is because you feel responsible for three other deaths—for Alfred Hampton and Mollie Mac-Lean and a young woman named Julie Loren who never got to be a bride."

"Stop it!" She put her hands over her ears. "Don't be brutal."

Pulling her hands down, he held both of them in his

own. His eyes were warm and concerned. "Face it, Karen, and hold on. I'm about to exorcise your ghosts. When you and the doctor couldn't come to grips with this I decided I'd better take a hand. Where do you think I've been for the past two weeks?"

"You said in Eastern Canada, in Montreal."

"Eastern Canada, yes. Montreal, no. I went back to Hampton—"

"Hampton!"

He squeezed her hands. "You really must stop this deplorable habit of interrupting. Yes, I went back to Hampton and I talked with Chief Barnes, Dr. Jim Miles, and a butcher. Uh-huh, I can see your mouth opening. No interrupting! Now, you feel that if you never had returned to Hampton, if Cassie hadn't seen you in that hot clinch with the doctor, those three people would still be alive. Is that about it?"

"They wouldn't have died," she cried. "Cassie would probably have married Jim and lived a long peaceful life being a good wife and doing good deeds. I was the one who changed her, who made a murderer of her!"

"You didn't change her, Karen. Cassie killed two people long before you set foot in Hampton. There's a good chance she would have killed more. The Cassies of this world don't just start butchering people so skillfully without some experience. Chief Barnes knew it before you left; he said he started to tell you and then decided there was no sense in upsetting you further. When I told him how you are suffering, and Jamie too, he told all."

"I don't believe it. Theo told me the only murder in Hampton had been that of a shoemaker axing his wife."

"Stop talking and I'll prove it. For openers, Cassie killed her own mother. You must have heard how Laura Saunders died."

261

"Jim told me about it. She died from a heart attack brought on by eating too much."

"Did he tell you that Laura was bedridden—she weighed about three hundred pounds—and that daughter Cassie was her sole nurse, companion, and slave? Did he tell you who went down to the butcher's and bought the forbidden pork and cooked a big meal? When Jim was called, Laura was already gone. Guess who sat by her bed and enjoyed every minute of her mother's death. Good Lord, Karen, you were sitting in Barnes's office when he asked Jim if he would ever have married Cassie, and Jim said no *because of Laura* and Barnes agreed with him. Everyone in Hampton suspected that Cassie had killed her mother, but nobody did anything or said anything because they sympathized with the daughter and figured the old woman got what she deserved. It's a close-knit little town and they protect their own, but Jim Miles wasn't about to wed and bed a wench capable of that."

Karen was staring at him wide-eyed. "Then why didn't they think of Cassie the minute they heard what was happening to Jamie and me, when you and Jamie were nearly killed?"

"Because, dear heart, clever little Cassie had erected an image in their minds that virtually wiped out her mother's death. She was a 'fine woman,' a woman who helped old people and children. A Sunday school teacher, for God's sake! Why didn't Alfred Hampton fear her? Why did Mac keep the fact she was in your house that night a secret and go trustingly along to the dying room? Cassie did volunteer work at the hospital. Julie Loren worked with her and liked her. Julie wasn't at all afraid of good old Cassie, so she unlocked the door and got a knife in her back."

He drew a deep breath.

"It was only after Barnes knew she was a killer that he

tied up the second murder to her. Alfred must have been one jump ahead of him; he probably guessed it the day you appealed to him for help. Alfred wasn't about to expose the town saint, but no doubt he threatened to hold it over her head to make her lay off Jamie and you. And what did Alfred get? A broken back. Let's face it, Cassie was a homicidal maniac who also happened to be a wonderful actress."

Karen was clinging to his hands and hers dripped with moisture. "What second murder?"

"Maybelle Cross. Ed Cross's niece, a girl who had lived most of her life in Toronto and was going to the university there, taking a course in journalism. She came to Hampton to spend a summer working on her uncle's paper."

"Maybelle? Uncle Alfred mentioned that name, and I thought it was an old romance of his. He said she looked like me."

"She did. I couldn't get a picture of her but I got a description. Maybelle was twenty-two but looked younger. Everyone I spoke with said she looked about sixteen. She was five-six, slender, had long pale-blond hair and brown eyes. She was popular, intelligent, and had a great personality. She came to town the summer after Laura Saunders died and immediately became smitten with young Dr. Miles. Apparently her interest was reciprocated, because Jim was wining and dining and courting her. And then she was killed."

"If there was another murder in Hampton, why didn't Theo Barnes tell me?"

"At the time it didn't look as though this one was connected with Hampton. Like many young ones then, Maybelle had a habit of ignoring the dangers of hitchhiking, often thumbing a ride instead of taking a bus or train. She was hitchhiking to Toronto for a weekend and went missing. A couple of boys found her body in a field on the outskirts of Katoma. She'd been hacked to bits, seventeen knife wounds in her body. Everybody in Hampton was shocked, but they figured she'd been picked up by a pervert, had resisted his advances, and been killed. After Cassie died, Theo Barnes started mulling over Maybelle Cross—how much she had looked like you, the way she had been stabbed with a knife—and he came to the conclusion that the car that picked her up could have been driven by Cassie Saunders."

Karen's head drooped again. "This doesn't actually prove anything. It's all guesswork. Even Laura's death—well, she might have forced Cassie to cook the meal for her."

"Chief Barnes wasn't guessing. The case on Maybelle Cross is now officially closed. When the girl's body was found in the field there were a couple of short black hairs clutched in her hand. After Cassie died, Barnes sent a sample of her hair to Katoma for comparison. They matched. Cassie Saunders killed the girl, again very cleverly."

"Hindsight. That's what Theo said."

"But it established a pattern. As long as Jim Miles was unattached and attentive to her she was fine, but nothing and no one was going to get between them. Even if he had married her—which is doubtful—what would have happened to the first blond girl who showed an interest in him? It could have been one of his patients, a kid growing up in town, or even a stranger. She killed three people just to avenge herself on you. Think of the number she might have killed if she hadn't been unmasked. No, Cassie had a taste for it. She liked to kill. You didn't *start* her, you *stopped* her. Now, darling, think about that."

"I will. I'm dazed. It will take time to adjust."

Getting to his feet, he pulled her up and put his arms around her. "I've a hunch your ordeal is over. Remember

264

this. If you hadn't gone back to Hampton you'd never have met *me*. Think what a loss that would have been."

The dog was nuzzling her robe, and she could hear the patter of Jamie's feet as she ran along the hall toward the kitchen. She smiled up at her husband. "You're extremely modest."

"And you—in Jamie's own words—are extremely pul-chri-tu-di-nous."